DESIGNS ON THE DUKE

Suddenly a Duke Series
Book Four

Alexa Aston

© Copyright 2023 by Alexa Aston
Text by Alexa Aston
Cover by Dar Albert

Dragonblade Publishing, Inc. is an imprint of Kathryn Le Veque Novels, Inc.
P.O. Box 23
Moreno Valley, CA 92556
ceo@dragonbladepublishing.com

Produced in the United States of America

First Edition June 2023
Print Edition

Reproduction of any kind except where it pertains to short quotes in relation to advertising or promotion is strictly prohibited.

All Rights Reserved.

The characters and events portrayed in this book are fictitious. Any similarity to real persons, living or dead, is purely coincidental and not intended by the author.

ARE YOU SIGNED UP FOR DRAGONBLADE'S BLOG?

You'll get the latest news and information on exclusive giveaways, exclusive excerpts, coming releases, sales, free books, cover reveals and more.

Check out our complete list of authors, too!

No spam, no junk. That's a promise!

Sign Up Here

www.dragonbladepublishing.com

Dearest Reader;

Thank you for your support of a small press. At Dragonblade Publishing, we strive to bring you the highest quality Historical Romance from some of the best authors in the business. Without your support, there is no 'us', so we sincerely hope you adore these stories and find some new favorite authors along the way.

Happy Reading!

CEO, Dragonblade Publishing

Additional Dragonblade books by Author Alexa Aston

Suddenly a Duke Series
Portrait of the Duke
Music for the Duke
Polishing the Duke
Designs on the Duke

Second Sons of London Series
Educated By The Earl
Debating With The Duke
Empowered By The Earl
Made for the Marquess
Dubious about the Duke
Valued by the Viscount
Meant for the Marquess

Dukes Done Wrong Series
Discouraging the Duke
Deflecting the Duke
Disrupting the Duke
Delighting the Duke
Destiny with a Duke

Dukes of Distinction Series
Duke of Renown
Duke of Charm
Duke of Disrepute
Duke of Arrogance
Duke of Honor
The Duke That I Want

The St. Clairs Series
Devoted to the Duke
Midnight with the Marquess
Embracing the Earl
Defending the Duke
Suddenly a St. Clair
Starlight Night (Novella)
The Twelve Days of Love (Novella)

Soldiers & Soulmates Series
To Heal an Earl
To Tame a Rogue
To Trust a Duke
To Save a Love
To Win a Widow
Yuletide at Gillingham (Novella)

The Lyon's Den Series
The Lyon's Lady Love

King's Cousins Series
The Pawn
The Heir
The Bastard

Medieval Runaway Wives
Song of the Heart
A Promise of Tomorrow
Destined for Love

Knights of Honor Series
Word of Honor
Marked by Honor
Code of Honor
Journey to Honor
Heart of Honor

Bold in Honor
Love and Honor
Gift of Honor
Path to Honor
Return to Honor

Pirates of Britannia Series
God of the Seas

De Wolfe Pack: The Series
Rise of de Wolfe

The de Wolfes of Esterley Castle
Diana
Derek
Thea

Also from Alexa Aston
The Bridge to Love
One Magic Night

PROLOGUE

Morville—1801

ABIGAIL TRENT AWOKE and despair immediately filled her.

This might be the day Papa left this earth.

Her throat thickened with unshed tears as she worried not only about her beloved father, but what would happen to her when he passed. She was an only child who had lost her mother when she was only two and had been raised by her carefree, loving father. He was charming but certainly had his faults. Managing money and his estate had been his downfall. His charm had won him the hand of the daughter of an earl. The couple had impulsively eloped to Gretna Green when her grandfather had denied her father's suit. Even back then, the viscount's coffers were fairly empty.

Because of that impulsive elopement, there had been no marriage settlements drawn up. Her grandfather had refused to award the dowry her mother would have brought into the marriage since he did not approve of their union. Abby barely remembered Mama, only a shadowy figure with a voice that used to sing to her as she rocked Abby to sleep. Mama had died in childbirth, along with an infant son, and Abby's father had raised her. She had never had a governess. Papa had taught her himself. She was talented at maths and knew much about history, while being able to translate any passage she was given into Latin or French.

But what good would those skills do her when her father was gone? She supposed she would follow the path of many impoverished gentlewomen before her and become a governess. How she was to do that, however, was unknown, especially since she was only four and ten. Once Papa passed, the title and estate would revert to the crown since no male heirs existed. She wondered how long she would have before a representative of the king arrived and booted her from the place.

Not that there was much here to begin with. Over the years, her father had sold off almost everything of value within the house, from furniture to paintings to carpets. Servants had been let go at regular intervals, and this past year when Papa had become bedridden and the servants could not be paid at all, all but his valet had left. Abby had taught herself how to cook for them and did all the cleaning of the house on her own. She did what she could with the estate's bookkeeping when the estate's steward left. She had even planted a small garden, and they ate from it, while she occasionally wrung the neck of a chicken and plucked its feathers before boiling it, stretching the fowl's meat and broth for as long as she could between the three of them. Papa barely ate anything nowadays.

Abby rose and washed and dressed for the day. She went to the kitchen and started a fire, another one of those skills she had taught herself by trial and error. She put on a kettle to boil the water for tea and soon Jackson showed up.

The valet had been with her father since Papa was a young man and had remained loyal throughout the years as times grew lean. Abby had explained to Jackson that she had no money to pension him off upon her father's death. The servant had told her he was too old to find a new position once the viscount went to meet his Maker and hinted that he might be doing the same himself. She had heard him hacking and wondered if his cough meant that he also would meet his demise soon. Jackson had grown almost as gaunt as Papa had, and it took the both of them to move him from the bed when she stripped the bedclothes and put fresh ones on.

She and Jackson drank a cup of tea and ate the hard crusts of the last of the loaves she had baked three days ago, no butter or jam to spread upon them. No flour or yeast was left, and Abby didn't know what they would eat come tomorrow.

She made a cup of tea for Papa, and Jackson accompanied her upstairs to the viscount's bedchamber. Papa had soiled the bedclothes again, and she went downstairs to retrieve a bucket of water and cloths to clean him, knowing Jackson didn't have the strength to haul the items up the stairs himself. Abby promised herself she would not cry. She had shed no tears in a long time, knowing they never improved a situation.

They cleaned her father, and she stripped the bed, taking the bedclothes downstairs to be washed later. Of all the tasks she had learned to do, washing was by far the most time-consuming and difficult. She wouldn't think about the hours of work which lay ahead. She would go and be with Papa, knowing today might be his last.

Jackson helped her make the bed again and between the two of them, they got Papa back into it.

"His lordship drank some of his tea, Miss Trent," the valet said.

She smiled brightly. "That is good news. Do you think you could drink some more now, Papa?"

"No," he said weakly and then glanced at the servant. "Leave us."

Abby pulled up a chair to the bed and took Papa's hands in hers. He was so cold even though it was midsummer. She gave thanks that they weren't in the midst of winter because she was not very good at swinging an ax and chopping wood. She knew Papa would not make it to the autumn, much less winter, and wondered what might be in store for her come the first snowfall.

He mustered a smile and said, "I have written to Ladiwyck. It took a few times, but I managed to finish the letter over several days' time. I had Jackson send it some time ago."

Abby had heard stories her entire life of Lord Ladiwyck, her father's closest friend, who was an earl and adventurer.

"Has he returned to England?" she asked. "Might he be able to come and visit you?"

She had never laid eyes upon the earl, though her father spoke of the man with great fondness. Lord Ladiwyck did write regularly, however, even sending items from his travels as gifts. Abby used a shawl he had gifted to her mother from one of his visits to India. Other items Lord Ladiwyck had sent, she sold in the nearby village for whatever she could get.

"I told him my time draws near and asked him to come and take responsibility for you."

His words surprised her. She had wondered who might take her in, supposing the vicar and his wife would on a temporary basis until something was decided, or she was old enough to earn a living on her own.

"I received a letter from him just yesterday," Papa revealed.

Hurt this had been kept from her, Abby asked, "Did Jackson bring it to you?"

"He did. I did not want you to know what I had asked of Magnus until I heard from him. He is not a family man, but a world traveler and adventurer at heart. Magnus is willing, however, to make you his ward. When I am gone, I am certain he will send you to school and help you in making your come-out."

Sadness filled Papa's face. "I am sorry I have no dowry to give you, Abby. Unfortunately, that is what most gentlemen seek. You are fair of face, however, and have a sweet spirit about you. Perhaps there will be some gentleman, low on the rung of Polite Society, who might offer for you. It is my greatest hope that this happens."

Her father began coughing, and she quickly grabbed one of the cloths that sat beside the bed, holding it under his mouth. It quickly soaked with blood.

He fell back into the pillows, exhausted. "We will talk more of this later," he promised, patting her hand.

Papa closed his eyes, and she saw he drifted off. Abby should get up. There was so much to do. Washing the soiled bedclothes and his nightshirts. Finding something for her and Jackson to eat. But a voice inside her told Abby to stay where she was.

She placed her hand over Papa's, knowing he was breathing his last.

When the end came, he went quietly, never awakening again. She felt the hot hand beneath hers grow warm. Then cool. And finally, cold. She remained with him until Jackson entered the bedchamber again.

"He is gone," she told the valet. "No more suffering."

Jackson winced. "His lordship was a good man, Miss Trent. Full of life and laughter. No one had a sunnier nature than the viscount."

"But not one much for responsibility, I am afraid. Nor did he have a head for figures. We must alert his solicitor, Jackson. I will write to him today. He will need to notify the crown of Papa's death."

"There is someone here to see you, Miss Trent. That is why I came upstairs."

"No, tell them Papa has just passed. I need to wash his body. Find something for him to wear. He has lost so much weight in this past year. Most of his clothes swallow him."

"You must see this visitor, Miss Trent. It is the Earl of Ladiwyck."

Abby sighed. "Send him in."

She watched the valet leave and then return moments later, guessing the earl had been waiting in the corridor for admittance to the bedchamber. Abby moved to greet him.

As Ladiwyck entered the room, he looked larger than life. He was several inches above six feet and with a robust look about him that let all know he was in good health and even better spirits. He stepped toward her and offered his hand, and she curtseyed and took it.

"Good afternoon, Lord Ladiwyck. I am sorry, but you have arrived too late. Papa passed about an hour ago."

The earl's eyes went to the bed and then back to her. "I am deeply sorry for your loss, Abby."

He enveloped her, making her feel small and yet safe at the same time. Tears slid down her cheeks as the earl rubbed her back in comfort.

Finally, Lord Ladiwyck released her and asked, "May I have a few moments alone with my dear friend?"

"Of course, my lord. I will wait for you in the drawing room."

She and Jackson left the bedchamber, and she told the valet to wait for Lord Ladiwyck and bring him to the drawing room. She knew it would be teatime soon but had nothing to offer their guest other than a cup of tea. Abby recalled there was some madeira in her father's study and went there. Retrieving it, she took it to the drawing room and waited for the earl to appear.

When he did, she asked if she could pour him a glass, and he agreed.

They sat in silence for a moment on the lone settee in the room, and then Abby said, "Papa told me that you would make me your ward. He said you might possibly send me to school."

"I haven't had much time to think about it. I will admit that the idea of having a ward and being responsible for you is a bit overwhelming to me."

Anger rippled through her, and Abby did not mince words. "I know you gallivant about the world, my lord. If it is inconvenient for you to become a guardian to me, then I am perfectly capable of making my way in the world."

Amusement flickered in his eyes, riling her even further.

"How old are you, Abby?"

"Abby was Papa's nickname for me," she snapped. "We do not know one another, my lord. I am Miss Trent—or possibly Abigail—to you."

The earl did not bother to hide his smile. "Ah, you are as spirited as your mother was."

Immediately, she deflated. "You knew Mama?"

"I most certainly did. I even tried to court her—but she only had eyes for your father. Perhaps she saw the wanderlust within me and knew I would never be good at settling down. I haven't in all these years. Settled down. My title will go to a cousin or his son. I have enjoyed a life of privilege and traveled the globe."

He paused. "Yet I would have liked to have done so with your mother."

"Did you love Mama?" Abby asked.

"It was such a long time ago. Perhaps I did—and she spoiled me for any other woman. You do favor her in looks, though I see a bit of your father in you, as well."

He reached and took her hands in his. "I do not think I would be much of a father figure to you, Abigail. But I would like to be your friend. I would be happy to help guide you. I am going to give you a choice now. How old are you?"

"Four and ten, my lord."

His eyes flickered about the room and then landed upon her. "It looks as if not much is here."

"We are destitute," she admitted. "Anything of value—even gifts you have sent over the years—has been sold off. The only servant is Jackson, Papa's valet, whom you have met. We could not pay our servants or our bills."

"And you have been managing everything, haven't you?"

"I have, my lord. I learned to cook and clean and have taken care of the estate as best I could."

"Did you have a governess? Or did you go away to school at some point?" he asked.

"There was never enough money for such a luxury. Papa taught me himself, though. If you do send me to school, I would not be far behind the other girls. In fact, I think I might run circles about them."

"Confident. I like that. I said that I would give you a choice, Abigail. I think you are mature enough to make the decision yourself. I will do as your father asked and become the guardian that sends you off to school and helps you make your debut into Polite Society when the time comes. I will even provide a dowry for you so that some young swain might snatch you up. It would be the conventional life of a young woman in the *ton*."

She had not dreamed of being able to take her place among the *ton*, knowing of her financial situation. Yet curiosity filled her, and Abby asked, "And what would the second choice be, Lord Ladiwyck?"

He smiled broadly. "It would be to become my traveling companion. I am not one to stay in one place for too long. It would be a nomadic life. You would see the world. Experience new countries and different cultures."

His gaze bored into her, as if he could see into her very soul.

"It is your choice, Abigail. Follow the typical route of a lady in Polite Society—or see places others never will and be educated by your experiences in the world."

The choice boggled her mind. She hesitated a brief moment, weighing the options.

And then made the decision which would change the course of her life.

"There is no choice to make, my lord," Abby said with confidence. "I want a life others only dream of. I want to see the world by your side."

Lord Ladiwyck squeezed her hands. "I think you have made the wisest decision, Abigail."

She smiled up at him. "Why don't you call me Abby?"

Chapter One

Ciudad Rodrigo, Spain—19 January 1812

Major Elijah Young left Wellington's tent with his brother, Captain Gilford Young. They trailed after their commanding officer, Major-General Sir Robert Craufurd, known as Black Bob by the men of the Light Division. Although a strict disciplinarian, Craufurd had a violent temper and cursed heavily when he lost it. The nickname referred to Craufurd's black moods as much as it did his dark, heavy facial stubble. Despite the moniker, both Youngs found their leader brilliant and had been thrilled when Craufurd had been given command of the Light Division two years ago. The company was an elite group of foot soldiers and had been a stalwart of the Peninsular War, a shining light for Wellington in his quest to rid Spain of the French forces of Bonaparte.

Major-General Craufurd now paused, pivoting to look at the twins. "What do you think of our battle orders?"

Picton's Third Division had been ordered to storm the greater breach on the northwest side of the French garrison, while the Light Division would go against the lesser breach on the north.

"We will notch a victory with ease," predicted Gil airily, always one to speak and act quickly.

Elijah proved the more thoughtful of the twins, preferring to mull over things before he spoke.

"And you, Major? Do you agree with your brother?"

"The fortress is second class in every regard, Major-General. The walls may be just over thirty feet high, but they are composed of poor masonry and weak parapets. The narrow ramparts will also give the French trouble when we attack."

"True," Craufurd said, his hands linked behind his back. "Go now. Prepare the men. We must be in place within half an hour for the attack at seven o'clock."

As the Young brothers hurried away, Elijah knew night attacks were notorious for heavy casualties. He worried not for himself but for his twin, who seemed to always be in the thick of the fighting, no matter what his orders were, taking unnecessary risks that one day might very well cost Gil his life.

Elijah placed his hands on Gil's shoulders. "Be careful tonight," he cautioned.

"We are fortunate that we have good men under us, Eli. They are seasoned soldiers and would follow us to the ends of the earth. They will support us this night."

He embraced his brother, feeling as if they were one spirit in two bodies, clapping Gil hard on the back before stepping back.

In unison, they said, "For God. For country. For us and Mama," the words they repeated before going into every battle.

"Good luck," Gil said, smiling.

"You know I do not believe in luck," Elijah replied. "We are prepared. Well trained and supplied."

Gil laughed. "Well, I say we have God *and* Wellington on our side."

They parted, each to go to gather his own troops.

Soon, Elijah had his men formed in their battle lines, ready to march. They headed to the fort, the winter's dark night having come a little over an hour earlier. He looked down the lines and saw Gil, nodding at his twin. Gil waved back and then turned toward his men.

The battle commenced. Elijah was glad Denis Pack's Portuguese brigade would attack on the east, testing the defenses at the San Pelayo Gate. It would be an added distraction. In total, Wellington would be using close to eleven thousand men in this assault. It had taken almost ten days of fighting leading up to this moment, with the Greater and Lesser Tesons being captured prior to tonight's attack.

The signal came, and Elijah moved quickly, his men following. Fighting proved fierce, but the Light Division overran the fortress' lesser breach. He tried not to think of the deaths at his hands as he wiped the blood from his sword and sheathed it.

As his men rounded up captives, Gil appeared at Elijah's side.

"Picton's having a harder go of it," his brother said. "But our soldiers can push through the fort now and help smooth the way. Be safe."

Gil motioned for his troops to continue moving deeper within the fort.

Two hours later, news traveled quickly that the fort had fallen. Elijah asked for a status report from an arriving lieutenant.

"Casualties were on the heavy side, Major Young, especially a significant number among the Light Division. It looks as if almost two hundred Allies were lost. The early count also has nine hundred wounded." The officer paused. "Major-General Mackinnon was killed in action. Major-General Craufurd was hit in the lung. Lieutenant Shaw, his staff officer, carried him from the action."

"Is he alive?" Elijah demanded, knowing a shot to the lung would eventually be fatal.

"Barely," the lieutenant replied. "It is said he was mortally wounded, Major."

Anger sizzled through him, but he kept it in check. "Thank you, Lieutenant."

"Eli!"

He looked over his shoulder and saw his twin approaching, a grim look on his face.

"Did you hear about Craufurd?"

Elijah nodded. "Mackinnon was lost, as well." He glanced around. "There should be more men here, even with the numerous casualties."

"The looting has begun," his brother said. "That is what I came to tell you. With Craufurd out of action, we need to quell it as quickly as possible."

Though not sanctioned, British soldiers, often from the lowest class of society, would sack a city after a victory, despite the best efforts of the officers to prevent this from happening. This instance should be different, with the people of Cuidad Rodrigo being their allies. Still, Elijah knew the soldiers would pillage, nonetheless.

"Let's go and try to stop as much as we can," he said, dreading the new fight ahead, one where he would go head-to-head with his own countrymen.

Fires had already been started throughout the city. British soldiers ran wild, emerging from houses ladened with sacks that held their spoils of war, everything from money and clothes to food and works of art. The twins did their best to stop the looting but were overwhelmed by the sheer number of men feeling entitled after a victory.

Above the shouts, a scream sounded. Both brothers looked up to a burning house, seeing a woman at the window, a babe in her arms.

"*Ayúdeme!*" she cried.

"I'll get her and the child," Gil said impulsively.

Before Elijah could stop his brother, Gil had raced across the street and inside the house, flames licking the doorway where he entered.

"Gil!" he cried fruitlessly, knowing his brother had no fear of death.

Then he heard a shriek nearby and raced to the alley. He saw a soldier with a young girl of twelve or thirteen, pressed against the brick wall. The soldier held his forearm against her throat and yanked up her skirts as she cried.

Racing to the pair, Elijah knocked the private away, and the man sprawled on the ground. The girl collapsed, tears streaming down her cheeks. A sudden rage filled him, and he yanked out his sword and thrust it into the private lying there. He withdrew it and stabbed the soldier a second time. A third.

Finally, his anger subsided. The private stared lifelessly up at him.

Stumbling away, he went to the girl and bent, taking her elbow. She shrieked in terror.

"I won't hurt you," he said gently, only knowing a few words of Spanish, hoping his gentle tone would convey that he meant her no harm. "I will take you home. To your *casa*. To your *madre* and *padre*."

Slowly, he guided her to her feet. They left the alley, and she pointed to the house that Gil had rashly run into.

"*Mi casa*," she told him.

The house was now engulfed in flames. Elijah stood looking at it, tears welling in his eyes.

"*Madre!*" the girl cried, breaking away from him.

He followed her, seeing her fall into the arms of the woman who had appeared at the window with the babe. If she got out, surely Gil had also been able to do so. He turned wildly in circles and spied his brother, sitting on the ground across the street from the burning structure. He rushed to his brother.

Gil had a blanket wrapped about him. His face was dark with soot, and he was coughing deeply. Elijah knelt next to his twin.

"Are you all right?" he asked, worried not only about the hacking cough but the confusion he saw in Gil's eyes.

"Where are they?" Gil asked, his voice hoarse and his breathing noisy. "The woman and child."

Putting an arm about Gil, Elijah sat next to him. "They got out. You saved them both. They are fine."

"Good."

Another coughing spell erupted, with Gil spitting out dark mucus. Elijah tightened his hold on his twin, feeling helpless as Gil continued to cough and wheeze.

"Where is Mama?" his brother asked, frowning, his eyes glazed.

"Mama is at home. In England. We are in Spain, Gil. Fighting for the crown," he said, stroking his brother's hair in comfort, cold fear pooling in his belly as he began to realize his brother's muddled thoughts and disorientation indicated he was physically worse than Elijah had first believed.

"My hands. They hurt," Gil said, raising them and looking at them dully.

Elijah saw the burns on them, even as he heard Gil rasping, his breath labored and weak.

"Stay with me, Brother," he urged, tears beginning to stream down his face as he recognized he only had moments remaining with his twin. "Don't leave me."

In a moment of clarity, Gil met his gaze. "You will be duke someday, Eli. Be a . . . good one . . ."

Gil's voice trailed off, and his eyes went glassy. He coughed again, dark mucus dribbling down his chin.

"No, don't go," he begged. "I cannot do this without you."

His brother shuddered. His body went limp. Elijah knew Gil was gone. He continued to hold his twin, though, as the chaos raged on about them. He could only think that Gil had died a hero. Perhaps not on the battlefield, but a hero all the same. A mother and her child would live instead of being placed in early graves.

Eventually, more officers arrived. Soldiers came to their senses and began leaving the town, ready to return to the outskirts of Cuidad Rodrigo, where their camp was. He watched everything unfold, feeling nothing. Then he rose, scooping up his brother's body into his arms.

Passing the woman and babe Gil had saved, as well as the girl

Elijah had helped, he saw them huddled together, their home and possessions now gone. Still, they lived.

While his twin was dead.

He slowly made his way along the streets filled with debris and came upon an abandoned flower cart. He placed Gil amidst the flowers and began rolling it back to camp, ignoring everything around him. He steered the cart to the medical tent, knowing the physicians could do nothing. Elijah collapsed beside the cart, his mournful wail filling the night.

Soldiers came. Some of his own men. They led him away, promising to care for Gil's body, and returned him to the tent he had shared with his twin. Stumbling inside, he fell upon Gil's cot and curled into a ball, the pain of losing his brother engulfing him. He lay there throughout the night, thinking of their lives together. Sharing meals with Mama. Fishing in a nearby stream. Going to the local clergyman's parsonage for lessons. Leaving for war.

He had nothing to live for now that his twin was gone. How would he look Mama in the eyes and tell her this horrible news? She had told him to protect Gil. Sweet, rash, impulsive, goodhearted Gil.

Dawn came. With it, he knew they would soon be on the move once the area had been secured. Wellington's plans had hinged on a victory at Ciudad Rodrigo. That having occurred, they would now proceed to march to Badajoz. Elijah no longer had the heart—or the stomach—for war. Yet he was a commissioned officer, one who needed to continue to lead his men.

And a future duke.

That thought made him grow nauseous. He rolled from the cot and vomited on the ground next to it, the stench making him queasy. He stepped outside the tent, dawn just beginning to break on the horizon. He watched the sunrise and the camp come to life again, melancholy filling him at the thought of writing to Mama.

He would not write to Bradford. Their father had washed his

hands of the three of them only a few months after he wed Mama. The duke had been thirty-five years Mama's senior, while she was a girl of eighteen making her come-out. Somehow, the duke came to believe that Mama had been unfaithful to him and banished her from Marblebridge, his ducal seat in Surrey. He sent her to his only estate in the north. She had given birth to the duke's twins there. Not in the duke's house, but rather in the small cottage on the estate in Norfolk where he had exiled Mama. She might have been a duchess—but they lived as paupers.

Mama never told them why her husband thought her unfaithful, only that he believed the twins were not his issue. Bradford had nothing to do with them over the years as they struggled to make ends meet. Elijah thought it a joke when others addressed him as Lord Elijah, such as the clergyman whom they'd taken lessons with. Mama did the man's laundry in exchange for teaching her boys, having no spare coin to give.

While Mama took in sewing to provide some income, Elijah and Gil had gone to work at ten, toiling at a variety of odd jobs from chopping firewood to painting until they turned eighteen. Mama had told them her favorite aunt had died and left her a bequeathal. Instead of spending it on herself, she insisted upon buying a commission for both her boys. They had been at war ever since.

Until now. When he must write her and tell her of Gil's death.

Elijah would make certain Mama knew Gil died a hero, saving a woman and her babe from a burning building. Without meaning to, Mama had always favored Gil. He looked to be the male version of her, with blond hair and brown eyes. Elijah assumed he resembled the duke, and that small thing slightly influenced his mother's behavior toward her younger son. Still, he knew she loved him fiercely.

Would she still love him now that he had let Gil die?

"Major Young?"

He glanced up and saw a young private with a bundle of letters in his hand.

"For you and Captain Young," the soldier said, handing over two letters.

He accepted them, seeing Mama's handwriting on each. His gut churned, knowing one was for Gil.

He sat on the ground, the letters in his lap. Finally, he opened the one addressed to him.

My dear Elijah —

I hope this finds you well. As always, I have followed news of the war in the newspapers and pray for you and Gil each night, hoping God will keep my boys safe. Thank you for your last letter. I hope Wellington will find success in Spain, and you will be able to move on from there. Oh, how I hope this war will end someday soon!

I must now share news with you that is not entirely unexpected. The Duke of Bradford is no more. He would have turned one and eighty recently. That means that your brother is no longer the heir apparent; he is the new Duke of Bradford. I have written to him separately but wanted you to know, as well. Gil should inform Major-General Craufurd as soon as possible of the change in his circumstances. He must sell his commission and return to England in order to assume his seat in the House of Lords and his place at Marblebridge.

I know you have always felt a strong sense of duty, Elijah, and will think you should remain and continue to fight against the French. I am asking that you also sell your commission and return with your brother. Gil will need your guidance in the weeks and months ahead. He can be impulsive—even a bit reckless at times—and will need your calming influence upon him. Gil may hold the ducal title—but he will need your advice as he becomes the Duke of Bradford and learns to fulfill all his responsivities. You are so organized and intelligent. He might make you his secretary or even the steward at Marblebridge.

I know I am asking a lot of you, Elijah. I always seem to do so, especially when it concerns your brother. He will need you more than your men now do, however. Navigating Polite Society and running several estates is no easy task. Gil will do well to have you by his side. Though there is no title for you, you are Lord Elijah Young, brother to a duke. The two of you should assume your places in Polite Society together. I would be delighted if you both attended the upcoming Season and found ladies to wed. We could all live together at Marblebridge as a family.

Support Gil now in all that you do. Help him in speaking with your commanding officer and ridding yourselves of your commissions. Come home to England—to me—and we'll be together again. I will be waiting in Norfolk for you both. From there, we can travel to London to meet with Bradford's solicitor and gain a clearer picture of the situation.

I have missed you, Elijah. You and Gil. I am ready now for you both to have all that you missed out on, thanks to your father's misguided beliefs. You and Gil will be shining lights in Polite Society, my son.

My love to you always.
Your Loving Mama

Elijah's throat tightened with emotion, making it hard to breathe. He was now the Duke of Bradford. A title which was never supposed to be his.

One he would not be able to reject.

Chapter Two

February—London

Abby raised her face to the sun, letting the rays wash over her. The warmth spread through her. She shielded her eyes and looked at the pyramid again, awed by its splendor.

Then something distracted her. She frowned. A cloud hid the sun, and the warmth fled.

She awoke with a start, confused at first. Then she realized she was back in England—and had been since early last summer.

Her days of traveling were behind her. At least, for now. Her focus after living abroad for almost a decade would remain on her new business. Bits and pieces of the dream, which receded quickly, caused her to leap from bed. She located her sketchpad and rushed to capture what she could before the idea dissipated. When she finished, she took a moment to study her drawing. Incorporating the sphinx into the chairback's design worked. It was small and in the center, subtle and yet a bold statement. She thought it would look best in ebony, but mahogany was a close second choice.

Setting down her pencil, she rang for Ethel, and the maid helped Abby dress for the day. Her life seemed so normal now, so routine, unlike the years spent outside England with Magnus, moving from country to country. Her guardian had opened the world to Abby, taking her to several continents. She had tasted local cuisines, dining on exotic fare such as caruru in South America and smoked ham and clam chowder in the United States to vada pav in India and zalabyas while in Turkey. Wherever she and Magnus journeyed, they had studied architecture, history, and art.

Abby had fancied herself an artist at one time, in those years before Papa died. She had sketched objects and even people, thinking that one day she might become a famous painter. Her drawing skills had paid off in a way she never would have thought.

Furniture.

The more she traveled, the more she had been drawn to the furniture they saw. She began drawing various pieces in sketchbooks, filling them and starting others, until now she had hundreds of them. Once she had studied furniture in different countries and from varying eras, she started designing her own furniture. That had led her to her life's ambition.

Opening her own furniture shop.

Magnus had escorted her back to England and put Mr. Peak, his solicitor, at Abby's disposal. Her guardian took off again for Eastern Europe, while she met many hours with Mr. Peak. He had drawn up the papers making Magnus and Abby partners in her venture. For now, Magnus funded her. His generosity had allowed her to rent a place for her furniture designs to come to life, as well as pay the salaries for the craftsmen who did so. It also had provided funds to rent a shop in Mayfair amidst several fashionable shops. Madame Planche, a famous modiste was on one side of her soon-to-open shop and a shirtmaker was on the other. Across the street was one of London's largest bookshops.

She would be opening the doors to her shop in a week's time, the realization of all the months of hard work by her and others on her behalf.

"Thank you, Ethel," she said, dismissing the maid.

Abby sat at her dressing table and brushed her long, dark blond locks, twisting and pinning them up. She remembered how years ago Magnus had given her a choice—either have a conventional life as a lady of the *ton* or become an adventurer with him.

She had never regretted the decision to follow him around the world.

Of course, it meant a different kind of life for her. Magnus had been her only steady companion for all those years. Yes, they had made friends wherever they went in countries near and wide. Eventually, they left those friends behind, sometimes never seeing them again. When they had finally returned to England early last June, Magnus had only stayed ten days and then was off again. Abby knew no one in London. She had no time to make friends because she was eager to begin the foundation for her new business.

No, she would never be one for the *ton*. She would never attend social affairs held by members of Polite Society. Never gossip with women her own age. She would never marry and raise a family.

But she would continue to live a life that others might envy. She was her own woman, capable of running her own business. She had always been good with maths and could keep her own ledgers. She would design her furniture and slowly build a client base.

Already, she had studied some of the more famous furniture designers of the day in England, leaning toward the work of Thomas Sheraton and to a lesser degree, Thomas Hope. Abby had devoured Sheraton's written works, especially *The Cabinet-maker and Upholsterer's Drawing Book* and his later *The Cabinet-maker, Upholsterer and General Artists' Encyclopaedia*.

One day she hoped to write her own encyclopaedia and inspire future designers. Until then, she had plenty to keep her busy.

She went downstairs to the breakfast room, and Feathers greeted her.

"What might you like this morning, Miss Trent?"

"I believe I will have two poached eggs and some toast points, Feathers."

"I will inform Cook of your decision." The butler left the room.

She liked that the room was now empty. Magnus did not employ a group of servants since he was so rarely at his townhouse. Instead, he left things to Feathers and Cook. They could hire help to come in on a weekly or monthly basis to clean the townhouse or do the laundry. Because of that, no footmen hovered in the background as she ate her meals. Ethel had been hired to help take care of Abby and also do light cleaning about the house. She was the only new addition to the household ever since Magnus had become the Earl of Ladiwyck when he turned twenty.

Feathers returned with her breakfast and the one newspaper Abby subscribed to. She liked to peruse the articles and see what was going on in the world as she wondered where Magnus might be. One day, she believed Britain and her allies would best Bonaparte and send him into exile. If so, she knew she and Magnus would be on the first ship bound across the English Channel for France. Magnus had seen Paris before the war began. Abby had only seen the great city through books. She couldn't wait to travel the French countryside, sampling its cuisine and going to the great museums in Paris.

As she turned the page, Feathers entered the room again. "Miss Trent, we have a surprise guest."

She couldn't for the life of her imagine who would be calling, since no visitors had done so since she had lived here.

Then Magnus rounded the corner, and she let out a cry of joy, leaping to her feet and racing to him, falling into his arms.

"I am so happy to see you!" she exclaimed. "Why didn't you give us notice of your arrival?"

He released her, clasping her hands as he looked her up and down. "England suits you, Abby. And you know how letters go astray when one travels. I thought a surprise might be nice."

She smiled at him but took in his appearance. He was thinner than the last time she had seen him. The silver gracing his temples was now threaded through his hair, so much so that she couldn't tell where the silver began and the blond ended.

"Come have a seat. Feathers, bring Lord Ladiwyck some breakfast. And coffee, not tea. Also, have Ethel make up his bed and see that his rooms are prepared for his stay."

"Yes, Miss Trent," the butler said, leaving them alone.

They went and sat at the table. "I still cannot believe you are here."

"One of your letters did reach me," he told her. "From it, I knew your shop would be opening soon. I wanted to be back in time for that."

Her eyes misted with tears. She took his hand and squeezed it. "That is very thoughtful of you. I must thank you for the loan of Mr. Peak. He has been most helpful in all my endeavors."

Magnus chuckled. "He should be most accommodating. I pay him an enormous amount of money for him to manage my affairs and yours now, as well."

"Mr. Peak helped me to find places to rent in order to have space to have my furniture built and a shop in which to sell it. I cannot wait to show you both." She paused. "You look tired, though. Perhaps you can rest today, and I will take you out tomorrow."

"No, I am fully rested. I arrived in town last night. It was late, so I stayed at my club. I did not want to bother anyone. Please, squire me about today. I want to see what your business looks like."

"Our business," Abby corrected. "We are partners. True, you have given the capital for me to establish things. Hopefully, once I open my doors, I will start making money and be able to return your investment."

"What have you been working on recently?" he asked.

She spent several minutes telling him of her latest designs as he ate. She even showed him the cards she had made up to hand out to those who called at the shop.

Magnus fingered the card and read, "*Trent Furnishings. Simplicity and Elegance.* I like it, Abby."

"I am so happy you will be here for the opening. How long do you plan to stay in England?"

"I believe I will be here through the Season," he replied.

His answer dumbfounded her. "Through the Season? Why would you do that? You haven't attended the Season since you courted Mama and lost her to Papa."

He chuckled. "Yes, your mother's rejection sent me on my travels about the world. But I intend to stay and attend events to help you. It would be good for you to move about in Polite Society and have doors opened to you."

She snorted. "Or doors slammed in my face." She shook her head. "Magnus, I am a working woman. The *ton* is not interested in having someone such as me come to their events. Besides, women attend the Season to find themselves a husband. I have no need of one and can support myself. That does not even take into account that I am considered to be on the shelf. No, I cannot do so. Social affairs would take up too much of my time. I would miss too much work."

Taking her hand, he said, "You need to make the social connections, Abby. Your furniture is of high quality and can only be afforded by members of the *ton*. I believe there is no harm in trying to meet others and build relationships with those who would patronize your shop."

Bewilderment filled her. "Who on earth would invite me, Magnus? Papa has been gone for years. No one knows who I am. I cannot make my come-out at five and twenty."

He smiled slyly. "They will invite me. I am a curiosity to them. They will want to hear a few of my stories. I will make certain that those invitations include you."

She thought a moment on his words. "I can see where having met members of Polite Society might help get them into my shop. The furniture would then speak for itself. The problem is that I have no wardrobe to wear to such events. Most of my gowns are older than the hills. I even wear trousers at times, especially when I am visiting the workspace."

Abby could only imagine how the *ton* would cringe, seeing a woman donning trousers. In her travels, she had viewed women in a variety of outfits, ones which suited their culture and stations in life. Again, she couldn't help but be a bit wary of how she would be received in English society—much less how she might fit in.

"You will have to have some new gowns made up anyway to wear at your shop, Abby. You cannot look like a pauper. To be successful, you must look successful to begin with."

"I had not thought of it that way. Good advice, Magnus."

"Your mother was always clad simply and elegantly. We will see if her modiste is still in business."

"Simple and elegant," she mused. "Like my furniture's lines!"

He set down his fork and took a last swallow of his coffee. "Take me around to the places you've rented."

"Let me fetch my reticule and bonnet. I will meet you in the foyer."

On the way to her room, she passed Feathers, who told her that he had finished unpacking Lord Ladiwyck's trunk and the earl's rooms were being prepared.

"We are off to see my spaces," she told the butler. "We probably will not return until teatime."

"Very good, Miss Trent."

She met Magnus in the foyer. "What is the weather like?"

"No rain. Cold and cloudy, though."

He took her arm and escorted her outside. "I suppose we will have to locate a hansom cab."

Since Magnus was rarely in England, he did not keep a carriage and horses, much less a coachman.

"I have taken to using Samuel quite frequently. He is usually parked around the corner."

They left the square and turned the corner. Sure enough, Samuel and his horse sat there.

"Good morning, Samuel," Abby called. "I would like to introduce you to Lord Ladiwyck."

The driver doffed his hat, his usual ready smile on his face. "Good day to you, my lord. Miss Trent has told me all about you and how you've financed her new shop. She'll make a go of things, my lord."

"You are an admirer of hers, Samuel?" Magnus asked.

"I am, my lord," the cabbie said enthusiastically. "I drive Miss Trent fairly often. She's invited me in to see the workspace. Her furniture is beautiful." He turned to Abby. "Let me help you up, Miss Trent. There you go."

As they traveled the streets of London, she asked, "Do you miss these sights and smells?"

"I actually do," her guardian admitted. "I spent a fair amount of time here and at our country estate. London does have a certain beauty that other large cities do not possess."

"Well, I had never been to town before you brought me all those years ago. We have only returned here sporadically, but I do know what you mean. I have been to so many fantastic places and yet London—and England—will always be home."

"I hadn't thought about all the traveling you have to do, from the townhouse to your rented spaces."

"It is no bother. Samuel is often waiting for me. I have come to trust him and also like him quite a bit."

They pulled up to the spot where her two furniture makers worked. Magnus exited the hansom cab first and then offered his hand to her.

"Shall I wait, my lord? Or I could come back at a later time. Sometimes, Miss Trent is here for several hours."

"I have a proposition for you, Samuel," Magnus said. "How would you like to drive Miss Trent around permanently? I do not have a carriage and team of horses so you would have to use your own horse for now."

The cabbie's smile widened. "Why, that would be ever so grand, my lord."

"The mews are empty except for the carriage I used long ago. You could keep your vehicle and horse there. I believe there is also space above the mews if you wish to live there. No rent would be required. You could take meals in the kitchen with Feathers and the maid."

"Thank you, my lord," Samuel said enthusiastically. "I'd be happy to work for you."

"Oh, it would be for Miss Trent. I am often gone, so you would have to answer to her."

Samuel smiled at a surprised Abby. "It would be an honor to work for you, Miss Trent."

"Why don't you move your things in today after you have finished driving us about?" Magnus fished in his pocket and presented Samuel with a guinea. "Hopefully, this would be enough to pay off your landlord. I should have asked—have you a wife and children?"

"No, my lord," the cabbie said, his countenance falling. "My wife passed on four years ago. Our only daughter is married and lives near Canterbury. It will only be me."

"Very well," Magnus said. Turning to Abby, he said, "Let us see what you have been up to, my dear."

"With pleasure."

She led him inside the building, saying, "I cannot thank you enough for providing me with my own transportation and driver, Magnus. It will be so helpful."

He smiled. "I am happy to do so. Now, show me everything."

"This part of the building is older but well maintained. The entire first floor is designated for storage. We can look at it later. I want you to meet Mr. Bauer and Mr. Alexander."

They went up the stairs to the large open space where the two furniture makers worked. Mr. Bauer had a saw in hand, while Mr. Alexander sanded a large section of wood.

"Greetings, gentlemen," Abby called, causing them both to cease what they were doing.

She introduced Magnus to them.

"Miss Trent is a very clever woman," Bauer praised. "It has been a pleasure bringing her designs to life."

"I have designed a few pieces during my day," Mr. Alexander added, "but none shine as Miss Trent's work does."

The two men led Magnus about, showing him the pieces they currently worked on and explaining some of the details to him. She noted that he seemed suitably impressed. Magnus was not one for effusive praise, so when he turned to her and told her how good he thought her work, she knew it must be outstanding.

"You have shared designs with me before, but these go far beyond the expectations I had for you, my dear."

"I soaked in everything I could on our travels and try to incorporate what I saw and learned into each piece."

"Your work is original. You also use different woods in unusual ways. I like that."

"Why don't you go downstairs and wander about what has been completed?" she suggested. "I have a few new sketches to go over with Mr. Alexander and Mr. Bauer."

Magnus left the room, and she pulled her drawings from her reticule. "These are for a secretaire, commode, blanket chest, and sideboard."

Abby shared her sketches, highlighting the parts that distinguished these pieces from other ones previously crafted. They discussed which woods to use and decided that Bauer would carve the commode and sideboard, while Alexander worked on the secretaire and blanket chest. Once the furniture was completed, the three of them would evaluate the work and see if the same design should be used again.

"Very well, gentlemen. I will be back tomorrow and stay longer. I want to show Lord Ladiwyck the actual shop now."

They bid her farewell, and she returned downstairs, finding Magnus studying a credenza.

"I am suitably impressed, Abby. To think all these pieces of furniture spring from your designs. I believe you will take the *ton* by storm."

She laughed. "I think that phrase is intended for beautiful women making their come-outs. The ones who turn the heads of all the rakes, as well as gentlemen truly in search of a bride."

He grew serious. "You are beautiful, Abby. You remind me even more of your mother than that day long ago when we first met. She could have wed any eligible gentleman that year. She chose your father. He was handsome. Carefree. Always happy." A shadow crossed his face. "I hope they enjoyed their time together."

"I believe they did, Magnus," she said quietly. "Papa only mentioned Mama now and then. When he did, his face always glowed, and his words praised her."

"He was a lucky man to have the both of you in his life."

Abby slipped her hand through his arm. "Come. We'll have Samuel drive us to Mayfair now. I am eager to get your opinion regarding my shop."

His brows arched. "I believe that is *our* shop," he teased.

"Our shop," she agreed. "If I earn enough, one day I might ask to buy you out."

He cupped her cheek. "What is mine, is yours, Abby. You have been a daughter to me and made my life richer for having come into it. I won't be able to leave you my country estate because it is entailed.

When the time comes, though, I will see you taken care of."

Her throat grew thick with tears, thinking of a time when Magnus might be gone. She swallowed and tried to make light of things. "I will take care of myself. *You* have taught me to do so."

He roared with laughter. "That I have. That I have."

They returned to Samuel's hansom cab, and he headed toward Mayfair.

Abby couldn't wait to hear what Magnus thought of Trent Furnishings.

Chapter Three

Norville—Norfolk

ELIJAH THANKED THE farmer who had given him a ride and hopped from the hay cart. He took a deep breath and then headed up the lane. He wouldn't go to the big house, which was the duke's. Or had been the duke's.

It was now his.

He wondered just how many houses he did own across England. So many questions plagued him. He would start getting answers from his mother. Gil had never pressed Mama about the past because he was so happy-go-lucky and figured whenever he became the Duke of Bradford, everything would magically fall into place. Elijah, on the other hand, had not asked Mama anything out of respect for her.

Yet there were many unanswered questions—and Mama would know the answer to more than a few of them. Now that he was the duke, he wanted to be prepared as much as possible for what lay ahead.

He crossed a meadow and then entered the woods on the other side of it, recalling the happy times he and Gil had played here. They never once had gone to the big house, always staying at the tiny cottage. At least living in those close quarters had better prepared him for life in the army. Countless complaints had sounded from officers who had led lives of ease. Usually, it was the second son of a family who had a commission bought for him. They hadn't worried about where their next meal might come from. A good majority of them had gone to university. Elijah would have enjoyed a university education. He was drawn to history and literature and would have found it fascinating to explore both in depth.

It wasn't meant to be, however. Gil and he were fortunate that Mama came into the inheritance she had and that she had willingly spent the bulk of it purchasing commissions for them. Being around other officers, Elijah had picked up quite a bit. It would help ease his transition in society.

The cottage came into view and he paused, a wave of emotions passing through him. This place had been home. Often, he had thought of it while away at war, thinking of Mama sitting with her sewing in her lap or stirring stew. Homesickness washed over him, and he pushed the distant memories of the past aside. He would never live in such a cramped place again. Never have to fight his twin for his half of the blanket. He would sleep in a bed with a feathered mattress instead of on the floor or in his army cot.

Everything would be different.

Instead of knocking, Elijah turned the handle and slipped into the cottage, wanting to surprise Mama. It was empty, though. An air of disuse blanketed it. No fire had burned in the grate for a while. No food was out.

Then he spied the single page on the table and went to it, reading it quickly.

Gil —

I have gone to the big house. No one can keep me out of it now that my son owns it. Hurry to me, my sweet boy. I do hope you bring Elijah with you.

Your loving mama,

A chill ran through him. She still didn't know Gil was gone.

Then he shook it off, thinking she had written this note soon after she had received word of her husband's death. Most likely, the letters she had written to her boys had been composed and sent from the big house, and she hadn't thought to return here. At least that was what Elijah hoped. It had been hard enough writing to her of Gil's death. If he had to tell her in person now, it might destroy them both.

Folding the note, he slipped it into his pocket and left the cottage for what he knew would be the last time. He didn't look back. Didn't pause and take it in. That life was over. It was the past.

He must continue to look to his future.

Elijah cut through the woods again, heading to the large stone edifice that dominated the landscape. He had never stepped inside it in the eighteen years he had spent on the property. He had been gone another nine years from England, fighting a war which seemed never-ending.

No one was outside the house. He approached the front door and paused, collecting himself, before knocking firmly. He would never need knock again. Servants would be watching for him, ready to wait on him hand and foot.

The door opened. From the dress of the man, he surmised this was his butler. The servant's staid expression changed in an instant. His eyes widened. His jaw dropped.

"Your Grace!" he said, more in shock than awe.

It confirmed everything Elijah had believed to be true. That he was like his father in looks.

The butler quickly recovered. "Won't you come inside, Your Grace? It is very cold today."

Elijah entered and then gazed about the huge foyer, taking in the chandelier. The paintings. The grandfather clock.

"My apologies, Your Grace. It is just that . . . well, you are so like him. Your father."

"Where is my mother?" he asked sharply, not wanting to hear how he resembled a dead man who had never bothered to meet his sons even once.

"Her Grace is in the drawing room. If you would follow me."

The butler moved up a grand staircase to the next floor. All along the corridor, they passed bits of furniture and paintings that were lavish. Even the thick carpet he trod upon was plush and obviously expensive. If this house were furnished so lavishly—and the duke never came here—then what would the other estates be like?

Pausing, the butler opened the door. "His Grace, the Duke of Bradford."

Elijah stepped into the room, saying, "Leave us," and sensing the door close behind him. His gaze went to the far side of the room, where a cheery fire burned in the grate. A woman rose from a chair near the fire, setting her book aside.

"Elijah!" Mama cried.

He crossed the room and wrapped her in his arms, holding her close. Then his hands settled on her waist, and he swung her about, hearing her laugh.

"Put me down," she told him.

He did as she asked, and they stared at one another, no words coming. Then tears welled in her eyes, and he knew she was thinking of Gil. Mama took his hands and squeezed them, leading him to a settee.

"Did you go to the cottage first?"

"I did. I found your note and came here straightaway."

"I wasn't going to spend one more night in that hovel," she said, venom in her voice.

Her words—and even more, her tone—took him aback. "I thought you loved our cottage."

"I hated it. I hated being exiled to it. Bradford was a stupid, obstinate fool. He condemned me to a life little more than a medieval serf. I was the daughter of an earl! I had been coddled my entire life. I had to learn how to cook and clean. Raise two boys on my own with no help from anyone."

Elijah shook his head. "You never for a single moment showed how miserable you were, Mama. You were always happy and smiling, making every day an adventure for us."

She cupped his cheek. "Because I had the two of you. You and Gil saved me. I had to go on because I had you. I knew no one would help me. I couldn't let you see my bitterness. I didn't want you to think me helpless. I had to learn to be a new person."

He took her hand and kissed it. "You did a magnificent job raising us in such horrible circumstances. Your optimism and joy are what I remember. Gil had a lot of you in him."

"Gil," she repeated quietly, tears starting to roll down her cheeks. "Oh, my darling boy. Gone."

Relief filled him. At least she had gotten his letter.

"I must apologize to you, Elijah."

"For what?" he asked, perplexed.

"I did favor Gil—and I knew you knew that I did. I couldn't help it. He was so sunny and carefree. It was obvious he was my child."

"While I looked like . . . him." Elijah couldn't even bring himself to say the duke's name.

"Yes, you did. From the beginning. Although I married Bradford when he was in his fifties, he was still a handsome man." She paused. "Looking at you, I can see now what he looked like in his prime."

"The butler looked as if he had seen a ghost when he opened the door."

Mama nodded. "You will get that from others, as well. Those who knew Bradford long ago." She wrung her hands in her lap. "If only he had pushed aside his pride for one minute and come to see you. He would have known you were his."

Elijah's gaze met hers. "Why did he think you had betrayed him, Mama?"

She glanced away. "It is in the past."

"I don't care," he said firmly, causing her to turn quickly to look at him again. "I have been respectful of you and your feelings, but I want answers now. I am the Duke of Bradford—and I deserve answers." Mama sucked in a quick breath. She nodded to herself, as if reaching a conclusion.

"You do, Elijah. You most certainly do. When I looked at you, I saw Bradford every time. It was as if he mocked me through you." She captured his hands in hers. "I do love you, Elijah. I always have. On a daily basis, I forced myself to look past your physical attributes. Then I could always see your caring heart and kindness. Your intelligence and willingness to look after your brother and me."

His jaw stiffened. "I didn't do a good job of that now, didn't I? Gil is dead."

"It was war, Elijah! I know I asked the impossible of you when I begged you to keep your brother safe. He was always so foolhardy. He would act without thinking. I did not mean to place such a burden upon you. I understand the enemy was all around you. You are only human, Elijah. You could not stop bullets from flying."

"You know it wasn't a bullet which killed Gil, Mama. I wrote to you of the circumstances."

She bit her trembling lip. "I know what happened. Gil saw someone in trouble and went to her aid. Short of tackling him to the ground and binding his ankles and wrists, you could not have stopped him, my sweet boy. You wrote that he did save that mother and her babe."

Unshed tears made his throat grow tight. "He did, Mama. I saw her just before I left Spain. I gave her twenty pounds to help her find a new place to live. She had another child, a daughter who was twelve. The three of them were going to take the money and return to the village she came from. Her husband had been killed days before."

"Then it is a good thing Gil saved her and her child," Mama said.

"The doctors told me sometimes a person escapes a fire, but their lungs suffer damage. That is what killed Gil."

"Did he suffer much?" she asked.

Elijah would always see his twin gasping for those last few breaths of air. "I was with him, Mama. He died in my arms. He was at peace. It was as if he went to sleep."

Better her think that than truly know how horrifying those last moments were.

"This will be wrong of me to say, but I will voice it nonetheless." Mama paused, searching his face as if she looked for something. "You will make for a better duke than your brother, Elijah. You have a steadfastness about you. You have a deep sense of responsibility and will see your tenants cared for. Gil would have assumed the title and then make light of it. He would have spent lavishly and enjoyed himself."

"That is a harsh assessment, Mama."

"It is," she agreed. "It does not mean I loved my firstborn less. I could see his failings, though. You will step up and be the good man you always have been, Elijah. I expect you to be a remarkable Duke of Bradford. You will take your place in Polite Society and the House of Lords. You will become familiar with the workings of all your estates, particularly Marblebridge. It is your ducal seat in Surrey. You will sire an heir and a spare and see that your line continues."

She smiled brightly. "We will go to town and meet with your solicitor. His name is Soames. He is the one who wrote to me and told me of Bradford's passing. There is no reason to stay in Norfolk any longer. I suggest we leave tomorrow morning. Once we've met with Soames and have a clearer idea of your situation, we can then go on to Surrey."

"I would ask for one day here, Mama, before we leave. I would like to see this house. Speak to the steward. Get to know Norville in a way

I never did during those years I grew up here. I may not return to the north for a good while. I might as well learn something about my estate before I am gone."

"That is wise, Elijah. See, I said you would make for an excellent duke. Would you like me to ring for some tea now? I would like us to catch up."

She stood and did so, taking her seat again. The butler appeared, and Mama asked for tea to be sent up.

"At once, Your Grace."

After the butler left, Elijah said, "It is odd hearing you being referred to in such a manner."

"It is my title by right. I should have been called so all along."

He looked at her steadily. "That is my question which you never really answered, Mama. Why did the duke think that Gil and I were fathered by another man?"

Tears misted her eyes. "Because I did love someone else. Long ago." She swallowed. "Perhaps I still do."

"Who?"

She shook her head, sorrow causing her to slump. "He was a steward. My father's steward. His name was Paul Baxter. I fancied myself madly in love with him. We had dreams of running away together and actually got part of the way to Gretna Green."

He frowned. "I don't know what that is."

"It is just across the border in Scotland. Couples who do not have their parents' blessings elope there. Scotland's laws regarding marriage differ from those in England. Paul and I were of age and could have wed at Gretna Green without parental consent."

Mama stood and began pacing the room. "We took two horses from the stables and were going to ride to London, where we would catch a mail coach to Scotland. Somehow, my father got word of our plans and chased us down in his carriage. Poor Paul was dismissed on the spot, dismissed without a reference. I was dragged home and told never to speak of the incident again. If I had, I would have been ruined."

She returned to the settee. "Instead, I made my come-out six months later. My heart still loved Paul, but I knew we could never be together. I actually had several gentlemen courting me when my father announced that I would wed the Duke of Bradford." She sighed. "I was eighteen. He was thirty-five years my senior. He had been married twice before. The first marriage resulted in three girls. The second produced no children. I was his third wife—and greatest hope for an heir."

"How did he learn of Paul? Did he come to see you?"

"No. That is what was so ridiculous about the entire matter. Yes, I was a fool and kept letters which Paul had written to me. Bradford hired a lady's maid for me. She was loyal to him and not me. She snooped through my things and found those letters, taking them to the duke. He read them and then summoned me. I had told him the month before that I was with child. He had been overjoyed, telling me that he knew this time he would get his heir."

"He confronted you about your lover?"

"He did, raging at me. Telling me that I was already much too large and that I had gotten with child before our wedding. How I had fooled him and that my father must have been in on the ruse, pawning me off when I already carried another man's child. I wept. I begged him to listen to me. I had not lain with Paul. He had not wanted us to do so before we were legally man and wife. Bradford, however, refused to listen. He had the maid pack my things and told me he was sending me as far away from him as he could, to an estate he rarely visited and where the weather was terrible."

Mama brushed away her tears. "I know now that because I carried twins, I did appear to be further along. I wrote Bradford once a few months had passed and the midwife here told me I was almost certain to produce twins. Even after I gave birth to you and Gil and saw you were Bradford's spitting image, even as a babe, my letters to my husband remained unanswered. He believed the worst of me. Nothing would sway him. He wanted nothing to do with me or the two of you."

"It was his loss," Elijah said. "I am only sorry you loved another and were forced to wed Bradford."

"It is in the past, my boy. We must look to the future."

He agreed but could still hear Mama say that she might still love Paul Baxter. She had suffered for so many years, stripped of her place in society and forced to live in poverty.

When they reached London, Elijah would do everything in his power to see if he might be able to locate this man.

And right the wrongs done to his mother so long ago.

Chapter Four

Elijah and his mother arrived in London on a mail coach. Norville had no ducal carriage—nor a carriage of any kind. The few times the Duke of Bradford had visited the estate had been years earlier, and he had always come via his own coach. The Norville butler explained to Elijah that a private carriage could be rented in Norwich. It would involve numerous stops and the need to locate a new team of horses each time, as well as replacing the driver.

He told Mama that a mail coach would be much faster, leaving out that it would be uncomfortable. Elijah had traveled from Spain to London by ship and then taken a mail carriage to Norwich. She had gone along with his decision, packing a trunk. He had no luggage beyond a small satchel containing a few personal items, such as a fresh shirt and his razor and comb. He continued to wear his military uniform. He would need to see a tailor and have civilian clothes made up for him as soon as possible, as well as have Mama see a dressmaker.

He noted that she was slightly better dressed than she had been during his childhood and supposed she had spent a bit of the money he and Gil had sent home on herself. Still, she was a duchess and needed a vast improvement in what she wore. She had talked to him about taking his place among the *ton*, but it truly was the last thing he wished to do. He hated them. Everything about them. How shallow the people were. How no one had come to his mother's aid after she had been cast aside by her husband—not even her own family. They had cut off all contact with her, taking Bradford's side. Elijah dreaded the day he ran into anyone related to Mama and would have to control his temper. He didn't think punching out anyone was a good idea, much less in a London ballroom.

Not only did he not wish to be a part of the *ton*, he had no plans to marry. Mama had already begun talking to him about the upcoming Season. From what he gathered, members of Polite Society came together for social events to gossip, dance, play cards, and look for a suitable mate. He cared nothing for gossip. He didn't know how to dance. Cards were a mere distraction. And as for finding a mate? He would not do so. He loathed his father and the fact that he now followed in the man's footsteps. If he did not wed, then he would not produce an heir. Bradford had been so eager to marry Mama because he had no other living male relatives who could inherit the dukedom. If Elijah did not provide an heir, the title would revert to the crown.

And he was perfectly happy with that occurring.

Mama would hate it, of course. She would want him to dress in finery and choose a woman to become his duchess. Elijah simply didn't have it in him. He still felt half-complete with Gil being gone, as if part of him was missing and always would be. It wouldn't be fair to marry and be a ghost in a marriage, which is how he felt. He would do his duty and take his seat in the House of Lords. Learn everything he could about his estates and care for his tenants. But the ducal title would end with him. He would brook no argument on that topic. All he had to do now was inform Mama of his decision.

All bloody hell would break loose when he did.

He retrieved her trunk and brought it to her. "Should we go see Soames now?"

"We have no appointment, Elijah," Mama said.

"I am a duke," he said gruffly. "I would think I wouldn't need an appointment."

"True, but it would be nice to freshen up a bit before we do so. We should take a hansom cab to your townhouse."

"I don't even know where it is, Mama."

"I do," she said, her eyes gleaming. "It is one of the grandest places in town."

They located a hansom cab and gave the driver the address.

"Home from the war, Major?" the coachman asked, recognizing his rank.

"Yes," he replied, helping the man lift Mama's trunk.

"I've a brother fighting. In Spain. He says he's afraid it'll be another Hundred Years War."

Elijah shuddered. "Let's hope not."

The cabbie took up his reins. Mama kept a running dialogue going, telling Elijah about the different places they passed and what various areas of town were called. She looked so happy to be back in London. He had never thought about what her exile had meant. She had always been optimistic and cheerful around Gil and him. Though they had struggled to make ends meet, he had never felt deprived in any way.

Now, he realized just how miserable she had been. Mama had been a young, beautiful, entitled woman who'd had everything ripped from her. She had been banished from the world she had always known, with no family or friends to support her. At least she would soon be back in her element. The least he could do was see her restored to her old life. Or actually, her new one. She would be a duchess and free to do as she pleased. He knew clothes would be important and would see her properly garbed.

He sensed the excitement in Mama as she said, "This is Mayfair, Elijah. The most prestigious part of the city. We will soon be home."

He wondered how she could refer to it as home when she had only lived in the townhouse a few months. Then the hansom cab slowed as they turned into a square, and he saw what had to be his. A grand house. This was no home. This was a palace, one fit for a king.

He thought of his humble beginnings and the life he had led in the tiny, one-room cottage. The fact he not only owned this property, but would also live in it, boggled his mind.

"Here we are, Major," the cabbie called. He bounded down from his seat and said, "Let me help you with the trunk."

Elijah left the vehicle and handed down Mama and then allowed the cab driver to assist him in bringing the trunk to the front door. He paid the man, who doffed his hat and then returned to his cab.

Elijah faced Mama. "I suppose we should knock," he said, his belly churning.

"Yes, please do so."

He stepped to the door and rapped on it before moving back two paces.

Nothing happened.

Frowning, he moved to the door again and knocked even harder.

"This is extremely odd," Mama said. "A footman should be stationed by the front door at all times. I do not understand why no one is responding."

"Might I help you?" a voice called.

Looking over Mama's shoulder, he saw a man of about six feet tall and thirty years of age.

"Yes," he replied. "No one seems to be answering our knock."

His words seemed to stun the man. Then he said, "*You* are the new duke. The Duke of Bradford."

"I am."

A pained expression crossed the stranger's face. "I'm afraid you will not find anyone at home, Your Grace. All but a handful of the servants were dismissed months ago. The others left service once His Grace passed."

"What do you mean—left service?" Mama demanded. "A new duke was coming. Servants should be here, ready to greet us."

Reluctance filled the man's face, and Elijah knew that this man held the key to more than a few mysteries.

"Might I inquire as to whom you might be?" he asked.

"I am Nelson—like the admiral—and I am a footman next door for Lord Ritter. Servants gossip. That's a fact. I know quite a bit about your household, Your Graces, and the situation." He paused. "It is not pleasant."

"You aren't dressed as a footman," Elijah said.

"Lord Ritter allows the butler to give each footman and maid one afternoon a month off. In the past, I have visited my mother in Cheapside for a few hours. I lost her just before Christmas past, however."

"Do you have plans today, Nelson?" he asked.

"I like to walk in the park, Your Grace. It's always nice to get out for some fresh air. Sometimes, I even go to a bookstore. One of the housemaids and I enjoy reading. We pool our money and buy a book every now and then for the two of us to share."

"I will pay you for your time today, Nelson, if you come inside with us and share everything you know. I have just returned from the Peninsular War, and Her Grace and I arrived in London not an hour ago. We would appreciate your help."

He saw the footman mull over things a moment, and then Nelson said, "All right, Your Grace. I will be happy to tell you all that I know. We should go in through the kitchens, I would think. Follow me."

He looked to Mama, who nodded at him. Then he lifted her trunk, placing it on his shoulder. The two of them followed Nelson along the pavement and down a set of stairs, where Elijah assumed the kitchens were.

"I'll have to break a window, Your Grace. There is no other way to get inside your property unless you go to your solicitor and obtain a key."

"He is our next stop, but we are here now. Get us in however you can. We can see to the damage later."

The footman removed a handkerchief and wrapped it about his hand before slamming his fist several times into a window. Once the glass broke, he reached inside and turned a lock. Nelson swung open the kitchen door and entered, holding it in place.

"Your Graces?"

Mama swept inside, and Elijah followed, setting the trunk onto the floor as Nelson closed the door. The kitchens were enormous. Then again, he knew it would take many servants to run such a large establishment. The amount of food prepared for the family and these servants would be tremendous.

"Perhaps we should go into the drawing room, Nelson. You can tell us what you know," Mama said.

The footman winced. "Your Grace, we may head to the drawing room, but I don't believe you would wish to stay there."

"Why on earth not?" Mama asked.

"Because I doubt you will find anyplace to sit upon."

Nelson's words baffled Elijah and his mother. "Why would a drawing room not have a place to sit?" he demanded.

"May I have permission to speak frankly, Your Grace?"

He nodded. "I need to know as much as possible, Nelson. Hold nothing back."

"Very well, Your Grace." The footman swallowed. "It is common knowledge among the *ton* and their servants that the former duke believed his young wife cuckolded him and the two sons she bore were not of his blood."

It was bad enough knowing the duke had banished Mama for believing that, but for it to be public knowledge in Polite Society upset Elijah to no end.

"That being said," the footman continued, "that will be dispelled the moment you are out and about. You see, you greatly resemble your father. Once people see you, there will be no doubt that the old duke had been mistaken—and dreadfully wronged you and your mother. Your brother, as well."

"My brother died in the war recently," Elijah said tersely.

Sympathy filled the footman's face. "I am very sorry for your loss, Your Grace. I, too, lost my brother to the war. He served over seven years for His Majesty."

"My condolences to you, as well. Go on."

"The former duke's health had declined for a few years," Nelson explained. "Gradually, he no longer set foot outside his townhouse. Servants were dismissed, left and right, until only His Grace's cook and valet remained. His Grace, believing a man not of his blood would take his place, wanted to make things . . . difficult for you. He ordered that everything in the house be sold off."

"*Sold off?*" Mama asked. "I am not certain I understand, Nelson."

"His Grace . . . wanted things to be uncomfortable, Your Grace. My understanding is that every stick of furniture in the place was sold, except for the duke's bed. The valet and cook slept on cots. I don't know how many rooms the house has—probably seventy-five or more—and you won't find anything within them. Every piece of furniture, every carpet, every painting and work of art is gone. We saw them being carted away."

"Gone," Elijah echoed, rage filling him. "Do you know what happened to the money from the sales?"

"That I cannot answer, Your Grace. You will have to speak with your solicitor regarding that matter. You will need to refurnish the entire house, this one and your country estates, as well. I heard the duke had everyone let go at all of those houses, as well. Only the stewards remained employed in order to oversee the estates and their tenants."

Nelson brightened. "The good news is that you and Her Grace may refurnish all your homes however you wish."

Elijah could not imagine what it would take to refurnish not only this enormous townhouse, but however many houses he owned in the country. It was cruel of his father to have done something of this nature. It not only affected him, but also the hundreds of servants who had lost their positions due to one man's pettiness.

"Thank you for sharing this information, Nelson," he said. "It is a lot to take in."

"I'm sorry you will have to go through so much trouble, Your Graces. I can recommend an inn nearby that you might stay at while you work on refurnishing your home. I also know of an employment agency where you might begin looking in order to compile a staff in town. I assume you will remain for the Season and the session in the House of Lords."

This man had been quite helpful, and Elijah wanted to reward him. Instead of offering money to the footman, he had an idea.

"Are you happy in your position with Lord Ritter? Do you have higher aspirations beyond being a footman?"

"Every servant worth his salt aspires to move up within a household, Your Grace. Why do you ask?"

"Because I am going to be in need of a great number of servants. I will need someone whom I trust."

"I currently am a footman and have a chance to become the head footman by year's end when Lord Ritter's head footman retires. I would be honored, Your Grace, to become *your* head footman and train those footmen you hire to their positions."

Elijah looked to Mama, who must have read his mind, because she nodded encouragingly. He turned back to Nelson.

"I had a different position in mind for you. I would like for you to be my butler."

The footman's eyes grew round. "You aren't jesting, are you? I am only thirty years of age."

"Do you think you have the skills needed in order to manage this household? Could you handle a large staff of servants?"

"Given the opportunity, I will tell you in no uncertain terms that I am up for the challenge. It would be an honor to serve you and Her Grace."

"Then you must put in notice at once at Lord Ritter's. I hope I will not have alienated my new neighbor by stealing his soon-to-be head footman."

Nelson chuckled. "I doubt Lord Ritter would care. He comes to town infrequently. We received word only yesterday that he would not be attending the Season this year. Perhaps the only person who might get his nose out of joint will be the butler."

"Then I will accompany you to see him now. I would like you to start immediately, Nelson."

The newly-named butler beamed with pride. "I would be happy to do so, Your Grace."

Elijah turned to Mama. "Would you like to look over the house while we are gone?"

"No. You won't be gone long, Bradford. I will wait here in the kitchens for you so that we may view your house together."

Sadness washed over him as he realized Mama would forever address him as Bradford in front of others from now on. She had explained to him that would be the case. Hearing it come from her lips for the first time let him know the door to his past was now firmly shut, and the new one to his future opened.

Chapter Five

Elijah accompanied Nelson next door, and they approached the front door. Their knock was responded to immediately, and a footman showed them in, puzzled why Nelson accompanied the new Duke of Bradford.

"I wish to speak to your butler at once," Elijah said.

The butler appeared moments later, and Elijah introduced himself. The same look that Nelson had given Elijah surfaced on the butler's face as he realized the new Duke of Bradford extremely favored the former one.

"Since I have no servants, I am in need of an entire staff," he said crisply. "I have met Nelson, here, and he is to be my new butler. I have told him to give his notice at once. He's to pack his things now and come next door. Is that understood?"

He had spoken firmly, as he had with his men when he addressed them. The butler seemed gobsmacked and merely nodded.

"Good. Nelson, go pack and come next door as soon as you have finished."

"Yes, Your Grace," his new butler responded, jauntily walking away, a spring in his step.

"Thank you," Elijah said to the butler, leaving the house and returning next door once more through the kitchens where Mama waited.

"Ready to give me a tour?" he asked.

"I am happy to do so, Bradford."

"Must you address me in such a manner even when we are alone, Mama?"

She looked perplexed. "It is the done thing." She paused. "You will always be Elijah in my heart, my boy, but we are in a new world now and must play by its rules." She slipped her arm through his. "Come."

They started at the top of the house and worked their way downward. Every room was bare. No curtains hung at the windows. No rugs rested on the floors. Not a piece of furniture was in any room, save for the duke's rooms. Only a massive bed sat there, rumpled bedclothes still on it. He supposed with the duke's death that the valet knew he would no longer be paid and left everything as it was. A cot was in the corner, and he assumed the valet had slept on it.

They went through a room which Mama said was the duke's dressing room. It, too, was bare. The fact the man had been so spiteful that he had even gotten rid of his entire wardrobe irked Elijah. At the same time, he was glad that all traces of Bradford were gone. He decided he would dispose of the bed, not wanting to sleep where the old bastard had.

Nelson joined them, having quickly packed his things and placing them in the butler's room. He accompanied them for the rest of their tour. Between Mama and Nelson, Elijah got a better idea of the house. There was a billiard room with no table. A study with no desk. A library which held no books. How petty of the duke to have even sold every book.

"We will head to Mr. Soames' offices now," Elijah informed his new butler. "You will need to begin working on hiring my staff."

"Might I ask one thing before I do so, Your Grace?"

"Of course. I want as much transparency as possible between us. I will be very clear on my end regarding my expectations. I have been an army officer for many years and preferred being direct and succinct with my men. It will be the same with you. I hope you will appreciate my forthrightness."

Nelson nodded. "I couldn't agree with you more. If I—and others—are to serve you, I prefer to have clear instructions to pass along." He paused. "I would like to first add a housekeeper to the staff and work with her on all the rest of the hirings. I have someone in mind."

Elijah guessed, "Would it be the housemaid you previously mentioned?"

The servant's cheeks pinkened. "Yes, Your Grace. I have every intention of marrying her. We will be a good team together and serve you well."

"I think it an excellent idea," Mama chimed in. "As housekeeper, your wife will have a huge say-so in how the household will be run. Having her advice as you build the staff will be wise. When will you wed?"

Nelson gave her a sheepish smile. "Actually, we already have, Your Grace. We did so a few weeks before Christmas. My mother was ill, and we decided to go ahead and do so."

Mama smiled at their new butler. "I am certain it made it easier for her to leave, knowing you had someone to be with you."

"No one knows," Nelson revealed. "We haven't told a soul, but I would like to have her serve as our housekeeper. She is bright and organized and will keep me *and* your household in good order."

"Then go next door and see that you bring back your bride, Nelson," Elijah declared. "There was a second cot in the cook's room off the kitchen. You can retrieve it and the one in the bedchamber and sleep on those until I can purchase a bed for the two of you to sleep upon." He sighed. "This is going to be a massive project."

Mama patted his forearm. "We can take it one room at a time, Bradford. Nelson and Mrs. Nelson will be invaluable in the process. Retrieve your wife and then begin making a list of servants you believe to be necessary in order to run this household. We can meet tomorrow morning and discuss it. Ten o'clock."

"Yes, Your Grace," said the butler. "Our list will be ready."

Nelson shared the name of the inn he had suggested and said he would go there now and reserve rooms for them for the next week.

"No, we can go directly there ourselves," Elijah said. "It is more important for you to extract Mrs. Nelson from Lord Ritter's house. We will see you tomorrow morning."

"Thank you, Your Grace," Nelson said, his face earnest. "I realize you are taking a chance by hiring us both, especially since we do not have the experience in the positions we are being hired for. I promise you this. We will not let you down. You shall always get the best from us both."

He nodded. "Thank you for your candor, Nelson. I assume the duke sold his carriage and horses?"

"Not the carriage, Your Grace. Just the horses. We will see about getting you a coachman first, and then you can go to Tattersall's to purchase a team."

At least he knew something about horseflesh after his time in the army, so selecting horses wouldn't be as frightening as the rest of the myriad of things he had to do.

"See to finding us a hansom cab, then. I'll retrieve the trunk."

"Let me do both, Your Grace."

Seeing it was important to Nelson, he agreed. Soon, they were in a cab on the way to his solicitor's, Mama's trunk and his satchel along for the ride.

When they arrived, he asked the cabbie to wait with the trunk, telling him they would then head to an inn. He paid the man double for the completed leg, and the driver was perfectly content to wait for him to return.

They entered Soames' offices, and he told the clerk who he was and that he must speak to Mr. Soames at once.

"Yes, Your Grace," the young man said, awe in his eyes. "I'll be right back."

In less than a minute, a portly man strode into the receiving room. He stopped in his tracks, taken aback a moment, then recovered. "Your Graces. I am Mr. Soames. Please, won't you come this way?"

The solicitor led them to a large office and had them sit, offering them a cup of tea. They accepted, and the clerk was sent to bring it to them.

"We have much to discuss, Your Graces." Soames paused. "My condolences to you both."

"We do not need or want them," Elijah said. "I never laid eyes on the duke, and Her Grace hadn't seen him in years."

"Of course," Soames corrected. "Thank you for coming. We have much to discuss."

"Such as how much money was raised selling every bit of furniture in each house I now own?"

The solicitor cleared his throat, clearly uncomfortable. "A most unfortunate thing. I spoke to His Grace at length, hoping to convince him to change his mind. He was bound and determined, however, to make life as difficult as he could for his heir."

"Actually, I was not his heir," Elijah said. "I am the second-born brother. My twin, Gilford Young, was older by a few minutes." He paused. "Gil was lost to us at Cuidad Rodrigo."

Soames visibly trembled at the news. "That is most disheartening news, Your Grace. My sympathies to both of you."

"Thank you," Mama said quietly. "I had not seen my elder son in over nine years. It is a painful loss to endure. Thankfully, my other boy has come home to me and assumed the title." She hesitated and then said, "It may be for the best. We have been informed of the gossip which has spread among the *ton* over the years. I had hoped that my husband would not be so foolish as to air his false lies, but it seems that is not the case. All of Polite Society's eyes will be upon the new Bradford—and there is no way he will be mistaken for anyone other than his father's son. Gilford took his looks after me. There would always have been questions when he assumed the title because of that."

"No one could deny that His Grace is anyone but his father's son," Soames assured them. "The resemblance between the two of you is remarkable. Her Grace is correct in saying that will sway Polite Society's opinion. You—and your mother—will be welcomed with open arms."

"In the meantime, I have not a chair to sit upon, nor a cook to bring me even a cup of tea," Elijah said disagreeably.

"I have the funds from all the sales, Your Grace," Soames told them. "It was a massive undertaking in the last months of the duke's life. Everything was sold in town. At Marblebridge, your country seat. At three other estates. The only place not touched was the house in Norfolk and that is simply because time ran out, and it was the farthest away. Once everything there had been sold, I was instructed to give away all the monies to various charities. His Grace did not want his heir to have access to any of the proceeds."

"I assume it is in my bank account," he said.

"It is, Your Grace. Let us spend an hour now discussing your various holdings and investments. It will be a mere overview in order to acquaint you with your financial position. We will need to spend hours, at a later date, and make certain you have a good understanding of what you possess."

"Go ahead," Elijah encouraged.

It was closer to two hours by the time Soames finished. Elijah teetered on the edge of being addlepated with so much thrown at him.

"You can see that you are secure financially, Your Grace," the solicitor said. "In fact, you are one of the richest men in England."

"I suppose I can afford a few pieces of furniture," he said drily.

Soames laughed aloud. "Oh, you can certainly fill your homes again with whatever pieces you choose. Her Grace will be most helpful in redecorating the properties and selecting the artwork for them."

"I will do some of it," Mama declared. "Here in town is most important. My son will wed soon, though, in order to secure the ducal line. His duchess should be the one to select the furnishings for Marblebridge and the other estates."

Elijah knew now was not the time to reveal that he had no intentions of ever wedding. Rising, he said, "Thank you for your time, Mr. Soames. We will schedule another meeting soon. I will be in touch."

"Very well, Your Grace. Let me know how I can help."

The solicitor gave Elijah the keys to his townhouse and walked them to the receiving area and opened the door. "I look forward to our next meeting."

As Mama walked through the open door, he turned back to Soames. "Draw up a list of suitable dressmakers. Tailors, as well. Send that to me as soon as possible. It is important that if Mama is to rejoin Polite Society that she look the part of a duchess."

He stepped through the door and as he turned his head forward again, Elijah collided hard with someone.

"I beg your pardon," he said, reaching out and grabbing on to a falling woman. Trying to right her, he only managed to force her forward, and she crashed into him.

"Oh!" she exclaimed, her ample breasts pressed against his chest as he clutched her upper arms.

Oh, indeed.

She was a very beautiful woman. One with dark blond hair and a willowy frame. From where she stood against him, he judged her to be about five inches over five feet. And she smelled divine. Her scent was rich and sweet. Intoxicating.

"What is the scent you wear?" he asked, his gaze meeting large, blue eyes.

"Jasmine," she said, her voice low and sultry. "Legend has it that a

Tuscan gardener guarded his treasured jasmine plant and would not allow anyone to cut from it. When it eventually bloomed, he gave it to the woman he loved. She was so enchanted by his gesture that she decided to marry him."

Elijah's heart began pounding against his ribs. "It is mesmerizing."

"My brief story . . . or my perfume?" the woman asked, a teasing light in her eyes.

He became aware he still held her close, her breasts pushed into his chest. He quickly released his grasp on her, taking a step back, the heady scent of jasmine still in his nostrils.

"Both," he said, smiling.

She returned his smile. "I know this is an awkward meeting, my lord, but allow me to introduce us."

"Us?" he echoed and looked around, spying Mama standing next to an older gentleman.

He desperately hoped this man was her father.

And not her husband.

The woman said, "This is the Earl of Ladiwyck. He served as my guardian for many years and is now my closest friend."

Relief swept through Elijah. He offered his hand to the man. "Good afternoon, my lord. I am the Duke of Bradford." He turned. "And this is my mother, the Duchess of Bradford."

Ladiwyck bowed to Mama. "A pleasure to meet you, Your Graces. May I present Miss Abigail Trent? As she said, I was once her guardian." He grinned. "Though she kept me in line far more than I did her, from Egypt to Greece to North America."

Miss Abigail Trent . . .

"Ah, so you have traveled extensively," Mama said.

"We did for a decade," Lord Ladiwyck said. "We are back in England for now. Miss Trent is putting down roots and starting a business. I plan to remain a while and support her efforts. At least until the spirt of wanderlust takes root in me again, and I feel the need to travel once more."

Elijah found his voice. "A business. How interesting. I don't know many ladies who start their own business."

Miss Trent laughed, sending goosebumps along his arms. "I daresay you don't know many ladies, Your Grace. If you are still wearing a uniform, I suppose you are new to your title and only recently back from the war."

"You guessed correctly, Miss Trent," he said. "Mama and I arrived in London today. But I would be most interested to hear about your venture." It was the only thing he could think of to be able to spend more time with her.

"Then come to tea with us, Your Grace," Lord Ladiwyck said. "We were just leaving our solicitor's office and heading home."

"We, too, were leaving my solicitor's office." He looked to Mama. "Would you like to go to tea at Lord Ladiwyck's?"

"That would be delightful," she proclaimed.

Ladiwyck shared his address, and Elijah said, "We are in that hansom cab. Perhaps the driver can follow you to your home."

"You have no carriage of your own, Your Grace?" Miss Trent asked. "I have never heard of a duke without a carriage."

"I discovered that I do have one. I simply don't have the horses to pull it," he said, laughing.

"Then you are welcome to ride with us," Miss Trent said.

"My trunk," Mama reminded him. "It is with the cabbie."

"You truly did just arrive in town," Miss Trent exclaimed. "Why don't you have the driver follow us and bring it along? After tea, Magnus—that is, Lord Ladiwyck—can give you use of his carriage to return home." She paused, mischief in her eyes. "That is, if you actually know where your home is."

Elijah laughed. "Oh, we have been there, Miss Trent. That was our first stop. It is an interesting story."

"Then please tell it to us over tea."

"I will give the driver my address, Your Grace, if you will accompany the ladies to my carriage," the earl said.

He did so, handing up Mama and then taking Miss Trent's hand. Even gloved, he felt the heat in her fingers.

And suddenly, wanted to kiss her. Very badly.

He waited for Lord Ladiwyck, who climbed into the vehicle. Elijah followed—and saw the open spot was beside Miss Trent. He took it. Immediately, the subtle scent of jasmine tickled his nose.

Curiosity filled him. He wanted to learn everything he could about this woman.

Chapter Six

ABBY WANTED TO kiss this duke in the worst way possible. The thought surprised her because kissing had not been of interest to her in the past. Yes, she had kissed a few men in their various travels. An Italian conte. An Egyptian tour guide. Even the Administrator of Ontario. None of these men and their kisses had tempted her to move beyond the kiss.

What was it about this man? A duke, of all people, who appealed to her so much.

Perhaps it was the uniform he wore—and how well he wore it. The snug trousers displayed his muscled thighs to perfection. He was around six feet tall, lean but muscular, filling out the rest of his uniform nicely. She liked how today's sun brought out golden highlights in his brown hair. His hazel eyes had changed color as they had spoken, revealing that he, too, might be interested in her. He brimmed with confidence, a very appealing quality to her. Though his manners had been polite, she sensed a bit of rough and tumble about him, chalking that up to his army years being ones at constant war.

Since he was back, she assumed he had not been the heir apparent, rather a second son who had inherited the title by default.

Looking to the duke, she asked, "Where were you stationed, Your Grace?"

"I had been fighting in Spain under the leadership of Major-

General Craufurd. Wellington was our overall commander. The final battle I participated in was at Cuidad Rodrigo last month."

"I read of that battle in the newspapers recently," Magnus said. "Wellington was made an earl and gained a healthy pension for his efforts. Taking that French garrison will surely allow our troops to push south, I would imagine."

"Yes, my lord," said the duke. "You are correct. My guess is that British forces and their Spanish and Portuguese allies will now move to Badajoz and take it. The victory at Cuidad Rodrigo also allowed for a northern gateway to open from Portugal into the French-dominated portion of Spain."

Curious, Abby asked, "Will you miss the fighting? I mean to say that you look to be a major to me, which indicates you have been at war for a good while now, Your Grace. Will you find the transition back to Polite Society difficult?"

She watched as he mulled over his answer before speaking and liked that about him even more. Too many people were rash as they spoke, not putting any thought behind what they said.

"I will miss the life itself," the duke shared. "Mama purchased my commission when I was but eight and ten years of age. I left England after a few weeks of training. I have spent my entire adult life at war."

She thought it interesting that he said his mother purchased the commission and not his father or family.

"The life was fairly regimented. I trained with my men, and then we would receive our orders and march to the next encounter. My men became as family to me, and I do worry for their safety and wellbeing, as well as that of my fellow officers."

"How do you climb the ladder, so to speak?" she asked. "A major is a high rank to attain for one of your age."

"I am seven and twenty. Proving yourself—your leadership, the way you handle your men, the skills you possess—they all factor into promotions. Unfortunately, the more officers killed by our enemy, the easier it becomes to climb this so-called ladder you speak of. As far as fitting into society? I have never been a part of it and may yet choose to remain separate from it."

The duchess clucked her tongue. "This is all new to my son. I am certain once he gets his bearings that he will be a full participant in Polite Society. After all, he will need to wed and provide an heir."

Surprise filled Abby as she saw anger spark in the duke's eyes. His jaw tightened, and he looked as if he wanted to say something but chose to remain silent. Something told her that he and his mother were going to have a future conversation about her remarks. Perhaps the duke had left a sweetheart behind all those years ago and might try to connect with her again. It was none of Abby's business, though.

Even if the urge to kiss him had yet to subside.

She looked to the duchess. "Since you have your trunk with you, Your Grace, I assume that you were not living in town during your son's years away. Where have you been residing? At the ducal country estate?"

"I have been living in Norfolk, close to Norwich, where my husband had an estate. We were estranged for many years. I brought my sons up there."

Intrigue now filled her. She knew oftentimes marriages of convenience in the *ton* were most inconvenient ones. That couples lived apart for many years. It was interesting, however, that the duchess said she had raised her sons herself. Usually, male children remained with their fathers, especially those who would inherit a title.

"Where are you other sons, Your Grace?" Abby asked politely.

A pained expression crossed the duchess' face. "My older boy recently was lost to me."

The duke added, "It was the day of the Battle of Cuidad Rodrigo. Once I brought Gil's body back to camp, the letter from Mama was delivered, letting us know the Duke of Bradford was gone." He sighed. "My brother was a duke for a short while and did not even know it."

Part of this made more sense to her. It was common for second sons to enter the army since the firstborn would receive the title, wealth, and lands. For the heir to a duke to have also gone to war, knowing the dangers of battle, shocked her.

The duchess cleared her throat. "Since you have been gone from England for many years on your travels, you may not know of the gossip that plagues us."

Magnus gently said, "You owe us no explanation, Your Grace. The *ton* forms their opinions. Often, they are wrong."

The duchess nodded. "They were in this case. Bradford accused me of infidelity shortly after I became with child. He sent me away. I never saw him again, only receiving news of his death last month by letter. That is when I wrote the twins in order to let them know they should return to England. Little did I know that Gil would not come home to me."

Magnus offered the duchess his handkerchief, and she dabbed her eyes with it.

Turning to the duke, Abby said, "As an only child, I can only imagine how difficult it must be to lose a brother. To lose your twin must be excruciating."

"It is as if I am missing half of me," he said. "I assumed one day Gil would become the Duke of Bradford, and I would remain in His Majesty's army. Little did I know in a cruel twist of fate that I would lose my brother and inherit a title I never wanted nor cared for."

She could understand some of his feelings, hearing both the vehemence and hurt in his voice. To know one's own father had accused his mother of infidelity and rejected her and the sons she bore, never seeing his children, must be incredibly painful. Losing a beloved brother and having to take on responsibilities that never should have been his would prove to be difficult.

Abby's heart ached for this man.

The carriage came to a halt, and Magnus said, "A good cup of tea can always make things seem better." He climbed from the carriage, and Abby allowed the duchess to go first.

Before she stood, the duke placed a hand on her forearm, causing her belly to flip over twice. "Do not think I won't carry out my duties, Miss Trent. I am committed to do so, if only in the name of my brother."

She quietly said, "I can well understand that, Your Grace," and then exited the carriage.

They entered the foyer, and Feathers greeted them.

"Tea in the drawing room for the four of us, Feathers," she said, leading their guests upstairs.

As they entered, she couldn't help but look at the duke as his eyes passed over the various items she and Magnus had collected over the years, as well as ones Magnus had brought home from his various travels.

"You have a most impressive drawing room, my lord," the duke said.

"I never seemed to fit into my family," Magnus revealed. "From the time I was young, I had the urge to explore. I began my travels upon graduation from university and rarely have I set foot in England since then."

Abby directed them to two settees near the fire, and Magnus sat next to the duchess, leaving her to sit beside the duke.

"Was it what you read that made you want to see the world?" the duchess asked.

"Reading did spark my interest, Your Grace. Even as a boy, I wandered our country estate far and wide and knew it much better than my own father or the steward who ran it. I became the earl a few months before leaving university. With both my parents gone and no siblings, I indulged my desire to roam the earth."

"You must have come back at some point for Miss Trent," the duke pointed out.

"Yes, I did return periodically to England." Magnus waved a hand. "You can see some of the treasures I have collected over the years. I would have them shipped back to this house and would return here for brief sojourns before heading out on my next adventure. My closest friend was Miss Trent's father and when he passed, he asked that he take her into my care. I gave Abby the choice of attending school here in England and then making her come-out as a proper young lady should—or joining me as I moved about."

"That was a brave choice on your part, Miss Trent," the duke said, admiration in his eyes.

"I agree," the duchess added. "I cannot think of a single girl from my own come-out Season who would have put aside entering the *ton* in order to travel."

"I suppose my upbringing was a bit unconventional," Abby said. "My mother died in childbirth when I was quite young, and so my father took it upon himself to educate me. I never had a governess. Instead, Papa saw the world as my oyster. He himself taught me to read and write, and then tutored me in a variety of subjects."

"When did you lose him?" the duke asked.

"I was fourteen years of age. Thankfully, Lord Ladiwyck saw I was a mature four and ten and gave me the choice he did. My education continued as we went abroad. We have seen the Great Pyramids of Egypt. The Taj Mahal in India. Saint Basil's Cathedral in Moscow. Roamed the hills of Tuscany and the Acropolis in Athens. Even ventured more than once across the Atlantic to our former colonies. New York and Boston are both thriving cities, and Lord Ladiwyck enjoyed meeting various political figures in Washington, D.C. We even dined with the man who was president at the time of our visit, a visionary named Jefferson. He is a scholar, writer, and inventor. I would enjoy returning to America at some point, but it looks as if war is on the horizon with the Americans, making it impossible."

She looked to the duke. "I feel it is foolish for Britain to split His

Majesty's forces and fight both in Europe against Bonaparte and three thousand miles away. What are your views, Your Grace?"

The duke grew thoughtful. "I believe America will be a better trading partner to us in the long run than an enemy. Men surrounding King George believe they can break America and bring her to her knees, forcing her back under British rule. I feel that is a foolish notion. The colonists stood up to us once before, and they will do so again in this coming war, even more united than previously. I hope our war department will come to its senses and if they do start a war overseas, decide to sign a quick peace with our American cousins so that those soldiers and officers who would fight in America could return. Until they do, Bonaparte will still have a slight advantage."

He shifted slightly. "Don't misunderstand what I say," he cautioned. "We have brilliant strategists on our side, Wellington, in particular. I have never been more impressed by a commander than Wellington. But he can only do so much with what he is given. And if troops and supplies are syphoned off to fight an unwinnable war in America, it will take even longer to defeat Bonaparte."

"So, you do envision a day when Bonaparte is taken down?" Abby pressed.

"I do, Miss Trent."

Tea arrived, and the conversation lightened considerably, with Abby and Magnus sharing a bit about their travels throughout the years and pointing out various objects to enhance their stories. The duke even laughed a few times, his laughter filling her with a fuzzy warmth that she had never experienced before. She knew intellectually that it was a physical response to the man himself and still wondered if one day she might tease a kiss from him.

The teapot empty, the duchess said, "I feel we have taken up far too much of your day. It was kind of you to invite us to tea and devote so much time to unexpected guests."

"Nonsense," Magnus told her. "We have enjoyed your company

very much. Unfortunately, because we are gone so often, we do not have many friends in town. I only arrived recently, but Miss Trent has been here since early last summer."

The duke's eyes lit with interest. "Have you been working on your business venture all these months, Miss Trent?"

"Yes, I have, Your Grace. You see, I always used to enjoy sketching as a young girl. Once I came under Lord Ladiwyck's wing and traveled with him, he encouraged my art. Over the years, I developed a keen interest in furniture design."

"Furniture?" the duke asked, doubt in his voice.

"Yes. My business is called Trent Furnishings and will be opening tomorrow. I have used my travels and all the furniture I have seen in the many countries that we visited as inspiration. I incorporate bits and pieces from other countries into my designs. I have hired two furniture makers to make those designs a reality. They work off my drawings, and I have my own shop in Mayfair where I have sample pieces on display for the public to view."

"This is marvelous," the duchess declared. "It is fate that we have met you today, Miss Trent. Don't you think so, Bradford?"

The duke nodded solemnly. "We are in need of furniture."

"Oh, do you have a certain piece or two in mind? I could either show you some of my designs or you are welcome to come to the opening of my shop at the edge of Mayfair tomorrow. There you could see examples of my work in person."

The duke chuckled. "Oh, I am in need of more than a piece or two, Miss Trent." He paused. "I am in need of an entire household of furniture. Several households, in fact. Might you be interested in taking on such a large project?"

Chapter Seven

ELIJAH HELD HIS breath, waiting for a response from Abby Trent. He liked that Lord Ladiwyck had revealed her Christian name and called her Abby. Miss Trent was so . . . severe.

Abby . . . was so warm.

He tried his best to keep his gaze from her mouth. He had watched it the entire time she had spoken about the exotic places she had been. Her lips reminded him of a rosebud. Pink. Succulent. Soft. He longed to brush his against hers and see what she tasted like. Already, that faint jasmine scent that clung to her drove him mad. He could understand how the woman in the legend she had told had rewarded the man who adored her and gave her the jasmine vine by marrying him.

Thoughts of marriage soured him, though. He did not wish to wed. He did not want his line carried on. Already, he was burdened, having to carry the Bradford name. He would not do that to his son. No, there would be no sons or daughters. No children at all.

Then he looked at Abby Trent's mouth again and weakened.

A woman such as her might not wish to settle down. Already, she had seen a good portion of the world, and now she was on the brink of opening her own business. Surely, she would not want to give everything up for marriage and children. Would she be interested, though, in a brief, torrid affair? He knew enough not to give her children. There were ways to prevent such a thing.

Elijah looked to her now, waiting for her reply. He liked how she had not immediately given him a yes or no. That her response would be careful and not a hasty one.

"That is a remarkable proposition, Your Grace. Of course, it is only natural for you to wish to put your own mark on your various houses, both here and in the country. Might I ask what you have done with the furnishings in these homes? Or if you wish to sell them? I could always take on the pieces in good condition. The others, I could have my craftsmen reclaim the wood and use portions of it on other pieces."

He shook his head. "I am afraid it is all gone, Miss Trent."

"Gone?" she asked, her confusion obvious.

"Gone," he said cheerfully. "It seems the previous duke wanted to make life as difficult as he could for the man who inherited his title. He went to his grave believing the ducal title would go to a man not of his blood."

"If Bradford had even once come to see our boys, he would have known the truth," the duchess said fervently. "His Grace is the very image of his father, resembling him in both build and looks. Why, my son's hazel eyes even change color the way Bradford's did, depending upon his mood."

"You are saying Bradford... sold everything in his household?" asked Lord Ladiwyck, clearly in disbelief.

"Every single item," Elijah confirmed. "Mama and I toured the Bradford townhouse here in London several hours ago. Beyond the duke's bed and two cots for servants, not a piece of furniture exists in the place. Rooms were stripped of their curtains and rugs. No paintings are on the walls, nor are there books on the bookshelves. From what my butler has told us, the duke did the same to all his country houses in the south. He would have done the same to his estate in Norfolk but ran out of time when he died."

Miss Trent said, "I apologize for your treatment by this man, Your

Grace. It was a cruel thing to do. Not only did he ignore you and your twin your entire lives, but he is reaching out from the grave and taunting you."

"Then I shall mock him in return, Miss Trent. I can begin to do so if you promise you will work with Mama and me. More Mama, I think. She comes from the *ton* and has excellent taste."

"Oh, but it will be your house, Bradford," his mother protested. "And that of your duchess." She looked to Miss Trent. "My son and I had discussed simply refurnishing the townhouse so we have a place to live during the Season. I suggested he wait on refurbishing his country seat and other estates so that his wife could have a hand in that."

"Quit harping on about a wife, Mama," he said, more sternly than he wished.

"Eventually, you will need one to—"

"No, I won't," he told her, deciding he would inform her of his decision now and try to make peace with her later. "I will not wed. Ever."

Mama looked taken aback at his proclamation, while Miss Trent and the earl in unison asked, "Ever?"

"Yes," he said firmly, converting to a military mindset. "I cannot help if the blood of the worst man who ever walked the earth runs through me. I can keep from passing it on."

"You mean . . . you will not have children?" Mama asked, looking stricken.

"That is correct. I will handle my responsibilities as the Duke of Bradford. I have never been one to back down from a challenge—and a challenge it will be since I have no idea how to behave in society or run an estate, much less multiple ones. I draw the line at perpetuating this line. I have no desire to seek a bride."

Mama's face set in determination. "You will change your mind, Bradford. Although you could be a stubborn child, I believe you will find you need the companionship."

"I can get a mistress if I need companionship, Mama."

"Elijah!" She leaped to her feet. "How dare you speak of a mistress in front of me or his lordship and Miss Trent. You go too far." She turned to their hosts. "I apologize for my son. He was raised better than this."

"Perhaps it is my bad blood coming out," he commented sourly, thoroughly upset now, but knowing he had taken things too far. "My apologies. I have been in the rough company of soldiers for too long. I will understand if you choose not to work with Mama and me on restoring our townhouse to a livable state, Miss Trent."

"On the contrary, Your Grace, I would like to rise to this challenge. To completely furnish a house from top to bottom, room by room, is a dream come true. I am eager to see this blank canvas so that I know what is at stake and how I can begin to make it a place that not only you can inhabit, but one where you will feel truly at home."

"It grows late," Lord Ladiwyck pointed out. "It would be best to see His Grace's townhouse in the light of day."

"I agree, my lord," Miss Trent said. "And tomorrow is a very busy day for me with the opening of my shop. I still wish for you to come if you have the time. You can browse and study the various pieces on display up close. It will give you an idea of my work and if you wish to proceed with this enormous undertaking by partnering with me."

"What time do you open, Miss Trent?" he asked, knowing he had ruined his chances with her on a personal level with his admission of never marrying, but he still needed her on a professional one.

"Trent Furnishings opens at ten o'clock." She provided the address.

"Then we will be there," Elijah promised. He rose, and the others followed suit. "Thank you for a lovely teatime, Miss Trent, Lord Ladiwyck. We must be off."

"Where will you stay?" the earl asked. "After all, you have no beds to sleep in."

"Our new butler suggested an inn."

Ladiwyck said, "Nonsense. Why would you wish to stay in an inn? It could be months before Abby can finish furnishing your household."

"I suppose we could find a place to rent in the meantime," Mama mused.

"A few rooms at an inn will suffice," he said.

"I have a better idea," Ladiwyck said. "You must stay here."

"Stay . . . here?" Elijah said, thinking that to be a very bad idea.

Especially since he still had wicked thoughts regarding Abby Trent.

"We have plenty of bedchambers. Rooms that you could use for a study or sitting room. You are more than welcome to become our houseguests." The earl looked to his ward. "Isn't that right?"

Miss Trent licked her lips, drawing his attention to them once again. Yes, it would be unbearable being under the same roof as this woman, possibly even a few doors down from her bedchamber.

"Of course, Magnus. After all, it is your house. You may invite whomever you wish to stay with us. I will be gone the bulk of every day, moving between the workshop and the sales shop."

"Thank you for your kind offer, my lord," Mama said. "However, it would not be appropriate for both of us to stay here. After all, Miss Trent is an unmarried woman, and Bradford is single, as well."

Elijah sighed. This would be his excuse. "Then I insist that you stay here, Mama. You will be more comfortable. I will be happy as a clam at an inn. After all, I have lived in tents and slept on the ground a good portion of the last decade. I can call on you every day. We can also meet Miss Trent at our townhouse and watch her progress as she furnishes the place. What do you say?"

"I think it a good compromise, Your Grace," Lord Ladiwyck said. "His Grace is correct. You will have privacy and space here that you would not have at an inn. His Grace could visit you daily. I am sure you have missed him after so many years apart. In fact, he could breakfast with us each morning before we all start our day and also return for tea or dinner."

That would be a problem. Seeing Miss Trent first thing each day. But Elijah saw the hope shining in Mama's eyes and could not disappoint her.

"I think it a fine plan, my lord," he agreed. "I will also be stealing Mama away to take her to dress fittings. She will need an entire new wardrobe for the upcoming Season."

"We are to go to the Season?" Mama asked. "But you said you did not want a bride, Bradford."

"You have been denied the company of Polite Society for far too long, Mama. I will accompany you to events. You can renew old friendships and make new friends."

"I plan for Abby and I to attend the Season as well," the earl said. "She, too, is not interested in marriage, but I told her it would be important for her to meet prospective customers. Her furniture is of a very fine quality, and members of the *ton* will be the clients she would serve."

"Lord Ladiwyck sprang this idea upon me," Miss Trent said. "I have yet to see a modiste regarding a wardrobe. I know I will need several new gowns if I am to go to social affairs this Season. Perhaps we could find a dressmaker and go to her together, Your Grace."

"That would be lovely, Miss Trent," Mama said, stars now in her eyes as she radiated happiness.

"I will see your trunk is brought in, Mama," Elijah said. "Then I will go to the inn and book rooms for myself."

"Would you care to return for dinner, Your Grace?" Miss Trent asked.

"I believe I will pass on this occasion, Miss Trent," he told her. "I have many lists to make of things that need to be accomplished. I will return for breakfast, however, and then Mama and I will go to your shop. Thank you again for tea."

Elijah left the drawing room and realized that Miss Trent had followed him.

"Did you have something to ask of me, Miss Trent?"

She hesitated a moment and then said, "No, Your Grace. I merely wish to speak to Mrs. Feathers about which bedchamber to give to your mother and let Cook know we will be three for dinner tonight and possibly four in the future."

Then she paused, and he knew she had more to say. When she did, her words surprised him.

"Are you truly not interested in taking a wife?"

He replied with frankness. "Not in the least, Miss Trent. You heard my reasons for not doing so. Bradford was a vindictive, vicious man, sending Mama away in her delicate condition. I will share in confidence with you that she went to his Norfolk estate—but it was to a one-room cottage and not the duke's house. Gil and I were raised there, sometimes with barely enough to eat. Mama has suffered more than most women. I want her to be restored to the position in society that she deserves. That is the only reason I will accompany her to these events. I will let the *ton* see my face so that they know I am truly Bradford's issue. It will mean she will once again be accepted. I want her to be happy."

Miss Trent nodded sagely. "You are a good son, Your Grace. Thank you for your honesty. Because I would also like to exercise candor with you. In fact, I wish to ask a favor of you."

Her words piqued his interest. "You are helping us so much. I would be happy to do what I could for you, Miss Trent."

Such as kiss you.

"I, too, have no desire to wed. I have lived a life unrestricted, doing and going as I please. Marrying would mean giving up my freedom. I want my business to be a success. Once it is, I hope to still travel some. By law, a husband would merely take my profits and become the new owner of what I have built and then saddle me with children."

He chuckled. "You do not like children, Miss Trent?"

"Oh, I quite like them. I even wish I could have some of my own."

"Without the domineering husband," he quipped.

She laughed, and it washed over him again, like a clean rain.

"I suppose. Yet I do worry about being supposedly an eligible woman at these *ton* events. In effect, I will be making my come-out to society at the ripe old age of five and twenty. While most will consider me on the shelf—and I am happy for them to do so—there might be other men who would . . . pester me."

Oh, yes. There would be a considerable number of men who would want to spend time with this beauty.

"What I am asking is if—at least for this Season—that you might pretend to show interest in me. From what Magnus says, a duke's presence is revered. If the *ton* believed you and I had an affection for one another, then they would leave the both of us alone."

"You are suggesting a false romance?"

She grinned. "Well, it would be advantageous to us both. A single, eligible duke will have women flocking to him. And I truly do not wish to have men following me about. If Polite Society thought we were a couple, that would allow us to move among them freely." She paused. "I believe it would also help my business. If I am being perfectly honest with you, my association with a duke would not go unnoticed."

"Yes, I can see where it might steer business your way." He took a deep breath and slowly exhaled. "We would have to look as if we cared for one another, Miss Trent, or we will not fool anyone."

"I believe I can gaze adoringly at you for a few weeks, Your Grace," she said, mischief shining in her eyes. "Could you do the same?"

Elijah knew he was playing with fire and that being burnt was more probability than possibility. Still, to be able to be in Miss Trent's presence would be worth it. She might even agree to a few kisses to make their romance seem all the more real.

He thrust out a hand. "You have yourself a bargain, Miss Trent."

She took his hand in hers, and they shook. The touch between them was electrifying.

Yes, this would take no acting on his part.

At all.

Chapter Eight

Abby rose early and summoned Ethel to help her dress for the day. She allowed the maid to fuss over her, knowing she wished Abby to look her best for today's opening of Trent Furnishings. Ethel had suggested which gown Abby should wear and the way her hair should be dressed. She gave herself over to the maid and was pleased at the image reflected in the mirror when Ethel had finished.

"Thank you," she told the servant.

It was still early, and she decided to go sit in the gardens. She had always loved being outdoors and was glad the gardens offered a small sanctuary in London. Since last summer, she had spent many hours there, working on her sketches and dreaming of this day, the one in which her shop would open to the public. Abby went to the gardens now and strolled along the path until she reached the gazebo in the center. Seating herself there, she finally allowed herself to think of the Duke of Bradford.

And what she had asked of him.

She had surprised herself in asking him to strike a devil's bargain with her, one which she hoped would benefit them both. She knew Magnus was right, and she needed to meet others of the *ton* if she wanted to gain them as clients. She did not, however, want to waste time having men chase after her, seeking to court her. She had been open with the duke about that. British law did allow a woman to own property and have her own money if she remained single. If she married, though, everything—all her possessions and funds—became the property of her husband. Abby had been independent far too long to have a husband dictate to her, much less take everything from her.

And what if her husband did not wish for her to continue with her furniture business? She knew a working woman in the *ton* would be taboo. That was another reason she could not consider being a true part of Polite Society. She hoped to simply meet others and speak a bit about her new venture to them, knowing she would have to delicately choose her words so as not to put off anyone.

Having the Duke of Bradford pretending to be interested in her would add a layer of protection to her. It would also help circulate her name. Curiosity would fill others, and they would come to visit Trent Furnishings, hopefully leaving after having purchased something for their homes.

Was it wise to do this, especially when she was attracted to the duke? That question had yet to be answered.

At least the duke had been direct about not desiring to wed. She knew it would disappoint his mother greatly, but Abby could understand why he felt the way he did. The previous Duke of Bradford had obviously been a terrible man, abandoning his young wife and never seeing her again, much less bothering to meet his children. Much talk would be generated with Bradford and his mother entering society. If Abby were associated with the duke, it would further draw attention to her.

Of course, the two would go their separate ways soon. She had asked the duke only for a few weeks. Just enough time to raise her profile within the *ton* and hopefully gain the trust of Polite Society and win some of their business. She knew it would be a struggle at first because most homes were completely furnished, and a family might only need the occasional odd piece.

Then again there was the enormous project the duke had commissioned her to complete, one which thrilled her and would be an immense challenge. To furnish an entire house from top to bottom, much less more than one, could set up her business and secure her future and those of her employees for years to come. She might even have to hire more workers to craft pieces for this project. When word got out that she was furnishing Bradford's entire townhouse, it would cause quite a stir. Perhaps she could convince Bradford to hold a ball in order to allow members of Polite Society to come into his home and see what she had done with it.

She believed she would work closely with the duchess. The duke's mother seemed quite refined, despite her long absence from society, and she thought the woman would possess excellent taste. Between the two of them, they would make certain that Bradford's townhouse shone brightly.

Abby wandered the gardens another hour before returning to the house for breakfast. Entering the breakfast room, she saw Magnus already present.

"Are you excited about today?" he asked, his eyes twinkling.

"I am trying to temper my expectations," she told him. "I realize I may not get much foot traffic in my store today or in the weeks to come, despite the fact I have placed advertisements in all the London newspapers. The *ton* will be dribbling back into town during the next few weeks. I know I may have to wait until the Season begins before I see more people come to browse in my shop."

"What are your feelings in regard to taking on Bradford's townhouse?"

"I should be nervous, but the project excites me, Magnus. To put my mark on not only an entire room, but an entire house of rooms is beyond my wildest dreams. If I simply furnished His Grace's townhouse, I would think my business a success, and I could live off the profits for years."

"Bradford did mention other properties which need to be furnished as well," he pointed out.

"Yes, but I will merely focus on his London home for now. If he and his mother are pleased with my work, then we can move on to his other estates."

The Duchess of Bradford entered the breakfast room, and they both greeted her. Abby went through the buffet with the duchess. They had just seated themselves when the Duke of Bradford arrived.

"Good morning," he called to them, heading straight for the buffet. "I am famished."

Once his plate was filled and he had joined them, he asked, "How was your night, Mama? Have you settled in?"

"I have, Bradford. I am so grateful to Lord Ladiwyck and Miss Trent for extending the invitation for me to stay here."

"You may stay as long as you wish, Your Grace," Magnus said, smiling warmly at the widow.

Abby watched him carefully. It occurred to her that her guardian might actually be interested in the duchess. As a woman. Over the many years of their travels, Magnus had been discreet in the assignations he had formed in the places they had visited. She saw the duchess smiling at Magnus and wondered if she might be witnessing the beginning of a budding relationship. The duchess most likely was in her mid-forties, based upon the age of her son, though she could have passed for a decade younger. If she and Magnus were to wed, it would please Abby to no end. She had been a companion to him for all these years but knew the duchess could offer him things she could not.

"I have been given the name of both a reputable dressmaker and tailor," the duke informed them. "Miss Trent, you mentioned that you would need some new gowns for the upcoming Season. I know Mama needs an entire new wardrobe. Perhaps you might wish to share Madame Aubert."

"If she is willing to take on the both of us, I would be happy to do so," Abby replied. "I know most of my gowns are out of fashion since I have not updated them during our travels these past few years."

"I would be delighted to go to fittings with you, Miss Trent, and select the fabrics and styles for our gowns." The duchess looked to her son. "Who is the tailor, Bradford? It is imperative that you, too, have something to wear besides your uniform."

"Yes, Mama. I have the name of a tailor named Tibbets. Perhaps after we leave Miss Trent's shop today, we can call upon Tibbets and make arrangements with him."

They finished breakfast, and Abby asked, "Would you care to see the workshop where my men craft my designs? We could go there now since there is time before my shop officially opens."

"I would enjoy that very much, Miss Trent," the duke replied.

"Why don't you use my carriage for the day, Your Graces?" Magnus suggested. "I decided to rent one for the Season in order to escort Abby to events. If I need to go anywhere, I can use the vehicle and driver normally at her disposal."

"That is most thoughtful of you, my lord," the duchess said.

Magnus told the duke that he would be happy to accompany him to Tattersall's when they were open next Monday.

"They are only open the one day of the week until the Season begins. Then you can also go on Thursdays. It is the only place to purchase horseflesh," Magnus assured the duke. "You will need use of your own carriage to get about town and to *ton* affairs."

They traveled to her workshop, where she introduced the pair to Mr. Alexander and Mr. Bauer. The men were happy to show a few of the completed pieces from this week, as well as ones in progress. Mr. Bauer was working upon a credenza and showed them the sketch Abby had made.

"Miss Trent always meets with us and goes over each design thoroughly," Bauer explained. "That way, Mr. Alexander and I have a clear idea what is expected from us."

Mr. Alexander added, "We also have a storeroom downstairs

which is filled with completed work of the last several months. Some items from it have already been moved to Miss Trent's shop for today's opening."

"It is good to see your work," the duke said. "I have arranged with Miss Trent for her to create a fairly large number of furnishings for me."

Abby saw her workers' eyes light with interest and said, "I will need to tour His Grace's townhouse first. Then I will sit with Their Graces and talk about styles of furniture and their needs. If we can use some previously completed pieces to begin filling their order, we will do so. I think, however, that I will need to hire additional craftsmen. If you have anyone in mind, please give me his name. We can arrange for an appointment for me to interview him and see his work. For now, we must head to Trent Furnishings." She laughed. "I would not wish to miss my own opening."

They returned to Magnus' carriage and drove back to Mayfair. She proudly led them into her store and said, "I will let you move about freely and see for yourself what is on display. I must meet with my manager and clerk for a few minutes."

She left the pair browsing and went to see Mr. Hogan. He and their clerk, Mr. Nix, went to the office located in the rear of the store.

"Is everything ready for the opening?" she asked.

"Everything is exactly as you wished it to be, Miss Trent," Mr. Hogan replied. "What needs does His Grace have?"

Abby did not go into detail as to why the duke had an empty townhouse. She told her workers that he and his mother would need to fill an entire townhouse with furnishings.

"How many rooms are in this townhouse?" Mr. Nix asked.

"I have yet to see it, but he is a duke. I am expecting anywhere between fifty and one hundred rooms."

The two men gasped. "Why, that alone could keep us busy for a couple of years," Mr. Hogan said. "It will ensure the success of Trent

Furnishings."

"Yes, it will generate income to keep us afloat for many years," she assured them. "Of course, I also want to garner other clients beyond His Grace."

"If Polite Society learns that His Grace is using you exclusively to furnish his home, Miss Trent, they will flock here. It would mean a plethora of clients," Mr. Nix said.

"I am hoping that very thing," she said. Rising, she added, "Shall we return to the shop? It is almost time to open for business."

The three returned to the display area and Abby saw Their Graces standing near a desk. It was one of her favorites she had designed, with its clean lines and brass inlays and stringing.

She joined them and asked, "Do you like this piece?"

The duke nodded. "The design and craftsmanship are superb. It is the desk I want for my study. Can you tell me a bit about its features?"

Abby went into detail about her design, lovingly stroking the wood as she spoke.

"I want it," Bradford confirmed again.

She motioned to her clerk. Mr. Nix came quickly to them.

"His Grace wishes to purchase this desk. Could you please mark it as *sold*?"

"Of course, Miss Trent," the clerk said, smiling brightly.

"We found other pieces that we like quite a bit," Her Grace said.

"Show me which ones, and we can also designate them as reserved," Abby told the duchess. "Be sure, however, that you truly love a piece. I have yet to see your townhouse and will need to not only see the number of rooms, but the different types continued within it. Some owners like a more eclectic grouping of furniture, while others prefer a more cohesive look. Remember, I can design anything you wish. Even if a piece here sells, I can have it replicated if you like it since the design is my own creation."

"When would you like to see the townhouse, Miss Trent?" the

duke asked.

"As soon as possible," she told him. "I will need to have a good idea of its layout, as well as your personal tastes before I begin to furnish it. I have hundreds—no, thousands—of sketches you can peruse, as well. If that is too overwhelming, I can narrow it down for you once I get a feel for your preferences. You will need a great deal, however, Your Grace. Beds. Chests. Commodes. Settees. Wardrobes. Tables."

"Could you come this afternoon?" he asked. "I know today is the opening of your shop, but you do have staff on hand to handle your customers."

Abby glanced around. Only one gentleman was in the store now. She was right in thinking she wouldn't have many come in to browse before everyone returned to town for the Season. It would be easy to devote time to the duke's massive project in these early days before the store gained recognition.

"I would be happy to tour the townhouse this afternoon, Your Grace. Simply return here whenever you wish for me to accompany you. Please take Lord Ladiwyck's carriage. I won't be going anywhere until you return."

"We will do so," he promised. "For now, I need to see what hopefully will be my new tailor."

"Thank you for showing us your workshop and this showroom," the duchess said. "You are a most talented woman, Miss Trent. Bradford and I look forward to working with you."

The two left the shop, and Abby wandered over to the sole customer and introduced herself. After asking him a few questions, she excused herself and returned with her sketchbook.

"I will begin drawing what you wish for. We can create this secretaire for your wife together."

As her pencil glided across the page, she made adjustments based upon the gentleman's input. When they finished, he smiled broadly.

"My wife will be pleased with this, Miss Trent."

They discussed the type of wood to use, and she told him it could be finished in a week's time, having Nix write down the address where it should be delivered.

"A bill of sale will come with the piece," she told him. "If you are pleased, I do hope you will share where you purchased this birthday present, my lord."

"My wife will most likely have her friends over for tea and show it off," he told her. "That will do the trick."

Abby thanked him for coming in and as the door closed, she looked to her staff of two.

"Our first sale!" she exclaimed. "Hopefully, many more are to come."

Chapter Nine

Elijah couldn't stop thinking about Abby Trent. Ever since they had made their pact to pretend to be in a relationship, he kept wishing it could be a reality instead of fantasy. That was utterly ridiculous. He had made it perfectly clear that he had no interest in obtaining a wife. Miss Trent, too, was not in want of a husband. Elijah hadn't known the law would strip her of everything she owned, handing it over to the man she wed. No wonder she was loath to marry. Although he hardly knew the first thing about Polite Society, he believed any husband she did wed would not want her spending time creating designs for furniture and selling her goods to the *ton*. The practice would probably embarrass him. Of course, this imaginary husband would take all the profits she had earned before their marriage and tuck them away as his.

He couldn't understand a society which would allow such a thing to happen. He had seen his own mother work her fingers to the bone, sewing night and day, as she tried to put food on their table. Why shouldn't a woman work hard and be allowed to keep what she had earned? If he married Miss Trent, not only would he let her keep all her profits, but he would also encourage her to continue to work.

Oh, what a foolish notion that was.

"What are you thinking about?" Mama asked.

Glad she had broken the spell of daydreaming about Miss Trent, he said, "Only thoughts of all we have to do. Getting the house ready so that we might inhabit it. Hiring servants. Seeing to our wardrobes. And I have yet to go to Surrey. Before the Season begins, I must spend some time at Marblebridge, Mama. Who knows if the duke ignored it? I need to see who is its steward and learn about the property. It will be where we live after we leave London. I know most of the *ton* heads to the country after the Season. Lord Ladiwyck mentioned something of that nature to me."

"Yes, that is the usual custom. Hopefully, you will have offered and been accepted by some young lady, and the three of us can travel together to Marblebridge."

Elijah bit his tongue. He had already told his mother his reasons for not wishing to wed. It seems she was ignoring what he had shared. Of course, when he started paying Miss Trent particular attention, Mama would no doubt believe he had changed his mind. Under no circumstances did he intend to share with Mama the scheme Miss Trent had come up with—the very one Elijah had committed to—knowing it would shock his mother.

For now, he would keep quiet.

"I do like the carriage Lord Ladiwyck rented," he said, hoping a change of subject would steer the conversation in a new area.

"It was good of him to offer to go to Tattersall's with you. The earl is a very nice, interesting man."

He heard something in Mama's voice that he hadn't before now. Could she possibly be *interested* in Ladiwyck? After all, she was still a beautiful woman. Even once the *ton* learned she was blameless for the gossip Bradford had spread about her years ago, it might be hard to attract a gentleman of quality. That is, if she even wanted to do so. Ladiwyck, though, was certainly unconventional. He seemed to have no qualms extending his friendship to them, despite the cloud they were under. If Mama could find happiness with the earl, Elijah would encourage the match.

"I agree. Ladiwyck is a kind, unusual gentleman. Quite entertaining. I am glad we have made his acquaintance. It will be nice to know someone going into the Season."

Mama studied him. "What of Miss Trent? What do you think of her?"

Elijah could see the wheels turning in her head and had to stifle his laughter.

"I find her talented. We could not be in better hands than having Miss Trent remake our townhouse from top to bottom."

"But what do you think of *her*?" she pressed.

He decided to lay the groundwork now for what was to come. "She is a very attractive, interesting woman. I hope to see more of her."

"Good. Because I like her quite a bit myself. You know, we will be spending a good deal of time with her. Her advice on furnishing each room will be important. Miss Trent is an expert. You should allow her free rein in doing as she pleases."

He had to glance out the window to hide his smile, knowing that Mama believed a match between him and Miss Trent was in the making. If the townhouse were to be her new home, surely it would be wise to allow her to furnish it as she saw fit.

"You are right, Mama. Miss Trent has more experience in these matters than either you or I do. While I think we should tell her some of our preferences, I would rather see her have the freedom to decorate as she sees fit."

The carriage rolled to a halt, and Ladiwyck's footman opened the door. The earl was right. Traveling in a luxurious vehicle such as this was far better than a hansom cab. He would need to get horses as soon as he could in order to move about town easily.

They entered the tailor's shop, and a clerk came to them. He blinked. "Oh, Your Grace. It is good to see you."

Obviously, the previous Duke of Bradford had clothes made up here. Elijah pushed aside the prejudice he already felt against the tailor who had made the duke's clothes and asked, "Is Mr. Tibbets here?"

"He is with a customer, Your Grace. In fact, he has one now and another coming in for an appointment which will last most of the day," the clerk said apologetically.

"I have only arrived in town and merely wished to meet Mr. Tibbets. I would also like to schedule time with him if he is available to make up my wardrobe. As you can see, I have only recently left His Majesty's service and will need everything."

"Let me fetch him, Your Grace," the clerk said, crossing the store and disappearing behind some curtains.

The clerk returned, accompanied by the store's owner. Tibbets looked to be a jovial man and bowed to them.

"Your Graces, it is good of you to come and visit my tailoring shop."

"You came highly recommended to me, Mr. Tibbets. I gather you also provided clothing for the previous Duke of Bradford."

"I did, Your Grace, until he fell ill. I had not seen him in over a year. Probably closer to two. I am happy to be of service to you, however, if you see fit to use me."

Elijah indicated his uniform. "I will need everything. I am wearing what I own. Could we schedule time soon?"

The tailor turned to the clerk, who said, "Tomorrow is entirely open, Mr. Tibbets. We could devote the entire day to His Grace."

Tibbets asked, "Would that suit you, Your Grace? We could start tomorrow morning. Measure you. Discuss your wardrobe needs for everyday wear both in town and in the country, as well as what you will need for the Season. We could also view the bolts of material and select the cloths to use."

"That would be satisfactory," he replied. "I will return tomorrow morning. Good day, Mr. Tibbets."

"Good day, Your Graces," the tailor responded.

They returned to the carriage, and Elijah gave Ladiwyck's coachman the address of Madame Aubert.

"I am a bit nervous about seeing a new modiste," his mother confided. "The one who prepared my come-out wardrobe must be long retired by now." She glanced down at her gown. "I have made all my own clothes since then."

"You look wonderful, Mama," he told her, wanting to bolster her confidence. "You yourself have said that we must dress the part for our new roles. Or rather, my new role. You have always been a duchess, even if you were not treated as one." He took her hand and squeezed it. "I wish I could right the wrongs Bradford did to you."

"Actually, he did me a favor, Elijah," she said softly, calling him by his given name. "You see, Bradford was a . . . difficult man. He had already been wed twice before and counted upon me to produce his heir. He was . . ." Her voice trailed off. She swallowed. "The duke was . . . harsh in the bedroom. It was a blessing not to have to service him once I left. Yes, I was relegated to a small cottage—but I had you and Gil. You were my world."

She touched his cheek. "Oh, how hard it was to let the two of you go off to war. I knew, though, that you needed to see some of the world."

"You spent your inheritance on our commissions when we could have stayed home and worked to support you."

"I wanted you to be in the company of gentlemen. Being in the presence of other officers who came from fine families, I hoped a bit of their polish would rub off on you. You have matured into a fine man, my son. And you will make for a wonderful duke, husband, and father."

Regret stung him, knowing he would never sire children. For a brief moment, he wished he could have ones of his own. Then he shoved the thought aside and locked it away. He would not continue Bradford's line. Let the duke rail at him from the bowels of Hell.

The picture that came to mind put a smile on his face.

As the carriage slowed, Mama said, "Shouldn't we wait for Miss Trent? I thought the two of us were to see the modiste together."

"Let's at least meet with her, Mama, and see if you even find her suitable or not. If you do, the sooner she can start on the wardrobe you require, the better."

She sighed. "If you wish."

They entered the dressmaker's shop and immediately were met by a woman who barely stood five feet tall. Her red hair was an unusual shade, and Elijah suspected it was dyed.

"Madame Aubert?" he asked.

"Yes, I am she."

"I am the Duke of Bradford. This is my mother, the Duchess of Bradford."

A knowing look came into the dressmaker's eyes. "Ah, yes. You recently came into your title, Your Grace, if I am not mistaken."

"I did. My mother and I will be in town for the Season. She has need of a new wardrobe."

Madame Aubert turned to Mama, sizing up the gown she wore, peering at it with interest. "These stitches are quite fine, Your Grace."

"Thank you. I did them myself," Mama answered, pride evident in her voice. "I have made all my clothes for many years."

Immediately, the modiste began peppering his mother with questions. Elijah stepped aside, roaming the shop, as the two women talked fashion. Once he made a full circle of the shop, he returned to them.

"I will need Her Grace for the rest of today," Madame Aubert informed him. "At least until teatime. We have much to discuss. Material to consider. Sketches to look over. Measurements to take."

"Do you mind, Bradford?" Mama asked.

"Not at all, Mama." He kissed her cheek. "I can return for you at half-past three. That will give us time to return to Lord Ladiwyck's for tea."

"Madame has said she is also willing to take on Miss Trent," Mama told him.

"Then we will ask Miss Trent when it is convenient for her to come to the shop for her fittings. I will see you later."

Elijah left the dress shop and decided to go to his townhouse. Nelson answered his knock.

"Your Grace, it is good to see you. How is the inn? I hope it is to your liking."

He explained how he was staying there, but his mother was staying with friends.

"Come and meet my wife."

Nelson led them to the kitchen, where a woman in her mid-twenties scribbled with a pencil. Seeing him, she leaped to her feet and bobbed a quick curtsey.

"Your Grace. It is good of you to have hired me sight unseen." She paused. "I know I am young, but I promise that I will be an asset to you and Her Grace."

"Nelson assured me of that very thing, Mrs. Nelson. Tell me what progress has occurred."

The couple took turns discussing the list they had made of the various positions which needed to be filled. They had already presented it to the head of the employment agency they wished to use, one from which Mrs. Nelson had gained her most recent position.

"Even though we don't have a cook yet, I have begun restocking the larder with staples," the new housekeeper told him. "Flour. Sugar. Coffee. Tea."

"And I have contracted for wood and coal to be delivered on a regular basis," his butler added. "We meet this afternoon with the first of several candidates at the employment agency. How quickly do you wish for staff to be hired, Your Grace?"

"Hire anyone immediately whom you believe will do a good job and place them on the payroll. I have met with a furniture designer who will be furnishing the entire house. While her pieces are meant for the family rooms, you will need to see to the servants' quarters being refurbished. Once you have beds for staff, they can begin reporting. My preference is to hire a cook before anyone else. A coachman next."

"You might check at Tattersall's for a coachman, Your Grace," Nelson told him. "Sometimes, that is the best place to seek a driver. Grooms, as well."

"I have plans to go to Tattersall's early next week. I will keep that in mind. I will be returning with a Miss Trent today. She is the designer who will create the furniture to fill the townhouse. She wishes to tour the place."

"I can give her the tour, Your Grace," Mrs. Nelson said. "I would have to miss out on the first round of interviews, but Nelson can handle those himself."

The thought of having Abby Trent to himself was impossible to pass up. "No, I would prefer you accompanying your husband to these interviews, Mrs. Nelson. I think it is important for both of you to have equal input regarding the staff. I can lead Miss Trent about the house. We will talk about the purpose of each room. She is interested in learning of my taste, so I would need to be present at any rate."

"Very well, Your Grace," the housekeeper said.

Elijah took his leave and returned to the carriage. It was still too early to claim Miss Trent and so he asked the coachman if he would take him about Mayfair and the surrounding areas. He wanted to get the lay of the land and begin learning the streets about him.

Once an hour had passed, the driver returned him to Trent Furnishings. He was ready to give Miss Trent the tour of his home.

He also planned to kiss her. More than once if she allowed him to do so. If he could kiss her, he hoped he would discover that she was no different from any other woman he had kissed before. Miss Abby Trent had taken up far too many of his thoughts since they had met.

He would get this kiss out of the way, coming up with some excuse as to why he needed to do so. Perhaps using their false interest in one another might seem plausible.

With that in mind, he left the carriage and entered Trent Furnishings.

Chapter Ten

Abby watched the door, telling herself she was looking for new customers who might enter.

In reality, she was awaiting the Duke of Bradford's return.

She couldn't stop thinking of the man and had no idea why she was drawn to him. Certainly, he was extremely good-looking, with his sun-streaked, soft brown hair and ever-changing hazel eyes. Looks had never been that important to her, though. It definitely was not the title he held. She had been gone from England so long and seen so many different people and cultures around the world. True, she and Magnus had been entertained by everyone from heads of state to lowly peasants who shared a bowl of soup and crust of bread with them. She was interested more in a person and not a title, though she would have to be more aware of those if she wanted her establishment to thrive.

She suspected one thing that drew her to this duke was that he seemed a bit lost, not knowing his place in the new world he had been thrust into. Abby was certain he had been an excellent officer in His Majesty's army, but that life was his past. While he projected an air of confidence, she saw within him the lost little boy who had never known his father. She did not think Bradford had suffered from never meeting the man who sired him. The current duke had been raised in a stable home by a loving mother, even if they had lacked in material possessions. He now had the world at his feet, though, and she wondered if that might change him.

Abby still itched to kiss him and wondered how she might bring that about. It wasn't as if she could come out and boldly ask him to kiss her.

Or could she?

They would certainly need to be alone for that to occur. She didn't know if that would happen anytime soon. She would be in his company often in the coming days but assumed his mother—and even Magnus—might be present, leaving no privacy. Abby decided to let things take their natural course. If she were meant to kiss this man, the opportunity would present itself.

The bell above the door jingled again and this time, the duke himself walked through it. Excitement rushed through her just at the sight of him. She realized she must rein in these new feelings. She had yet to put a name to them and did not want him to guess she had them. Already, she felt he held a power over her that no man ever had.

Smiling brightly, she moved to greet him. "Your Grace, it is good to see you again. How did things go at the tailor's?"

"Mr. Tibbets was otherwise engaged today with two clients. I had known by not having an appointment that it might not be possible to see him today. However, I did meet with him briefly and liked him quite a bit. I am to return tomorrow morning. He and his tailors will devote the entire day to me."

"That sounds quite promising. Let me fetch my spencer and reticule. Then we can be off."

Abby went and told Mr. Hogan that she was going to see His Grace's townhouse to get a better idea as to his wants and needs. Mr. Nix was showing a customer a beautiful wardrobe, and she hoped the clerk might close the sale.

Joining the duke, she said, "I am ready if you are."

They went out to Magnus' carriage, and Bradford handed her up. She deliberately sat in the center of one seat, which would force him to sit opposite her. It had distracted her to no end sitting beside him previously and she wished to keep her wits about her.

He entered the carriage and she asked, "Where is Her Grace? I thought she would tour the townhouse with us."

His lips twitched in amusement. "Mama and Madame Aubert are already thick as thieves," he told her. "She is to remain with the dressmaker until I return for her at half-past three. I thought we could then come and take tea at Lord Ladiwyck's with you."

Abby realized that would give them over two hours in the townhouse, plenty of time for her to see the entire place and thoroughly discuss with the duke what he envisioned her doing.

"How was your day, Miss Trent? Did you make any sales?"

"As a matter of fact, we did. I helped a gentleman pick out a secretaire for his wife's upcoming birthday. He assured me she would show it off to her friends as they returned to town. Another gentleman commissioned a sideboard and dining table for eight. He liked the ones I had on display and asked for slight modifications. I quickly sketched something out, and he approved of my design. I sent Mr. Nix with the drawings to deliver to the workshop, with instructions for Mr. Alexander and Mr. Bauer to begin on the pieces at once."

"It sounds as if you had a most successful first day," he noted.

"Frankly, it was more than I hoped for. Especially with it being February. The *ton* sometimes dribbles back this month, but more of them will come in March. Then all will be present by the time April begins in order to attend the Season. My furniture is designed for people who possess a good deal of money, and so I know my clientele will be drawn from those members of Polite Society. If the two sales today are the only ones made this week, I will be satisfied."

They arrived at his townhouse, and Abby thought how beautiful the square was in which it rested upon. The house itself was grand, with its white stucco façade framed by matching columns. It looked to be twice the size of Magnus' London home. All the better, because it would mean more rooms which needed to be filled with furniture.

Her furniture.

They went to the door, and the duke withdrew a key, unlocking it.

"I thought you said you had a butler."

As they entered the foyer and he closed the door, Bradford said, "I do. A butler and a housekeeper." He grinned. "A married couple whom I stole from my next-door neighbor, Lord Ritter."

Abby gasped. "You enticed Lord Ritter's butler and housekeeper to come work for you, Bradford? That was not a very neighborly thing to do."

"First, I was told Lord Ritter rarely comes to town and has already sent word he will not attend this Season. Second, the couple were a footman and parlor maid."

"You put a footman and parlor maid in charge of running your household? That is taking a huge risk, Your Grace."

"It might be, but Nelson is intelligent and enterprising. Mrs. Nelson seems to be quite efficient and organized. They were eager to vault into a higher position, and I believe I have their loyalty."

"Then where are they?"

"At this moment, they are at an employment agency, interviewing prospective people for various positions within the household. I wanted them to do this together since they will be working closely on managing my household for me. Once they hire a staff, I have told them to see to getting beds for all of these new employees. I won't have them sleeping on the floor."

"I can work on furnishing the servants' quarters first if that is what you wish, Your Grace. The furniture there will be simpler to build. If you so choose, I even know of a place where you could purchase furniture for your servants."

"No, I want you to furnish my entire household. I realize the servants' quarters will not be nearly as grand as the rest of the house, but I trust you and your craftsmen to do quality work." He paused. "Shall we begin our tour?"

Abby withdrew a pad and pencil from her reticule, ready to take notes as they moved about the various rooms. "Let's explore the ground floor first. As we go, provide any insight you can as to what you might wish in that room."

"I can do so, but I am depending upon your expertise, Miss Trent." His eyes glowed warmly at her, causing tingles to run through her.

They went first to the kitchens, and she explained the kind of work tables the cook and scullery maids would need to work upon. She also said they would need a small table and chairs for the cook to sit and take a rest. They moved to the servants' dining hall, and she noted it was large enough for a table of sixteen. The butler's office and bedchamber were together, across from the housekeeper's sitting room and bedchamber.

"I assume since the Nelsons are married that they can share a bedchamber. The butler's is the larger of the two so I will designate that for them."

She explained how she would furnish it and Nelson's office.

"I will turn Mrs. Nelson's bedchamber into an office for her. The outer room can remain her sitting room. I find that it is more conducive as far as communication goes for the housekeeper to have a place to entertain the staff. Have them in for a cup of tea and a chat."

"That will do nicely," he said. "We should continue."

They moved throughout the rest of the ground floor. His study was large, and the desk he had chosen this morning would look good here. She described the type of carpet and curtains she would like placed in the room, as well as the sitting area adjacent to the fireplace. They went to the dining room next, an enormous room.

"I assume we will have a large table in here. What number do you suggest that we seat?"

"You are a duke and will be entertaining a great deal. I say we should have the table seat thirty-six." She explained what she was thinking and even drew a quick sketch of the table and a chair. The room would also contain several sideboards.

"That chandelier is quite filthy," she noted. "Your staff should clean it, and then I will look to see if it is suitable. If not, I can have it replaced."

They saw a breakfast room, where the duke said he would prefer taking his meals when no guests were expected. A winter parlor also could hold a table and chairs, as well as other furniture to sit upon.

"I can even make the table so that it can be converted into a chessboard," she told him. "You could have two to four eat at it, and once the dishes were cleared, it would rotate and reveal the chessboard."

"A very clever idea. If only I knew how to play chess."

"Oh, I could teach you. Magnus taught me once I came into his care. We have passed many an hour aboard a ship playing chess."

They moved upstairs and saw a variety of rooms. She told him the drawing room, next to his study, would be the first room she tackled.

"It is here where you will entertain your guests, as well as spend time with your mother and friends. As you see, the room is very large. I will do groups of seatings scattered about and even include a pianoforte since some of your guests will play and offer to entertain."

She walked the room with him, sharing what she would do, and he agreed with all her suggestions.

"You don't seem to be giving me much of your opinions, Your Grace. I suppose I will need to go through the house again with Her Grace and draw ideas from her."

"Mama will be happy with whatever you decide, Miss Trent. You may share what you want to do with her, but we have both decided to bow to your expertise."

"Then I will have Her Grace look at several sketches and give me her preferences."

They entered the library, and Abby felt a wave of anger sizzle through her, seeing the bare shelves.

"It is still beyond my comprehension that the Duke of Bradford would be so petty as to sell every single book contained here."

"Fortunately, his solicitor kept the monies from the sales of all the furnishings separately from other accounts. It is from that I will draw to pay you for your services, Miss Trent."

The duke glanced about the room. "As to how to replace all the books? I haven't the foggiest notion."

"We can talk with a bookseller about that, Your Grace."

"You would help me with even that?" he asked.

"When I am done, I want this place to be a home to you and Her Grace. That means every lamp, every book, every rug, every painting on the wall will make you happy. I would see these shelves filled with books which you will enjoy over your lifetime." She paused. "That is, *if* you enjoy reading."

He chuckled. "I have not read in a very long time, Miss Trent. Men at war do not have time for such pleasurable pursuits." His eyes darkened, the hazel turning to an angry green.

"I see," she said, quickly turning to head toward the door.

He caught up to her, taking her elbow and spinning her around so that she faced him. Abby's heart beat like the wings of a hummingbird as she looked up at him.

"Yes, Your Grace?" she asked, her voice wavering.

"I have been thinking about your proposition," he said. "The one where we will pursue a false engagement."

"Oh, no, Your Grace," Abby said quickly. "No engagement. That cannot be."

"Why not?"

"If we are engaged, then a marriage is expected. Since you and I both know one will not occur, there can be no engagement."

"I don't see why not. It would draw attention to the both of us and help your business."

She shook her head. "No, Your Grace, an engagement would have to be eventually broken. That is never good for a lady."

Curiosity filled his face even as heat rushed through her, his fingers still clasping her elbow. She wet her lips nervously.

"You see, if an engagement is broken, it reflects poorly on the lady involved in the relationship. If the gentleman is known to be the one who ended things, Polite Society questions what is wrong with his former betrothed."

"And if the lady breaks off things?" he asked softly.

She sighed. "The *ton* still blames her. She might have caught her fiancé being unfaithful to her. She may have learned he was a gambler, with debts stacked to the heavens. It does not matter the circumstances. Polite Society always blames the woman. I cannot afford to take that blame, Your Grace. A broken engagement would ostracize me from Polite Society. I need the exact opposite. I need them to want to come to my store."

Abby needed to put distance between them. The heat from his fingers holding her elbow was too much to bear. She turned slightly, hoping to break the contact between them, but the duke's grasp tightened slightly. She had to make him understand how preposterous—and dangerous—his idea was.

"Therefore, we will have no engagement between us. You are simply going to show an abundant interest in me. Dance with me several times. Come to dinner at Magnus' house. Perhaps even escort me to the theatre or opera once or twice. Your interest in me will draw the interest of others. After a few weeks, things can cool between us. My name will already be out there and hopefully, the *ton* will begin shopping at Trent Furnishings. You can turn your eye to others or simply stop attending events."

"What about Mama? She will want to continue going to social affairs."

"You could escort her to balls and merely head straight for the card room and remain there the entire evening without dancing."

"I see," he said, a thoughtful expression upon his face.

Abby couldn't help but admire the high cheekbones, so sharp they could cut glass, and the firm jaw.

And those sensual lips, which now drew her attention. She looked at them longingly.

"We still need to be comfortable in one another's presence," he told her. "I feel if we get to know one another better—beyond our business relationship—that we will be more believable in front of others."

She swallowed nervously. "And how do you think we should go about doing so, Your Grace?"

His eyes gleamed, burning a bright green now, causing her body to tremble. "I think by kissing."

Chapter Eleven

ELIJAH'S WORDS HUNG in the air. He still held Miss Trent's elbow, feeling the electricity flow between them.

Please say yes.

"Yes," she said, surprising him. "Yes," she repeated. "If we are to be believed, there should be an air of comfort between us."

She wet her lips, causing desire to flood him. He would have to be very careful and restrain himself so that he did not lose control of the kiss.

Something told him it would be incredibly hard to maintain control once his lips touched hers.

"Shall we begin?" she asked. "Is here a good place?"

He would kiss her in a desert. Under the shade of an oak. Beside a river. In a garden. Wherever she was.

"Here is fine," he agreed pleasantly, surprised by how normal he sounded.

She gazed up at him. A giggle slipped from her. "Forgive me, Your Grace. I have kissed a man before. I suppose I shouldn't admit to that. I simply never had a man ask me before, and I am not certain where we should begin."

"Leave that to me, Miss Trent."

"Why don't you call me Abby? After all, we are about to undertake something intimate. Miss Trent seems so formal."

"All right, Abby." He smiled down at her. "And you must call me Elijah."

"Elijah? Oh, that sounds so stern."

"My brother called me Eli," he told her. "He was the only one who did so."

"Then Eli should be reserved for your memories of him," she responded. "Here—now—I will call you Elijah. But only for the next minute or so. Our other encounters will be around others, and you must be Your Grace at all times. I must remain Miss Trent."

"For now, you are Abby," he said, hearing the rawness in his voice. He wondered if she knew that was need bubbling to the surface.

Her large, blue eyes studied him. "I am ready, Elijah. You may kiss me now."

How he wanted to do more than kiss her. But he would keep to a kiss. A simple kiss.

Elijah lowered his mouth to hers, his hands moving to her shoulders to steady her. Softly, he brushed his lips against hers, hot desire flooding him. He tightened his hold on her, afraid she might turn away.

He couldn't let that occur.

Slowly, he broke the kiss and began planting brief kisses on her mouth. Their lips would join, and he relished the moment before lifting his mouth from hers, only to continually return to it.

Her fingers gripped the lapels of his coat, guaranteeing that he, too, was going nowhere. He smiled and felt her smile against his lips.

His hands slipped upward, pushing into her hair. He felt it loosen, pins spilling to the floor. He stroked the soft waves and then pushed his fingers into her tresses, pulling her closer, needing her warmth.

His mouth now grew insistent, the kisses longer, harder, causing desire to ripple through him. She began making soft, mewling noises, even as he growled in satisfaction.

Elijah wanted more of her. He was already dazzled by this woman.

He must prove to himself she was just an ordinary woman.

He knew he lied to himself even as he coaxed her mouth open.

His tongue delved into her mouth, seeking something he couldn't name. He explored her leisurely, his arms wrapping about her, pinning her to him. His tongue stroked hers, and she began to answer his kiss, hesitantly at first, and then with more confidence.

Desire exploded, running through him as never before. He had told himself he would find she was no different from any woman he had kissed. Instead, he affirmed just how unique she was.

The only woman for him.

The thought frightened him more than anything leading up to this moment. Quickly, he broke the kiss, releasing her and stepping back, needing to put distance between them.

Panting, he said, "My apologies, Miss Trent. I took the kiss too far."

Her eyes burned with need. Her lips were swollen from their love play. Color flooded her cheeks, making Abby Trent the most enticing creature he had ever seen.

"And I don't believe you took it far enough, Elijah."

Her words shocked him. Thrilled him. Without thinking, he rushed toward her, yanking her against him. Their bodies collided at the same time their mouths did. Hungrily, he plunged his tongue into her mouth again, needing the taste of her.

She responded eagerly, her fingers pushing into his hair, kneading his scalp.

The kiss went on and on. Time stood still. There was only Abby. Only Abby. Elijah took and took and knew he would never get enough to satisfy himself.

She was the one who broke the kiss this time. Her eyes were glazed with passion, her lips rosy and swollen. She breathed heavily and tried to bring her breathing under control.

"*That* was a kiss, Elijah. The best of my life." She paused, running her fingers through her hair. "You surprised me."

"How?"

"You showed me you are full of fire and energy. If you direct that passion to your tenants and toward your ducal duties, you will be the greatest duke England has ever seen."

Abby dropped to her knees and began retrieving the pins scattered on the wooden floor. Elijah knelt and helped her collect them. He rose and took her elbow, guiding her to her feet.

"Hold these if you would," she said, handing him the pins in her hands.

Then she ran her fingers through her hair several times before twisting it. She beckoned for a pin, and he handed it over, continuing to do so until her hair once more was perfectly in place.

"How did you do that?" he asked. "With no maid or mirror?"

"I had to do without a maid all those years Magnus and I traveled the world, Elijah. I am most self-sufficient."

He studied her carefully. She seemed perfectly normal, as if nothing earthshattering had occurred between them.

How could she be so unaffected?

For him, it was as if the earth had moved beneath his feet, shifting everything, changing his world.

While Abby seemed exactly the same as before. Placid. Confident. In control of herself.

She retrieved the pencil and pad, also on the floor. "We should continue on our tour, Your Grace."

ABBY LEFT THE empty library on shaky legs. She might exude an air of confidence—but she was thoroughly rattled inside.

The Duke of Bradford had kissed her. *Really* kissed her. He had teased with her. Explored her. Touched her. Made her feel like a woman for the first time. When he had stopped, she had asserted herself in a way she never dreamed she would.

And found that heaven could be a place on earth.

With the right man.

Confusion now filled her. She didn't want a husband. She couldn't afford to take on a lover. Besides the thought of an unwanted child, she could not risk the gossip that might leak out if someone discovered they were involved. It was one thing to flirt a bit in front of others at a ball. It was entirely another thing for a man to be seen leaving your residence at an hour in which all should be sleeping. If she were to make a success of Trent Furnishings, she could not fathom taking him as a lover.

Yet after their many kisses, the thought of coupling with him now consumed her. She could still taste him. She knew she still smelled of him. Her body ached, yearning to be close to his again. Wanting more than kisses. Wanting him inside her.

Abby had grown up in the country. She had seen animals coupling. She had also attended events all over the world and seen couples retreating for stolen kisses in dark passageways or in darker gardens. She had never been tempted in the least to participate in something such as that.

Until now. Now, all she wanted was to have Elijah's lips on hers.

Or on other parts of her.

That thought caused her face to flame. She was glad she was walking ahead of him and tried to breathe slowly, in and out, hoping to regain her composure and have her red face calm once more.

She moved in and out of rooms—parlors, sittings rooms, what she thought might once have been a billiard room. She kept her tone professional, telling him how she would restore each room.

"I don't play billiards," he said flatly.

Abby finally faced him. "You do not need to play yourself. Many of your guests will. It is something you should take up, though. A game of both skill and strategy. Magnus could teach you," she volunteered. "He enjoys playing after dinner."

"Do you?"

She did—and was a far better player than her guardian. She had taken to the game quickly once he showed her how it was played.

"I have upon occasion. Women rarely indulge in the sport, however. At least in England. Or so I am told."

Turning to leave the room, Elijah caught her arm. "If you enjoy it, you should play it. I wouldn't think you were a woman who would let society's conventions get in your way."

Her gaze met his. A rush of heat filled her. "I will admit I have led an unconventional life ever since my father's death. Magnus allowed me an unusual amount of freedom. If I am to fit into the *ton*, however, I must play by their rules. I want their business so I will behave with decorum."

His fingers singed her arm, and Abby had to stop from flinging herself at him. She couldn't take another moment of his touch and stepped away, exiting the room.

They went upstairs and found the rooms designated for the Duchess of Bradford.

"I think I will walk these rooms with Her Grace," Abby said. "After all, they were originally hers and will now be so again. We can discuss wallpaper and rugs, as well as what pieces she will desire."

"They won't always be Mama's rooms," he said quietly.

Frowning, she said, "You told me you had no wish to wed. That you didn't want to carry on your father's line."

His face hardened. "True." The duke turned away, returning to the corridor.

His rooms were next. The first would be a private room to converse with his closest of friends, and she discussed how she would decorate it. The second was simply for his own pleasure, a place he could read or think and have time away from both family and servants.

The bedchamber was by far the largest she had ever seen. It surprised her to find a bed within it, though it was stripped of its bedclothes.

"I want this bed removed," Elijah said harshly. "It was his. I refuse to sleep where he did."

"I can have it moved to another room. One of the guest bedchambers, perhaps. Or I can have my craftsmen break it down and use the parts of it in other projects."

"Either."

They entered his dressing room, and she said, "I would like a large, padded bench in here. You could sit on it while you put on your stockings and boots."

He shrugged and continued into the bathing chamber.

The old duke had even had his tub removed. His spitefulness continued to amaze her.

"I do not design bathtubs, but I can find one for you, one long and deep so you will fit in it comfortably. A screen, as well, so that you might have some privacy if you wish."

Elijah nodded curtly and retreated. Abby stood there a moment, thinking of a clawfoot tub in the center of this room.

And the naked duke sitting in it.

She went hot all over and fanned herself with her hands as he called out, "Are you coming?"

They investigated several guest bedchambers, and she told him these would be the last rooms she touched.

"I prefer to first furnish the rooms you and Her Grace will use the most," she told him.

"Yes. The drawing room. My study. The breakfast room would be my next preference. And of course, I want the servants taken care of quickly."

She jotted down a note. "Then I will begin working on designs for your house, Your Grace. I can also let you look through my previous sketches and the furniture already completed. I believe you will find quite a few things in my storeroom to your liking."

"No, I have told you that you will have a free hand in order to do as you wish. The sooner you can complete the task, the better."

Hurt—mixed with anger—ran through her. "You sound as if you wish to wash your hands of me as soon as possible."

He turned quickly, meeting her gaze. "No, I did not mean that. I just want to be settled in what is to be my home. Mine and Mama's. I want her to make friends and have a place to entertain them."

"And what of you, Your Grace? Don't you wish to make friends, as well?"

His face grew stony. "Gil was my friend. My brother. My heart. Anyone who comes after him will be merely an acquaintance."

Abby believed Elijah did not realize the depth to which his twin's death had affected him. It was not her place, though, to give him advice, and she certainly wasn't going to be his friend.

Not when she wanted to leap into his arms and wrap her legs about him and kiss him until they both grew breathless. She had a vague idea of what lovemaking involved, and images of that filled her mind.

"I believe I have seen everything I need, Your Grace." She wanted to put some distance between them and resorted to more formality now.

They returned downstairs and to the foyer just as the front door swung open. A couple entered, laughing gaily, and stopped upon seeing the two of them.

"Nelson," the duke said. "How were the interviews?"

The butler closed the door. "They went very well, Your Grace." He smiled at his wife. "Mrs. Nelson asked far harder questions than I thought of."

"How many servants do I now have?" the duke asked.

"A cook. Two footmen. Three parlor maids. Two scullery maids," the new housekeeper replied. "We will need more but with the house empty, a skeleton staff can easily care for it."

"I am Miss Trent," she told the couple. "I will be furnishing His Grace's townhouse so you will be seeing me on a regular basis."

She explained to them what she wanted to do with the butler's two rooms and the housekeeper's two rooms, and the pair approved of her decision.

"I will see that you are taken care of straightaway," Abby promised. "Then I will begin working on the other servants' rooms."

"We should be leaving, Miss Trent," Bradford said. "It is close to the time I am to pick up Mama."

"Very well, Your Grace. It was lovely meeting you, Mr. and Mrs. Nelson."

"The same, Miss Trent," Nelson told her.

Abby and Elijah returned to Magnus' carriage. Once inside, neither spoke a word until they arrived at Madame Aubert's. He insisted that she come inside and meet the modiste, who was more than willing to take on Abby as a client as a favor to Their Graces.

"You can come tomorrow morning, Miss Trent," Madame Aubert said.

"Could we make it tomorrow afternoon, Madame? You see, I have just opened a shop of my own and wish to be there tomorrow morning."

The modiste eyed her with interest. "Yes, come tomorrow afternoon, Miss Trent. You, too, Your Grace. You have an excellent eye and could help Miss Trent make decisions about her wardrobe."

"I would be happy to do so," the duchess said. "That is, if you wish me to help, Miss Trent."

She laughed. "You are taking my advice on how to furnish your townhouse, Your Grace. I would be happy to reciprocate and allow you and Madame Aubert to dress me for the Season."

They returned to the carriage. The duchess chatted happily about the many new gowns the dressmaker would make up for her and even made some suggestions regarding styles Abby would look good in.

The duke sat in silence.

She would say he was sulking, but his face looked carved from stone. He gave away nothing, and she thought he would be an excellent card player.

When they arrived at Magnus' residence, the duke helped them from the carriage and then said, "I have other business to attend to now. I will see you at breakfast tomorrow. Enjoy your tea, ladies."

Irritation filled her, knowing he had previously said he would be at tea. She smiled sweetly at him, however. "Thank you for allowing me to see your home, Your Grace. I look forward to helping you furnish it."

With that, she took the duchess' arm and moved her to the front door. It took every bit of willpower she possessed not to look back.

Chapter Twelve

Lord Ladiwyck's coachman called down to Elijah, "Shall I take you back to the inn, Your Grace?"

"No, I think I will walk for a bit. Thank you, though."

The driver flicked his wrists, and the horses started up to return to the mews.

Elijah walked the length of the square and left it. He didn't want to brood over Miss Abby Trent and decided he would do something which he had been toying with ever since they had arrived in London.

Go to Bow Street.

He knew of Bow Street from one of the men under his command. The soldier had been a former member of the Horse Patrol, which guarded the streets of London as a type of police force. Elijah had also learned an entire division of Bow Street was dedicated to runners, men who helped solve crimes. He hoped one of their specialties might involve locating missing persons.

After Mama had admitted to him that she had been in love before her forced marriage to the Duke of Bradford, Elijah had thought to see if he might find her former love. He knew it was a long shot and that Paul Baxter might not even be alive. He felt he owed it to Mama to try and give her some kind of closure.

Hailing a hansom cab, he told the driver his destination and hopped into the vehicle. On the ride there, however, his thoughts returned to Miss Trent.

And those hot, wonderful kisses.

Elijah admitted to himself that he wanted her. Badly. She was different from any woman he had ever known. Miss Trent had goals and a purpose in life, as well as the talent to achieve whatever she set out to do. She had told him she was not interested in marriage. He had revealed the same to her.

And yet the thought of spending the rest of his life with Abby Trent was incredibly appealing.

He recalled how she mentioned that she did want children, despite her desire to remain unwed. That was reason enough not to pursue her further. He refused to continue the Duke of Bradford's line. Who knew what bad blood lingered within him, thanks to his devious father. No, Elijah needed to rid her from his thoughts and his heart. Perhaps he could find a willing widow and begin an affair with her to satisfy his needs.

They reached the Bow Street headquarters, and he paid the cabbie. Upon entering the building, he went to a receiving desk.

"I am afraid I do not have an appointment, but I would like to speak to someone in charge. I am the Duke of Bradford."

It was the first time Elijah had confidently tossed out his title, knowing he would receive immediate attention—and he did. Soon, he was seated in the office of a Mr. Franklin.

"How might Bow Street help you, Your Grace?"

"I need to have you locate someone for me. I only possess a small bit of information about him."

The man took up a pencil and said, "Tell me everything you can about this man. The more information we have, the better our chances are in locating the person whom you seek."

"His name is Paul Baxter. He was a steward on the estate of a Lord Longley in Kent, just northwest of Dover. This was many years ago, close to thirty. Mr. Baxter was dismissed from his position, dismissed without references. That is all I can tell you."

Mr. Franklin finished scribbling his notes. "Might I ask the reason this Mr. Baxter was dismissed? It could help in the search."

Elijah hesitated a moment and then decided this man wouldn't perpetuate gossip from decades ago. "He tried to elope with my mother. They aimed for a place in Scotland, the name which now escapes me, because I am unfamiliar with it."

Light filled Mr. Franklin's eyes. "Ah, Gretna Green."

"Yes, that is the name my mother spoke. Mama was in love with Mr. Baxter, and they set out for Scotland. Unfortunately, her father somehow learned of their plans and chased them down. Baxter was let go on the spot, and Mama returned home." He paused. "Six months later, she made her come-out and was forced to wed the Duke of Bradford."

Mr. Franklin nodded in understanding. "I see."

"I would somehow like to make amends to Baxter, despite it being decades later. Without my grandfather giving the man references, it must have been difficult for him to find a new position. My mother has thought about Mr. Baxter fondly over the years."

"Would you like to unite the pair?" Franklin asked.

"It is a distinct possibility. For now, I am hoping that you can locate him so that I could speak to him myself. My mother knows nothing of this request. I would not want to get her hopes up."

"Of course, Your Grace. I will put one of my best people on this case. She just completed a rather difficult assignment, but she is always up for the impossible."

"Your runner is . . . a woman?"

"The only one among our group," Franklin said, pride evident in his voice. "If you have time to meet with Miss Slade now, I will summon her."

"If you believe Miss Slade will get the job done, then by all means send for her."

"Excuse me, Your Grace."

Franklin was gone a good five minutes and in that time, Elijah wondered what would possess a woman to embark upon an occupation solely performed by men. Curiosity filled him, and he was eager to meet this female Bow Street runner.

Franklin returned with Miss Slade in hand. She was a tall woman, lean and small-breasted, her golden eyes rimmed with brown. He rose, and she offered him her hand instead of bowing to him, which he found amusing. He shook her hand and the three of them took a seat.

"Mr. Franklin tells me that you are in need of locating someone, Your Grace. Please tell me all the details so that I may record them myself. I know you have already spoken with Mr. Franklin, but sometimes a client recalls something that previously went unmentioned."

Once more, Elijah related what he knew about Paul Baxter and the circumstances of the steward's dismissal. Miss Slade took notes as he spoke.

When he finished, he said, "I wish I knew more to share with you, Miss Slade. I realize these events occurred long ago, and it might be difficult—if not impossible—to trace Mr. Baxter's movements, much less find him."

Miss Slade's eyes twinkled. "Finding people—even those who do not wish to be found—is a specialty of mine, Your Grace. That is why Mr. Franklin recommended me for this assignment. If you will give me your address, I will send you weekly reports. We can also meet in person if you so desire."

Elijah had been thinking how he needed to put distance between him and Miss Trent and so he said, "I will only be in London until early next week, Miss Slade. I am staying at an inn while my townhouse is being refurbished."

He gave her the location of the inn. "If we could meet next Monday afternoon, I would appreciate it. You see, I will be leaving for

Marblebridge, my ducal seat in Surrey, on Tuesday morning. I have recently assumed my title and need to visit the estate for the first time and learn what my responsibilities toward my tenants will be."

If his words surprised the runner, she did not show it. Instead, she said, "Very well, Your Grace. I will start immediately and see you at the inn next Monday. Shall we say two o'clock?"

"I will be there," he promised, hoping that his business at Tattersall's would be concluded by then. If not, for any reason, he could send word to the innkeeper and have Miss Slade wait until he arrived.

He rose and she offered her hand once more. He shook it. "Thank you for taking on this case, Miss Slade."

She smiled. "It is what I do, Your Grace. I only hope that I will be able to find Mr. Baxter and help your mother receive some closure. Might I walk you out?"

Elijah said goodbye to Mr. Franklin, and Miss Slade escorted him from the office in which they met to the receiving room and said, "Goodbye, Your Grace."

He left the headquarters and hailed another hansom cab, returning to the inn. He hoped Miss Slade would be able to find Paul Baxter. He wanted to do this for Mama and right the wrong that was done to the steward so many years ago.

ABBY ROSE EARLY the next morning and breakfasted alone. Since she was scheduled to meet with Madame Aubert this afternoon, she had much to do before that appointment.

She asked Feathers to have Samuel ready her vehicle, and the driver took her to her workshop, where she found Mr. Bauer had already arrived.

"It's quite early, Miss Trent. Have you more designs to drop off?"

"I came to see if any progress had been made on the drawings Mr.

Nix dropped off yesterday, both the secretaire meant as a birthday gift and the dining set."

Bauer nodded. "Yes, Miss Trent. Come with me."

He showed her what had been accomplished since her visit yesterday morning and then said, "We will definitely need more workers if you are to fill an entire townhouse for His Grace. Mr. Alexander and I cannot do this alone. I have two friends whom I asked to come by this morning, hoping you would stop by as you usually do. Would you have time to interview them? I have seen both their work and would urge you to hire the pair."

"Thank you for summoning them, Mr. Bauer. I would be delighted to meet with them after they arrive. I will be in the storeroom, checking on several items, and tagging the ones I want designated for His Grace's townhouse."

Abby worked for a good hour, combing through the completed furniture and making notes of which pieces she wanted reserved for Bradford. She recorded them all in her notebook, noting which piece would go to what room, and then placed signs on each one, reserving them so they would not be taken to her Mayfair shop.

When she emerged, she found Mr. Alexander had arrived, and two men were speaking with him. She assumed they were the craftsmen Mr. Bauer had spoken of.

Going toward them, she said, "Good morning, gentlemen. I am Miss Trent. Mr. Bauer told me you would be stopping by this morning."

The shorter and stockier of the two stepped forward. "Good morning, Miss Trent. I am Mr. Echols." He indicated his companion. "This is my brother-in-law, Mr. Hunt. We work together making cabinets, tables, and chairs for the most part. We don't have nearly as grand a workspace as this, however. Our quarters are quite cramped."

"Come to our storeroom," she suggested. "I can show you pieces Mr. Alexander and Mr. Bauer have completed and we can visit a bit."

She led the pair to the storeroom and let them wander about freely, asking for their opinions regarding the furniture on display. Within a few minutes, Abby knew both these men had extensive knowledge about different woods and furniture styles. They pointed out the items they liked best and the ones which they would enjoy working on. Abby showed them some of her most recent designs and then told them about her new project.

"It is a massive one," she explained. "The Duke of Bradford has an entire townhouse to fill from top to bottom. It currently sits empty of all furnishings. The pieces I have marked here are ones I will be using in his home. There are several others at my Mayfair shop which will be sent to His Grace's townhouse. Still, it leaves much to be created—and that does not include other business that might come in off the street or from word of mouth. Might you be interested in coming to work for Trent Furnishings?"

Mr. Hunt said, "I think I can speak for the both of us that we are eager to accept your offer of employment, Miss Trent. Your designs are intriguing, and we look forward to bringing your drawings to life."

"That is excellent news," she declared. "When might you be able to start?"

"We can start now, Miss Trent," Mr. Echols said. "At least once we've retrieved our tools. I presume you wish for us to work here instead of in our current space."

"Yes, I would like all my craftsmen under one roof for convenience."

She told the pair what their salary and work hours would be. Both claimed her to be most generous.

"I expect quality work, and I know it is important to pay a craftsman what he is worth. Once we have completed this order for the Duke of Bradford, I believe it will spur more business for us. Expect to be busy now and in the future, gentlemen."

Abby left the workshop and had Samuel drive her to Trent Furnishings. There, she had Mr. Nix follow her about, marking numerous pieces as reserved for the Duke of Bradford.

"By the time all this furniture is moved from the shop, Miss Trent, we will be more than half empty," the clerk said.

"I realize that, Mr. Nix. You and Mr. Hogan must work on rearranging the store once that occurs. I will also have other items brought over to supplement what is left here."

Mr. Hogan joined them, and she asked, "Have you made arrangements yet with a mover?"

"I have found someone who is quite reliable, Miss Trent," her manager said. "I assume you will be wanting to move pieces as soon as possible to His Grace's townhouse."

"Yes, that is correct. Engage the services of these movers at once. They will need to move everything that I have marked in the store, along with a good number of pieces at the workshop's storeroom. The sooner, the better, Mr. Hogan. I need to see how the pieces I've selected look in His Grace's townhouse. It will also help me decide how to move forward in the process."

"I will write to them immediately, Miss Trent. I can have Mr. Nix deliver the message and handle any business that comes into the store myself while he is gone."

"Thank you," she said. "I will be in the office working on some new designs if you need me."

Abby worked a few hours and then left the office, where Mr. Hogan told her, "I have received a reply. The movers can be here at Trent Furnishings tomorrow morning at eight o'clock, Miss Trent. They know they also will be going to the storeroom to pick up additional furniture."

"That is very good news. I will be here to supervise the moving and accompany them to His Grace's townhouse so that they might place the pieces where I wish."

She would have to ask His Grace for a key to the townhouse or see if the Nelsons would be present tomorrow morning.

Leaving Trent Furnishings, she walked the three blocks to where Madame Aubert's dress shop was located, telling Samuel she was tired of sitting. She sent him home, knowing she would return with the Duchess of Bradford. As Abby arrived at the modiste's shop, Magnus' rented carriage pulled up, and the Duchess of Bradford joined her.

"I had a marvelous time with Madame Aubert yesterday, Miss Trent. I am so happy that you asked me to come with you today to help choose materials for your new gowns." The duchess glowed with happiness, looking even younger than she had previously.

"I definitely need your advice, Your Grace. I have not kept up with London fashions while Magnus and I traveled the world, and I have been so involved with starting up my business that I fear my wardrobe is hopelessly out of date."

The duchess linked arms with Abby. "Then let us go remedy that, my dear."

Chapter Thirteen

Abby discovered that she actually enjoyed picking out styles and fabrics for the new gowns which Madame Aubert would make up for her. She had never had much of an interest in fashion, but she liked the designs that the modiste showed her and even took pencil to paper, sketching out an idea or two that she had. Madame was eager to use the designs Abby had created. She was to return to the shop in a week's time, along with the Duchess of Bradford, for their first fittings.

In the carriage, the duchess said, "Thank you again, my dear, for allowing me to accompany you to your appointment. It was almost like having a daughter."

The duchess' eyes misted and once again, Abby thought how cruel this woman's husband had been to her, banishing her from her marriage and Polite Society, leaving her to raise her children on her own.

"Are you excited about attending your first Season?" the duchess asked. "Oh, I still think of my own come-out Season so long ago. The wonderful parties and balls. The handsome, attentive gentlemen." Then her mouth grew hard. "Unfortunately, it ended badly for me."

"Your marriage may not have been a success, Your Grace, but you did gain two wonderful boys from the union."

"That is absolutely true, Miss Trent. I am so happy to have Elijah home. I only wish Gil would have accompanied him." She paused.

"Although I do believe Elijah makes for a better duke than my other son would have."

Her curiosity piqued, Abby asked, "Why do you say that?"

"Ah, Gil was such an easy child to love, perhaps because he resembled me so much. He was always laughing about something and never took life too seriously. I do not believe I have ever met a more carefree spirit than Gil. Elijah, on the other hand, was a quiet child. Always observing silently all that happened about him. Reflecting on what he saw. While both my sons were intelligent, Elijah had a much stronger sense of duty than his brother. I am not speaking of being in the army and loyalty toward king and crown. Gil could be a bit thoughtless and rarely considered others' feelings, while Elijah always knew what his responsibilities entailed. He tried to make life as easy as he could for me—and that was no simple task."

That little boy certainly sounded like the duke of today to Abby.

The duchess turned her gaze out the window as she continued to speak. "Bradford abandoned our marriage. I may have possessed the title of Duchess of Bradford upon my marriage, but when he sent me away, it was not to the house upon his estate. I lived in a one-room cottage on the property. That is where I raised my boys, Miss Trent. It was oftentimes hard to make ends meet, and I took in sewing. It was the only skill I had that would support us as a family. Growing up, Elijah and Gil did odd jobs in the village for others. Elijah did three times what his twin did. Half the time, Elijah had to finish Gil's chores for him. Elijah was the man of the family from the time he was a small boy."

Abby's heart ached, thinking of the little boy who had such a heavy burden placed upon his shoulders at such a young age.

The duchess turned back to Abby. "My family cut all ties with me, taking Bradford's side. Fortunately, I had an elderly aunt who had a bit of money and no love for my father, who had been unkind to her when they were children. When she passed, she bequeathed to me a small sum of money. Elijah insisted that I use the funds to secure my future, but I wanted more for my boys. I used the money to buy each of them a commission, knowing being officers in His Majesty's army would add a bit of polish to them and expose them to others of their class. In return, they sent almost all their salaries home to me. I no longer had to worry about having enough money to put food on the table, especially since it was only myself. I was able to be more selective in the clients I took on and began sewing for the local gentry in the neighborhood. While I could sew my own new wardrobe, it is a luxury to sit back and have Madame Aubert do so for me."

The duchess' words gave Abby greater insight into Elijah and how his childhood had formed the man he now was, especially since he had been given the added burden of unexpectedly becoming the duke his brother was meant to be.

"I went with Bradford this morning to see Mr. Tibbets. I wanted to meet the tailor who would turn my son into a true duke. The old saying *clothes make the man* is certainly true for members of the *ton*, especially a duke. I found Mr. Tibbets to be delightful and an expert. I did help select some fabrics for coats to be made up, but I was able to leave and do a bit of shopping on my own, knowing my son was in good hands with his tailor. We will have to shop again another day since it is almost teatime, Miss Trent. You will need gloves, hats, slippers, stockings, and undergarments. I would be happy to go with you when you choose these if you don't mind me coming along."

"I would be happy for you to do so, Your Grace. You referred to me as a daughter. I am beginning to look upon you as a mother. My own died in childbirth when I was but two years of age. I cannot recall what she looked like. I can, though, hear her voice in my head because she would sing me to sleep."

The duchess reached for Abby's hand and squeezed it. "Thank you, my dear, for sharing that with me."

They arrived at Magnus' townhouse and went straight to the

drawing room for tea. Abby's belly fluttered with butterflies as she caught sight of Elijah. No, His Grace. She had to think of him that way.

And not those delicious, delirious kisses.

"Ah, how was your visit with Madame Aubert?" Magnus asked. "I have just been hearing about His Grace's time with Mr. Tibbetts today."

"It went very well," she replied. "The duchess' help was invaluable in helping me select my new wardrobe."

Magnus turned to the duke. "Abby has not had new clothes in several years. She would pick up a gown or two wherever we were. Why, she even bought things from local merchants." Magnus looked back to her. "Remember the blue sari you purchased in Calcutta? How it brought out the blue of your eyes?"

"A sari would not be appropriate to wear in English society," she told him. "I will be outfitted, however, from head to toe by the time Her Grace and Madame Aubert finish with me."

The teacart arrived, and Abby asked the duchess to pour out, a small task which seemed to delight the older woman.

"Your Grace," she said to the duke, "I have a great deal of furniture that is being moved to your residence tomorrow morning. I needed to see if your butler or housekeeper would be present to let us in. If not, might I have a key?"

"They will be there in the morning," the duke told her. "They will return to the employment agency tomorrow afternoon for another round of interviews with potential servants." He paused. "Might I be allowed to come and see what arrives?"

She didn't want him there, but he was spending a great deal of money with her. It would be churlish to keep him away, so she said, "Of course. I have marked the items at my shop which you and Her Grace told me you liked, along with a few other pieces that I believe will fit the décor of your townhouse. I also went through my extensive storeroom and marked numerous items to be delivered. I think after tomorrow's deliveries, you will be surprised at the progress we will make."

"It will be interesting to see how a room comes together," Bradford remarked.

"Furniture is only one part of it. Every room needs paintings and knickknacks, along with curtains and rugs. Do you still wish for me to handle the entire room, or would you rather hire someone else to purchase the artwork and other items?"

"I am leaving my townhouse in your capable hands, Miss Trent. I am sure Mama will have a few suggestions to add to whatever you do." He smiled fondly at his mother.

"Then expect the first delivery between eight-thirty and nine o'clock tomorrow morning. There is so much to bring that it will take several trips throughout the day."

"I can be there at that time. I have no commitments tomorrow." The duke turned to Magnus. "Speaking of commitments, are you still willing to go to Tattersall's with me on Monday, Lord Ladiwyck? I need to purchase a team of horses for my carriage so it will be easier to get about town."

Magnus nodded. "I am delighted to accompany you, Your Grace. I myself might need to invest in a team of horses."

"Oh?" said the duke. "The horses which draw your carriage seem perfectly fine to me."

Magnus chuckled. "Those are rented, same as the carriage. Since I have decided to stay for the Season this year and Abigail's come-out, I believe I should purchase something a little more worthy of my station."

They finished their tea, and Abby found herself fidgeting nervously. She was not—and never had been—a fidgeter. Traveling the world and meeting so many people and being immersed in a variety of cultures had given her confidence. Around the Duke of Bradford, however, she seemed to lose that self-assurance she normally possessed.

"You seem a bit restless, Miss Trent," the duke observed. "Perhaps you have been inside too much today and would enjoy taking a stroll now. I would be happy to accompany you."

He was the last person she should be alone with, and yet she heard herself replying, "That would be delightful, Your Grace." She looked to the other two, hoping to entice them to come along. "Would you care to join us?"

The duchess chuckled. "I have had my fill of exercise today. I will sit and talk with Lord Ladiwyck. The two of you go and enjoy your walk."

They went downstairs, and Abby slipped into her spencer again. It was growing dark and though there was no wind, there was a chill in the air. She tied the ribbons of her bonnet beneath her chin, and they set out.

"You have not reconsidered the bargain we struck with one another," the duke said. "Or have you?"

"I should," she said frankly. "I do not know if it is in our best interests, after all, to pursue a false relationship."

"I see nothing false about it, Miss Trent. We are friends. We are also business owner and client. That is two layers to our relationship."

"There can be no more kissing!" she blurted out, turning her head to observe his reaction.

His sensual lips merely smiled at her indulgently. "I thought it was an excellent way for us to get to know one another better," he said huskily.

"I do not believe we need to know each other any better than we already do, Your Grace. I also need to tutor you in regard to some of the rules of Polite Society. One, walking alone with an unwed woman in public is unacceptable."

His smile deepened. "Then why are you doing it with me?"

"I shouldn't be. It is still early. Most have not returned from their country estates to town. It is also growing dark. I don't believe anyone would recognize either of us. Me, because I have been abroad for so many years and spent the last months buried in work, never socializing. You, because you have been at war for your entire adult life, and few know what the Duke of Bradford even looks like."

"I will correct that statement, Miss Trent. It seems that everywhere I go, I am almost immediately recognized because the person knew my father. Mama told me I resembled him, but you should see the downright shock on the faces of those I encounter. It is as if Bradford has risen from his grave."

"Then I suppose that is a good reason to cut our stroll short. We should head back. As we go, let me reiterate that you are not to be alone with a young, unmarried woman in the future. I am a bit different because I am considered on the shelf. I have told you my advance age makes it so."

"You have said you are five and twenty. I think that quite young. In fact, I suppose you will live for several decades more."

"Back to the point I am trying to make, Your Grace," she said sternly. "You are never to be alone with an unwed woman. Not in a carriage and not accompanying her on a walk—unless her maid is with you."

His brow furrowed. "I am to have a maid on one arm and a young lady on the other?"

A giggle escaped Abby. "No, silly. The maid will walk several paces behind the two of you. Now, if you walk in the park, it is permissible to actually walk alone or ride in an open carriage, especially during the social hour, which is from five to six o'clock during the Season. Many of the *ton* walk or ride through the park at that time and greet one another. Since it is a public place with many others around, that is acceptable.

"As to a house? Never, ever be alone with a woman. If you are hosting a dinner, make certain that several people leave the table and go to the drawing room with you. You are never to take a woman anywhere alone in a house. The same goes for social affairs that you attend. People are all around you, and so it is acceptable for you to eat or dance with a woman. Gentlemen have an advantage in that they may go to the card room for a respite. You are a duke, Your Grace, a highly prized commodity. I have told you that mothers will want to sink their claws into you and have you court and wed their daughters. You do not want to be found by others alone with a woman. If you are, she will be compromised—and you will have no choice except to wed her."

"You are saying if I happened to show a young lady my library, for instance, and someone else came in, that I would have to marry that lady. Even though I had not laid a finger upon her?"

Abby smiled grimly. "You are now beginning to understand the rules of the *ton*."

"I suppose it is just as well that I am leaving town soon," he told her.

"You are ... leaving?" Abby hated the tone of her voice as the question hung between them.

"I must go to Marblebridge. If I am to be here and escort Mama to the Season's events and pay special attention to you, I cannot neglect my primary estate now. Have your way with my townhouse, Miss Trent. Mama can be my eyes and ears and make recommendations to you. I would be happy if you would write me, however, once a week and tell me of the progress you have made."

They approached the door to Magnus' townhouse, and she said, "I would be happy to keep you informed, Your Grace."

Feathers let them in, and she asked if the duke might be staying for dinner.

"No, I have prior commitments."

She wondered what that involved—and suspected that he might

already have found a mistress.

"Then enjoy your evening, Your Grace," Abby said crisply, and went to her bedchamber.

She sat in a chair, brooding, angry at herself for doing so. Then she decided this was a blessing in disguise, after all. The Duke of Bradford would be gone for weeks—and she would be able to concentrate on her business. Everything was as it should be.

Despite the little voice in her head saying otherwise.

Chapter Fourteen

Elijah cursed under his breath as the carriage turned into the square, and he spied his townhouse.

"Did you say something, Bradford?" his mother asked.

"No, Mama. I merely cleared my throat."

"When are you going to admit that you have feelings for Miss Trent?"

"What?"

The horses came to a stop and moments later, a footman opened the door.

"Not now," he growled, glaring at the man, who quickly closed the door.

"Must you be so irritable with the servants?" Mama asked, looking at him innocently.

"I want to talk about what you said."

"Oh? About you and Miss Trent?" Mama smoothed her gown. "I have seen a spark between the two of you, Bradford. It would be hard for you to hide such a thing. I know you previously mentioned not wanting to wed. I can even understand your reason why. But you are a perfectly decent gentleman, and Miss Trent is simply lovely, both in looks and manners. If you are interested in her, it is quite all right to change your mind."

He couldn't believe his mother had picked up on the current between Miss Trent and him. He had tried to avoid spending too much time around Miss Trent. She was the main reason he was citing his duty to Marblebridge.

Because if he stayed in town much longer, he couldn't trust what might happen between them. Not after those shared kisses in his empty library.

Still, he would honor the arrangement they had made between them, which he was beginning to consider an unholy alliance. Elijah hadn't changed his mind. He was never going to marry and propagate the family line. He would follow through on the bargain, though, paying Miss Trent special attention for the beginning weeks of the Season. It would keep matchmaking mamas away from him and allow Miss Trent to make a favorable impression upon the *ton*.

If they were to be believable, then his own mother must think they were a couple. He supposed now would be the time to plant those seeds, especially since Mama already had spoken up.

"I find Miss Trent to be quite admirable," he began. "She has led an unusual life, being brought up away from England and the *ton*. She is clever and interesting."

The hopeful look on Mama's face almost did him in. "Will you pursue her now? Before the Season starts?"

"I cannot."

Briefly, he shared his plans with her, telling her it was important for him to spend time at Marblebridge.

"That will allow me to be back in time for the Season," he concluded.

"What of your wardrobe, Bradford?"

"I am to see Mr. Tibbets Tuesday next for fittings. Based upon those, he and his tailors will continue building my wardrobe. Mr. Tibbets has also promised he would bring much of it to Marblebridge for me to try on. After all, Surrey isn't all that far from London."

Mama sighed. "I suppose Miss Trent will be busy furnishing your townhouse. You would not get to see her much if you did stay in town." She paused. "Do you wish for me to accompany you to the country?"

Elijah could tell from her expression that was the last thing Mama wanted to do.

"No. You have too many dress fittings, both yours and Miss Trent's, to see to. You also will need to visit daily and see the progress occurring in the townhouse. I'm sure the Nelsons can help keep you apprised of the staff they have hired. You have my full authority to make any decisions you see fit, Mama. I trust you and Miss Trent in this grand undertaking."

"Then I would prefer staying in town, Bradford. I think I am being quite helpful to Miss Trent."

"I have also asked her to write to me weekly and advise me of her progress," he added. "Once I have a firm grasp on everything at Marblebridge, I will return in time to accompany you to the opening night of the Season. It will be then that I will decide if I wish to further my friendship with Miss Trent."

Mama beamed. "I am glad to hear that."

"I suppose we should go in and see what she is up to now."

Elijah opened the carriage door and descended the steps placed before the doorway. Turning, he handed Mama down.

The front door to the townhouse was open. Two large wagons were parked in front, men unloading furniture and carrying it into the house. He recognized Mr. Alexander and guided Mama in the craftsman's direction.

"Ah, Your Grace," Mr. Alexander said. "You can see we are quite busy this morning." He wheeled around abruptly. "No, use three men to carry that. Not two." Turning back to them, Alexander said, "Miss Trent is inside, supervising where each piece is to go."

"Then we will locate her. Carry on, Mr. Alexander."

He led Mama into the house, where Nelson greeted them.

"Your Graces. Quite a busy morning. Might I get you a cup of tea?"

"No, thank you, Nelson," Mama said. "I would like to speak with Mrs. Nelson, however, regarding the china." She looked to Elijah. "Bradford had all but two pots and two chipped plates sold. I need to work with Mrs. Nelson on equipping the entire kitchen again. I will look for you after we finish our conversation."

She headed toward the kitchens, and he asked, "Where might Miss Trent be?"

The butler chuckled. "She is everywhere, Your Grace. A true whirlwind. She was last in the drawing room, however."

"Then I will look for her there."

He stepped aside as two men carried a settee toward the stairs and let them get a flight up before he began climbing the stairs himself. Following the pair to the drawing room, he found Miss Trent there, sounding like a drill sergeant barking orders.

"Yes, there. Two inches to the left. No, make it three. Ah, yes. Perfect." She turned. "Move it a little bit to the right. No, that is too much. Wait. There. Yes, that is exactly where it should be."

Her cheeks were flushed with excitement, and Elijah thought she looked in her element.

Then she caught sight of him. Her smile faltered. Mentally, he kicked himself, knowing he had been abrupt with her when he left her yesterday. He had never felt the urge to pull a woman to him and yet thrust her away at the same time. He wanted to be next to her. He wanted to not even be in the same room with her. He wanted to drag her to an empty room and kiss her senseless.

Confusion reigned within him as never before.

"Your Grace," she said, coming to him and curtseying. "As you can see, things are moving along."

He glanced about the room. "I can see that your craftsmen already had many pieces of furniture completed that look quite handsome here."

"I did believe several of my designs which had already been finished would look good in this room. Of course, even filled with furniture, it will seem incomplete without all the trappings of a normal room. Rugs alone can warm a room considerably, making it feel grand and yet quite livable. I want to place all the furniture first, however. Then I will get to the rest."

Moving about the room, Elijah took note of what was already in place, pointing out the details on several pieces which he liked.

"This is coming together nicely," he noted.

"The drawing room will be the first room completed," Miss Trent told him. "Your study and the breakfast room will follow. I already have Mr. Bauer working on both rooms, along with two new craftsmen I have hired."

"What of the servants' quarters?"

"I had a suitable bed for the Nelsons already brought over. The former duke's bed was far too large for their room. It has been moved to a guest bedchamber, the largest one I could find in order to accommodate it."

"Thank you." He shuddered. "The thought of lying where he had . . . bothered me a great deal."

Miss Trent shared with him other things she would be doing, stopping every now and then to direct the movers in where they should place furnishings. A pianoforte arrived, and she had the movers try it in three locations before she was satisfied.

"You seem as if you will be quite busy the rest of the day. Will you be missed at your shop?"

She laughed, sending chills racing along his spine. "Not at all. I think the few people who came in opening day have had their curiosity satisfied. I doubt I will see any new pieces commissioned until next month or even April. It will give me time to focus on your needs."

"When does the Season start?"

She thought a moment, that small crease between her brows calling out to him. Elijah wished he could kiss it away.

"It will be seven weeks from this coming Monday," she informed him. "I hope you will return to town before then."

"I will. I won't let you or Mama down, Miss Trent."

She blushed, her cheeks as rosy as her lips. "I never said you would, Your Grace."

Suddenly, he knew he had to kiss her.

"Could we look at the library again, Miss Trent? I had a few ideas what to do in it."

Her brow furrowed again, indicating her displeasure with that idea. Still, she replied pleasantly. "Of course, Your Grace. One moment."

She went to the window and looked out it. He accompanied her, gazing over her shoulder. One wagon was now gone, and the other almost emptied of its cargo.

"Perfect timing. The movers will be returning to my storeroom for their next load. I have a good hour before they will return, since it will take time to load the wagons and return here.

An hour which Elijah believed could be put to very good use.

They left the drawing room and headed to the library. Miss Trent entered, and he closed the door behind them, quietly turning the lock. What he had in mind would be best enjoyed without interruption.

Moving to the middle of the room, Miss Trent stood, arms akimbo. Slowly, she turned in a circle, taking in the entire space.

"What do you have in mind, Your Grace? I believe a library should be a welcoming spot."

He walked to her. "First, tell me what you plan to do in here, Miss Trent."

She launched into a detailed explanation, obviously having put a great deal of thought into how to furnish the room and the placement of the furniture. What she envisioned was warm and inviting. He could imagine sitting near the fire, a book in hand.

And Abby Trent seated next to him.

That picture of domesticity shook him to his core. Once more, he cursed inwardly, not wanting to see himself in that position. He was neither husband nor father material and wouldn't pretend to be.

She moved to a large window. "Here, I will place cushions. I think a window seat should have the option of being another place in which to read."

"I would have liked such a place as a boy," he mused. "Somewhere comfortable to sit and full of light."

"Did you enjoy reading as a child?"

Elijah nodded. "I did. Life got in the way more often than not, though. I had chores to do around our cottage. Wood to chop and water to haul. Gil and I also helped out our various neighbors. We did everything from milk cows to help with the harvest. Perhaps now I will lead a more leisurely life, and I will have time for reading. For learning."

Understanding shone in her eyes. "I believe we are never too old to learn. I think of all the places I have traveled and what I was exposed to by going abroad. I hope you will enjoy having time to yourself, Your Grace. Of course, you will have tremendous responsibilities, as well, but I know you will plan your time wisely and be able to enjoy various pursuits."

All Elijah wanted was to pursue *her*.

Taking a step toward her, he clasped her elbow, turning her to face him. "I have told you I will be gone several weeks. Most likely, right up until the Season begins."

"Yes?" she said breathily, her scent wafting up to tempt him.

"Do you always wear jasmine, Miss Trent? The scent is almost . . . seductive."

She swallowed visibly. "Hindus and Muslims regard jasmine as the perfume of love. It is said to relax the body and lower emotional borders, something necessary when engaging in . . . intimacy." She bit her lip, sending a frisson of desire through him. "I doubt I will ever know love, but I do enjoy a bit of jasmine dabbed at my pulse and throat. It reminds me of my days abroad."

He bent, his nose brushing her neck as he inhaled deeply. "Ah, yes." He lifted his head, his mouth close to hers. "The heat of your body releases the scent. I find it most intoxicating."

"You do?" she asked, her lips trembling.

"You know I do," he said huskily, dipping his head and brushing his lips slowly against hers.

She sighed. He could feel her eyelashes fluttering against his own cheeks. Elijah broke the kiss. He slipped an arm about her and released her elbow, his hand moving to cup her face. Slowly, he stroked his thumb against her cheek, his gaze pinning hers.

"You are a very beautiful woman, Abby," he said, using her Christian name. "One who appeals greatly to me."

Her palms went to his chest, as if to hold him back. "I thought we said no more kissing."

"*You* said that. *I* didn't agree to anything of the kind."

"We already know something of each other," she protested weakly, her fingernails digging into his chest.

"True. There are things, however, which I would like to show you."

She looked puzzled. "That would help us know one another better?"

Her innocence touched him deep within. "Yes. I will be gone several weeks. I do not want to lose the closeness we have established. I want to leave you with something to remember me by."

"Another kiss?" she asked, her breath coming rapidly, like a hare caught in a trap.

"Yes. The kind of kiss you will not forget."

His mouth took hers then, knowing they were alone and it might be the last time that occurred. Elijah wanted more than a kiss from this woman. He wanted to touch her soul.

His arm held her to him while his hand left her cheek and cupped her nape, holding her in place as his assault on her mouth went beyond any kiss he had ever bestowed. Hungrily, he took from her, tasting her, reveling in her. The jasmine on her skin heated, the scent rising, filling him.

Still, he wanted more. More of her than he should. And he wanted to give her something to remember him by as the weeks kept them apart.

He maneuvered her so her back touched a wall, trapping her in his embrace. As he kissed her over and over, his hand lifted her skirts, slipping underneath them, sliding up her leg. He heard her breath catch as his fingers glided over silky skin, moving to her core. His fingers brushed along the seam of her sex, and she gasped into his mouth.

Elijah broke the kiss, his lips hovering above her own. "Trust me," he murmured.

"I do," she said without hesitation, causing him to pause a moment.

He pushed aside all doubts, wanting to touch her. Make her come. Make her want him as much as he wanted her.

She was already wet, not knowing it, and he easily slid a finger into her.

"Oh!" she said, part surprise, part moan.

"I am going to touch you, Abby. Touch you where no one has ever touched you. Make you feel things that only I can make you feel."

"Yes," she said hoarsely, her voice breaking.

Looping her arms about his neck, she held on tightly as his fingers teased her. The sound of her whimpers, her gasps, her low groans made Elijah feel powerful.

He kissed her deeply, his tongue mimicking what his fingers did, causing her body to tremble. Increasing the speed, he stroked her deeply, feeling her body tense, knowing what would soon come.

She didn't know, however, and he broke the kiss. "I am giving you pleasure, am I not?"

"Yes," she said, her breath coming in spurts.

"Something is building inside you as we speak."

"As *you* speak," she managed to say. "I can barely utter a word."

"Soon, you will be mindless with pleasure, Abby. Pleasure that *I* have brought you."

His mouth seized hers again, his fingers working their magic. Soon, she gripped him with the strength of ten men, her body shuddering, her breath ragged, his mouth capturing her scream.

He had brought many women to orgasm, but none had brought him the satisfaction Abby Trent did now.

When it ended, she became limp, her arms falling away from him. Elijah scooped her up and carried her to the window seat, sitting with her in his lap.

Looking into her dazed eyes, he smiled. "Do you think you will remember me now?"

Chapter Fifteen

Seven weeks later...

ELIJAH GLANCED OUT the window of the post chaise that returned him to London. He had journeyed to Surrey in his ducal carriage, pulled by his new team of matched bays, ones he had purchased from Tattersall's. He had also bought a horse to ride in the country, knowing it would be easier to get around by horseback when he visited his tenants. He had sent the carriage and coachman back to London so it would be at his mother's disposal in the weeks he was gone. It would give her the freedom to move about when she chose and not have to depend upon Lord Ladiwyck's carriage, especially if she moved to the ducal townhouse.

Mama had written to him twice a week during his absence, telling him about her dress fittings and how the townhouse was slowly turning into a home. As more of the *ton* returned from the country, Lord Ladiwyck had held a few dinners, helping introduce Mama back into Polite Society. Her letters were filled with exuberance, and Elijah was glad that she sounded so happy with her new life. If him becoming the Duke of Bradford brought joy to his mother, so be it.

He had kept busy during his sojourn at Marblebridge. The house had been bare, with neither a single piece of furniture nor a dish gracing the cabinets. Elijah had stayed the entire visit with Peabody, his steward, who had a large, comfortable cottage on the estate. He had grown close with his employee and learned as much as he could about estate management during his weeks in the country. Once the Season ended, he was determined to visit all his estates and get to know the people residing on these various properties.

Soames had come down twice to meet with Elijah, who now had a firm grasp on his holdings and finances. Tibbets had also traveled to Surrey twice for wardrobe fittings, leaving several items behind so that Elijah could finally retire his military uniform for good. The bulk of his clothing had been delivered to his townhouse, with Tibbets promising to come and see that all pieces pleased Elijah and fit him well once he returned to town.

Nelson had also written, telling him that the hiring of Elijah's London staff was now complete and that all servants were on the property, their quarters filled with furniture, as a good deal of the house was. When he'd bought his horseflesh at Tattersall's, Elijah had hired a driver and a groom. He would revisit Tattersall's soon and purchase a few more horses for riding in town, along with another groom to help care for the animals. As the Season progressed, he would work with the Nelsons on choosing employees for Marblebridge. Mama had told him that the Nelsons were to be left in town with the staff, while he would need a new butler and housekeeper for Marblebridge, as well as dozens of servants to help run the country estate. Elijah was of a mind to bring the Nelsons to Surrey with him if he could not find a new butler and housekeeper he could trust. That would be decided down the line, however.

He had met with Miss Slade before leaving town. The Bow Street runner had little to report at that time, having only been on the case for a few days. Since then, she had gone to Kent twice, speaking to various servants of the current Lord Longley, as she worked to track down Paul Baxter's whereabouts. She had sent Elijah weekly reports of her progress, having picked up Baxter's trail and following it through the years. Miss Slade assured him that she had every confidence that Mr. Baxter would be found.

Elijah still had not mentioned any of this to Mama. He wanted to meet with the man first—if indeed Miss Slade found him—and ascertain whether or not it would be a good idea to reunite the pair. If, once he met the steward, he thought it a poor idea, Elijah still would see if Baxter would allow him to award some type of compensation.

The carriage slowed a bit, and he focused on his surroundings, seeing they were now entering London. He was told this yellow bounder, the nickname for a hired post chaise, would deliver him directly to his doorstep.

He wondered if Abby Trent might be there.

Elijah had done his best to forget the woman during his time in the country. Not only did he spend long hours with his steward, going over ledgers and learning about husbandry and crop rotation, he also put in hours of physical labor on the property. He rode to each tenant's cottage, wanting to meet them in person. He had helped replace roofs. Mend fences. Even assisted in foaling a horse. Falling into bed each night, he went to sleep immediately from sheer physical exhaustion.

Yet Abby continued to haunt his dreams every night.

Miss Trent's letters appeared like clockwork each week, full of meticulous details regarding the headway she had made as she refurbished each room. With his arrival today, Elijah knew he would see all the public rooms complete, as well as the rooms he and his mother used individually. Mama had decided to wait and move into the townhouse once Elijah came back to town. From everything the two women shared in their correspondence, he knew he would be pleased with the results.

He leaned his head against the cushion, closing his eyes, finally allowing himself the luxury to call up Miss Trent's image. He'd done everything he could to put her from his mind in the weeks they'd been apart. Her weekly correspondence caused him to relapse each time. Elijah yearned to see her once more. To taste her. To touch her.

In that moment, he knew he could not live without Abby in his life.

Would she be willing to make a marriage without children? That was the question. She had admitted to him that she wanted them. Might she be willing to put aside that need in order for them to be together? He had promised himself the Bradford line would end with him.

It would be the end of *him* if he could not make Abby Trent his.

She might not consider marrying him at all. If a thriving business were important to her, it could replace a husband and children. He also knew she had mentioned wanting to travel again someday. Truth be told, Elijah didn't have much to offer Abby Trent that she didn't already have.

He decided he would pretend to keep with the bargain they had made—and hope she might fall in love with him.

Because for the first time, Elijah admitted to himself that he was in love with her.

Could he court her as Polite Society looked on and convince her they would be better together than apart?

The next few weeks would tell.

Opening his eyes, he watched as the streets passed by. He recognized Mayfair as they reached it, excitement filling him. Having never had much in the way of material possessions, it surprised him how much he looked forward to seeing his home now—and all Abby had done with it.

Elijah wondered if she had thought of him during his absence. He had not seen her since that day in his library, when he had brought her to the heights of pleasure. She had quickly regained her composure and returned to directing the movers as to where they should place different items of furniture. He had left, shaken by the experience, and then avoided seeing her over the next three days before he left for Marblebridge, even meeting Lord Ladiwyck at Tattersall's instead of going to the earl's townhouse.

A rush of emotions swept through him as the post chaise pulled up in front of his residence. Nelson quickly appeared, along with two footmen, who claimed the large portmanteau which Mr. Tibbet had thoughtfully provided on his last trip to Surrey.

"Your Grace, it is good to see you," Nelson said. "I hope you had a pleasant journey from Marblebridge."

Elijah looked around, seeing that Samuel, the man who drove Abby about, sat in his vehicle.

She was here . . .

"Yes," he said to his butler. "Everything was fine."

"Will you be needing anything else, Your Grace?" the postillion called.

"No, that will be it. Thank you."

The post chaise's guide doffed his cap to Elijah and clucked his tongue, starting up the horses and guiding them from the square.

"Take His Grace's portmanteau to his rooms," Nelson instructed the footmen. "Would you care for tea, Your Grace?"

"No. I think I'd rather see the house and what Miss Trent has done with it," he replied.

The butler's eyes lit up. "Ah, I believe you will be most pleased, Your Grace. I have Mrs. Nelson assembling your staff now. They are gathering in the foyer."

"Then I should meet them."

Elijah followed his butler into the townhouse, where several lines of servants were forming.

Miss Trent was nowhere in sight.

Disappointment filled him, but he would not let her leave this house without speaking to her first. In fact, he would insist that she take him on a tour of the entire place so he could see what she had accomplished during his absence. It would be the beginning of his campaign to try and win her over. Elijah knew he must be subtle. If she thought his interest in her was real, she might skitter away and refuse to attend *ton* affairs altogether.

"You Grace, we are so happy to have you back," Mrs. Nelson said warmly. "Please allow Nelson and me to introduce you to your new staff."

He deliberately took his time as he went down the various lines, asking for each servant's name and what they would be doing in the household. Thanks to some of the looks he received, he supposed this didn't often occur in houses of the gentry.

Once he finished, Elijah decided to address the staff. Though not one for speeches, he believed it would set the proper tone.

"Thank you for accepting a position in my household," he began. "Previously, I was a major in His Majesty's army and did not expect to be named the Duke of Bradford. I am new to this world, but will do my utmost to be a good employer to you. In return, I ask that you do your best in the position you've been hired for and be kind to all within the household."

"Well said, Your Grace," Nelson said.

Elijah looked at the eager faces and hoped that not only would he be happy with those in his household but they, in return, would be happy to be in service here.

"Please return to your posts," he added, and the large group assembled began to disperse.

That was when he saw her.

She stood at the top of the landing of the staircase, watching him. Their gazes met, and his heart thumped hard against his ribs. She moved gracefully down the stairs, her hand skimming the banister. He watched her make every step and then come to him.

"Miss Trent."

"Your Grace."

"I believe I need to see what has been done with my house." He turned to the Nelsons. "Miss Trent and I will tour the house and then take tea in the drawing room."

"Yes, Your Grace," the couple replied, leaving the foyer.

He was now alone with her and felt like a bashful schoolboy, at a loss for what to say.

She smiled brightly at him. "I suppose we can start on the ground floor, Your Grace. I hope you will be pleased with all that I have done. Her Grace added a few touches, here and there, but she left the bulk of decorating to me."

"Your letters were quite thorough, Miss Trent. Your descriptions have made me eager to see what you wrote about brought to life."

"Shall we start?"

Chapter Sixteen

Abby turned away from the duke, her smile falling, her heart beating so rapidly that she feared she might suffer a heart attack.

She had known this day was coming. The day Bradford would return from Surrey. And yet she still wasn't prepared to see him.

Every day, she had busied herself, filling every hour with tasks. She sketched her designs as Samuel drove her from place to place. Met daily with her craftsmen, checking their work and fine-tuning her drawings. She visited her shop each day, talking with customers as more and more came in to browse—or even place orders.

And then she had devoted ten, twelve, even fourteen hours a day to the Duke of Bradford's house. She had seen that rooms had an adequate amount of furniture and played with the placement of every piece that was carried through the front door. She had visited rug merchants, selecting rugs of the highest quality. She had purchased chandeliers and lamps, landscapes and still lifes for the walls, vases and snuff boxes and every manner of knickknack that would make this house a home.

She had asked the duchess for her opinions and advice in those early days, seeing the older woman preferred to trust Abby's design instincts. The two had spent a good deal of time together at dress fittings and shopping when Abby wasn't working. Now, she had a house to show the duke. Part of her prayed he would not bring up the last kiss between them. His kisses had rendered her senseless.

Not to mention what his touch had done to her.

Late at night, when she collapsed into bed, weary to the bone, her thoughts returned to those stolen moments in the library. His mouth on hers. His body pressed against hers. The heat of his fingers as they delved inside her. The physical feelings and emotions from that encounter.

Did he think of it, too? Or did men simply move on from such experiences without a second thought?

She feared the intimacies which had occurred between them had caused a deep yearning to fill her, one which bewitched her, putting her under his spell. She couldn't afford to be spellbound by the duke, however. She had a business to run and already made inroads as more of the curious *ton* visited her shop. Quick thinking had her leave a couple of pieces in her shop marked with the Duke of Bradford's name. Seeing a duke bought from her had encouraged others to do so. Soon, word-of-mouth would drive more traffic into her shop, and she thought she might not even need to attend but a handful of social events.

Yet a part of her longed for the attention the duke had promised to pay to her. Oh, she knew it to be false. He had plainly made his feelings known regarding marriage and children. But to have his gaze upon her, looking at her as if she were the only woman in the world, made her want to spend at least some time in his company in front of the *ton*.

Now, though, she had a house to show him. She would be professional and courteous. With servants about the house now, there would be no opportunity for him to do the things he had done to her previously. She would show him his house and then leave.

Abby led the duke through each room on the ground floor, all now furnished as if every item within had been present for years. She pointed out the various woods she had used in the furniture, from oak and walnut to cherry veneer and pine. For grander pieces, she had used exotic woods such as ebony, zebrawood, and rosewood. She made sure her craftsmen polished each piece to emphasize and highlight the grains in those woods so that they displayed a visually striking surface. The large dining room table featured mahogany flame grains and used ebony for its inlays. The duke merely nodded as she pointed out what she had done, keeping his thoughts to himself.

They moved to the first floor, with the drawing room being the most magnificently decorated of all the public rooms.

"I gave a great deal of thought to the arrangement within each room, in particular this drawing room. I wanted it to be functional and open, and remain warm and inviting at the same time. You can see the furniture in this room is elegant but with slender lines. It is not overly detailed. I have stayed away from tall cabinets and focused upon using shorter pieces. Lower furniture allows for a better display of paintings on the walls and sculptures or statutes upon the furniture itself."

"Is that brass?" he asked, the first time he had spoken in over half an hour.

"Yes, I like to use brass and ormolu for accents, such as where the doors on a wardrobe meet, or in the fluting of a chair's leg."

"I see." He kept his hands clasped behind his back as he paced the room. "And the art?"

"I have drawn from artists both well-known and not yet discovered," she told him. "The paintings are pastoral, for the most part, though I did purchase a few still lifes."

He merely nodded, and she decided they had seen enough of drawing room.

Abby showed him various parlors and sittings rooms, along his study and the library.

She indicated the shelves. "As you can see, Your Grace, th is still a work in progress. I have been in touch with booksellers. The shelves are already half-full. You might w some bookshops on your own, as well as art galleries, and place your own stamp on this room. I will continue to work with booksellers to help round out the look."

She showed him his mother's rooms and then led him to the ducal rooms. He took his time in them, studying everything carefully.

"What is the wood in this bedchamber?"

"It is actually oak which has been ebonized. That is a process which darkens wood so that it closely resembles ebony. It is stained several times and polished to give a sleek, black appearance to the wood. It is very masculine in nature, and I did not use it anywhere else in the house."

Abby pointed out different pieces in the bedchamber and then led him into his dressing room. She had placed several commodes within it, telling him these low chests of drawers contained various items of clothing in each, such as his shirts and cravats. In his bathing chamber, she had put the largest bathtub she could find, one in which he might stretch out his legs with ease and sink into the water.

"This tub is large enough for two people," he noted, causing her to think of being in it with him.

She turned quickly and left the room, her cheeks filled with heat. She went to a window and opened it, hoping some cool air might cause her blush to die down.

The carpet in the bedchamber was too thick to hear his footsteps, but Abby knew the duke had followed her into the room. She closed the window and turned to him.

"That is it, save for one guest bedchamber, the one I placed the previous duke's bed in."

"I have no need to see it," he said dismissively.

"I will be working to fill all your guest bedchambers in the next few weeks. They are the only rooms in the house still lacking in furniture, besides the schoolroom and nursery. They all contain rugs, however, since I found a merchant with quality items and purchased for the entire house from him. And Mrs. Nelson and some of the maids are sewing curtains for them." She paused. "I did not have you tour the servants' quarters, Your Grace, but they have been completed. Suffice it to say that each room is furnished appropriately, and Mrs. Nelson has approved everything I did there."

His steady gaze caused her to grow hot all over. "You have done a remarkable job, Abby. I had not expected to see so much complete. The speed in which you have worked has been nothing short of amazing."

"Do you *like* it?" she pressed. "You haven't really said much of anything."

Bradford smiled—and it was as if the sun came out from behind a cloud after a rain shower occurred. "Oh, very much. Every room is stylish and yet comfortable. Your concepts show how much thought went into each design in every room. I believe I will be the envy of the *ton*."

She swallowed and then worked up her courage to ask, "Have you thought about giving a ball, Your Grace?"

A quizzical expression crossed his face. "A ball? Whatever for?"

Abby couldn't help but laugh. "Well, you *are* a duke. A leader of Polite Society. Most dukes entertain quite a bit, and I daresay many of them host balls. It would be a way to display your home."

He smiled. "And show off your designs, no doubt."

"I would not be opposed to you hosting a ball, Your Grace, for that very reason."

He thought a moment. "How does one go about giving a ball?"

"Her Grace would be the one to speak to about such matters. I have never attended a ball. I can only assume much thought goes into the giving of one. The food. The decorations. Hiring an orchestra."

"Mama would like that," he mused. "It would also be an excellent way for Polite Society to become acquainted with your work." The duke paused. "Yes, I believe that is a splendid idea."

"What is a splendid idea?"

Abby turned and saw the duke's mother enter the room.

"I was hoping you had arrived in town as planned, Bradford," the duchess continued. "I had my maid pack up my things from Lord Ladiwyck's and bring them here. Miss Trent and Nelson assure me that the house is now ready to be inhabited."

"Have you seen it, Mama?" the duke asked.

His mother smiled. "Every day, Bradford. I think Miss Trent has done an outstanding job."

"I agree, so much that I am considering hosting a ball. That is what Miss Trent and I were discussing."

The duchess' face lit with happiness. "Oh, a ball! That would be wonderful, Bradford. There is so much to do, however."

"I would leave it in your capable hands, Mama."

"Come, let us go to the drawing room. I left Lord Ladiwyck there and told Nelson to bring us tea. We can discuss the ball together. When to hold it. If we should select a theme."

The duchess looped her arm through Abby's, leading her down the corridor as the duke followed them.

Magnus waited in the drawing room, and the moment he spied her, he said, "This is such a beautiful room, Abby. I have been going about, studying each piece of furniture at great length. It must be thrilling to know you have designed everything within it."

She chuckled. "Well, I merely chose the rugs and the art, but I will take credit for the furniture design."

"Bradford is going to host a ball," the duchess told Magnus. "We can talk about it over tea."

Two maids rolled in the teacart under Mrs. Nelson's watchful eye as they took seats.

"Why don't you pour out, Miss Trent?" Her Grace said.

"It is your house, Your Grace. Yours and His Grace's," Abby protested.

"It may be—but you have brought this house to life. I think you should do the honors of pouring out."

She did so, proud that her hand did not tremble as she passed the duke his cup and saucer.

They talked of the ball and the best time to give it, deciding to attend a few balls themselves and seeing how those were set up before beginning to think of when invitations might be issued for the Duke of Bradford's ball.

"You will need a secretary," the duchess told her son. "He can keep up with your social schedule and mine. He will be a tremendous help in the planning of our ball."

"Another servant?" the duke said, sounding slightly exasperated. "I already met dozens of my servants earlier today, including a valet who seems more opinionated than my former batman in the army."

"The Nelsons did a superb job in hiring your staff," the duchess said. "They even hired a lady's maid for me."

Abby watched the duke's expression soften. "I am glad to hear you are being spoiled, Mama. And what of your new wardrobe?"

Her Grace launched into a description of some of her favorite gowns, drawing Abby into the conversation, as well.

"Madame Aubert was so easy to work with," she said. "I look forward to wearing her creations."

"Well, the first ball is in two days," Magnus said. "Hosted by Lord and Lady Capwell."

"We must go together," Her Grace insisted. "It has been ages since I graced a ballroom. The same goes for you, my lord."

Magnus said, "An excellent idea. At least the four of us will know one another. It will be nice to be in good company. Of course, His Grace will certainly be an object of interest, being a duke whom most of Polite Society has yet to meet. He will be expected to dance the entire night away."

Abby felt Bradford stiffen beside her. She looked to him. "Is something wrong, Your Grace?"

"I do not know how to dance," he confessed.

CHAPTER SEVENTEEN

ELIJAH ALLOWED MONK, his valet, to finish tying the starched cravat. He had found the servant a bit bossy and figured Monk thought to whip him into shape as a duke. The valet had organized Elijah's dressing room and could find any item with ease. It was filled now, along with his various wardrobes and dressers, with all the clothing provided by Tibbets. The tailor had also had a shirtmaker sew three dozen shirts for Elijah and had thoughtfully measured Elijah's feet and calves, sending those measurements off to a bootmaker and cobbler. He didn't see how he would ever wear all the clothes he now owned, but trusted his tailor and knew the man only did his job.

Monk stepped back. "You will certainly be the best-dressed gentleman at tonight's ball, Your Grace."

He looked down at the elegant black evening clothes, set off by the snow-white shirt and cravat. Nervousness filled him, something he would never admit to. He knew word had gotten out by now and that the members of the *ton* were eager to size him up, knowing he was Bradford's true son. He decided he would speak as little as possible and let people continue to wonder about him. After all, he was a duke and had no need to idly chat with others. Elijah only hoped his lofty title would put up an invisible barrier between him and those present tonight. He certainly wasn't a social creature, unlike Mama, and only was going this evening to reintroduce her into society.

And pay special attention to Abby.

Her looks alone would guarantee that single gentlemen would swarm about her. She was much more than those looks, however. She was spirited and intelligent and even though he had yet to meet other women of the *ton*, Elijah knew Abby Trent was an original.

"Thank you, Monk," he said. "I feel as if I am prepared tonight, thanks to your ministrations."

"Don't smile," the valet advised. "Don't seek to meet anyone. Have others come to you, Your Grace. If you choose to pay a compliment, make that a rare practice. Only dance with the daughters of earls or a higher rank. You want the woman you select as your duchess to have impeccable breeding."

He coughed, covering his amusement. "Thank you for the advice, Monk."

The valet's brows rose. "I have been valet to a marquess. I know what I speak of, Your Grace. I know you have been away at war. That hardens a man—and makes him a bit rough about the edges. I don't seek to soften you. I simply wish to make you aware of your status. You are a duke, Your Grace. Keep your title in mind, and hold your head high."

"I will do so, Monk," he promised, still amused.

Elijah went downstairs, where Nelson and Mrs. Nelson waited in the foyer.

"Your carriage is ready, Your Grace," Nelson told him. "The coachman knows to call at Lord Ladiwyck's before taking you and Her Grace to the ball."

"Thank you, Nelson."

He turned and saw Mama coming down the stairs. She wore a gown the color of seafoam, complementing her skin. Her hair was piled high atop her head. Diamonds sparkled at her throat and dangled from her ears, thanks to Soames giving Elijah access to the family jewels. His mother looked every inch a duchess. Elijah's throat grew thick, wishing he could give her back all those lost years spent in obscurity, raising Gil and him.

She reached the landing and turned to come down the final flight of stairs. Elijah smiled, and she returned his smile. Then, suddenly she was tumbling down the stairs, a shriek coming from her. He raced to catch her.

"Mama!" he cried, reaching her as she arrived at the bottom step, hitting her head. "Mama!"

Her eyelashes fluttered a moment, and then she grew still. He scooped her up. "Fetch a doctor. Now!"

Elijah looked down, seeing how still she was. "Mama?" he asked, receiving no response.

He carried her to her bedchamber, Mrs. Nelson following, hovering on the other side of the bed as Elijah gently set her down. He ran his fingers along her head, finding a slight bump. That could mean a concussion. Quickly, he checked her arms and legs. She winced when he touched her right ankle.

"No broken bones," he muttered. "A sprained ankle, I think."

"That is a good sign, Your Grace," Mrs. Nelson said, removing Mama's slippers and covering her with a quilt.

"I have seen men in battle strike their heads in a similar manner. Usually, they are all right." He perched on the side of the bed, taking her hands in his. "We need to wake her. I am not sure of the reason, but that is what the physicians in the army recommended doing."

"I'll fetch the smelling salts," the housekeeper said.

By the time Mrs. Nelson returned, a physician accompanied her.

"I am Dr. Orr, Your Grace," the man said. "Tell me what happened."

"Mama was coming down the stairs. Then suddenly, she was falling. She struck her head when she reached the bottom. I believe she may have sprained her right ankle, but I found no broken bones."

The doctor motioned for the smelling salts and Mrs. Nelson handed them over. Waving them under Mama's nose, Elijah saw her nose wrinkle and then she shuddered, her eyes opening.

Dr. Orr handed the smelling salts to Mrs. Nelson and said, "Good evening, Your Grace. You took a tumble down the stairs. I am Dr. Orr, here to see to you."

Mama looked confused. "I fell?"

"You did, Your Grace."

"I don't remember that." She shifted and frowned. "Oh. My ankle hurts a bit. So does my head."

"May I examine you?" the physician asked.

"Of course," Mama said.

After his examination, Dr. Orr said, "It is a sprained ankle. Not too severe. A cold compress for now will help. I suggest staying off it a day or so and then putting some weight on it after that. Your body will tell you when it's ready to be up and walking. As for your head, you do have a small goose egg forming where it hit the step. It is possible that you have a concussion."

Mama frowned. "What is that?"

"It is when someone has taken a blow to the head. You may feel out of sorts for a few days. How is your vision?"

Elijah listened as Dr. Orr asked his mother several more questions. The physician seemed pleased by Mama's answers.

"Your coordination is good, Your Grace. You are having no vision or hearing problems. You have answered my questions without hesitation, so I doubt your memory has been affected. As you rest your ankle, you will also rest your brain."

The physician turned to him. "Everything looks well, Your Grace. I would have a maid sit with Her Grace tonight in case she has need of anything."

He shook hands with Dr. Orr. "Thank you for coming."

"I will return tomorrow afternoon and see how Her Grace fares. I bid you good evening."

Dr. Orr left, and Elijah returned to his mother's bedside and took her hands in his. "I am glad you are fine, Mama. We will keep a close eye on you."

"You must go, Bradford. To the opening ball. Lord Ladiwyck and Miss Trent must be wondering where we are."

The last thing he wanted to do was go to a large social gathering. "I will go to them now, Mama, but I do not plan on appearing at a ball unless you are on my arm. When you are well, we will meet Polite Society head on. Together."

⸻

ABBY READIED HERSELF with Ethel's help. She was wearing one of the many gowns from Madame Aubert, a particular favorite in periwinkle. She did her own hair as was her custom and then went downstairs.

Magnus awaited her in the foyer, looking dapper in his evening clothes. He, too, had seen Mr. Tibbets and had new clothes made up for the Season.

"I cannot think of a more handsome man to escort me to the Capwell ball," she praised.

"Ah, but I am the lucky one to have you on my arm, Abby." He kissed her cheek. "I will happily pay Madame Aubert's bills if you look like this each night."

"Well, I plan to pay those bills myself, thanks to His Grace," she told him. "If his townhouse were the only furniture I provided for a client this year, I would more than make a hefty profit."

"No, let me provide this wardrobe for you," Magnus insisted. "It's the least I can do for my traveling companion of many years. You have been a boon to me, Abby. I may not have wed, but you are as a daughter to me. Even better, you are my friend."

They talked for several minutes, and then Magnus called to Feathers, asking him to check for Bradford's carriage.

"I will, my lord, but I do have a footman stationed to let us know when Their Graces arrive."

Feathers stepped outside and returned. "Not a sign yet, my lord. Traffic must be quite heavy. It always is on the opening night of the Season."

Abby began to worry, though, when the duke and his mother did not show up after some minutes.

"Do you think they might have been involved in a carriage accident?" she asked anxiously.

She could see concern on Magnus' face, as well. "I don't know. I'm of a mind to send a servant to them to see."

The footman from outside rushed into the foyer. "The carriage is here!"

She and Magnus went out the open door, only to see the duke bound from the carriage and hurry toward them. Just seeing him caused her heart to beat rapidly.

"I apologize for how late it is," he began. "Mama had a fall coming down the stairs. She twisted her ankle and banged her head. The doctor has just left."

"How is she?" Magnus asked, his concern obvious.

"She will be well in two or three days. Until then, she needs rest," Bradford replied. "She urged me to attend the ball without her. I cannot do so. When I meet Polite Society, it will be with her proudly by my side."

"I understand, Your Grace," Magnus said, "and admire you for waiting."

"I am leaving my carriage at your disposal, my lord," Bradford continued. "It would take too long to have your own prepared, and you are late enough as it is to the ball. Please go and enjoy yourselves."

Abby deflated at his words. While she certainly was concerned about the duchess' health, Abby had wanted to be with him as they entered the Capwells' ballroom. She had chosen this gown tonight because she wanted to look good. Not for the *ton*.

For him . . .

"That is most gracious of you, Your Grace," Magnus said. "May we drop you at your townhouse first?"

"No. It is only a few short blocks. You should get going." The duke paused. "Might I say you look quite lovely tonight, Miss Trent?"

"Thank you, Your Grace," she said demurely, glad he at least had noticed her.

The duke walked them to his carriage and offered her his hand.

"Try not to attract too many suitors, Miss Trent," he teased. "I know how you don't wish for anything to interfere with your business."

"I am not certain if I will even dance this evening," she replied. "I merely wish for Magnus to introduce me to a few others."

"Enjoy yourself," he said, his eyes searching her face as if he wished her to say more.

Abby stepped into the carriage, and Magnus followed behind her, a footman closing the door. She glanced out the window and gave a wave to the duke, dressed in his exquisite evening clothes. He would have stolen many hearts at tonight's ball.

"It is a pity that Her Grace injured herself. We must call on her tomorrow," Magnus said.

She studied her companion a moment. "Do you have feelings for Her Grace?"

He smiled wryly. "Am I that obvious?"

"No, not at all. But I know you better than anyone, and I have sensed something between the two of you for some time now."

"I will admit I have not felt feelings such as these since the time I was interested in your mother. Actually, my feelings are stronger than then."

"Have you shared them with Her Grace?"

Sadly, he shook his head. "No. I did not want to cage such a beautiful bird. She needs to step back into society and shine. I will bide my time. For now."

"Will you make your feelings known during the Season?"

He chuckled. "We will see how jealous I become when she begins to receive the attention I predict will come her way."

"Would you remain in England if you wed?" Abby pressed.

"Oh, you are being premature, my dear. Just because I am interested in the duchess does not mean she reciprocates that interest."

"I believe she would if you shared your feelings, Magnus."

"We will see."

The carriage delivered them to the Capwells' townhouse, and they went inside. Magnus had told her that a receiving line was always held to allow hosts to greet their guests, but none was formed. She supposed they had already missed it. As they mounted the stairs, she could hear music playing, and they slipped into the ballroom, dancers already in motion.

"Do my eyes deceive me?" a voice said. "Surely, it cannot be Ladiwyck."

Abby turned and saw a man close to Magnus' age approaching.

"Motwell? Is that you?"

The man grinned, and they shook hands. Magnus turned to her. "Miss Trent, this is Viscount Motwell, who was a friend of your father's, as well as mine. Motwell, Miss Trent is Morton's daughter."

He bowed to her. "The last time I saw you, Miss Trent, you were a pert six-year-old when I called at Morville. You were mad for the Greek gods. Poseidon was your favorite, if I recall."

She laughed. "I did go through a phase where the Greeks and Romans fascinated me, my lord. I am sorry I do not recall your visit."

The viscount waved a hand. "It was long ago, mostly likely two decades ago. I must say you have turned out to be a most lovely woman." Motwell paused. "I heard about your father's death. He was a good man. Always full of laughter—and a bit of mischief."

Lord Motwell took them around the ballroom, introducing them to several members of the *ton*. Many were interested in their travels, and Magnus told a few stories, entertaining a group that gathered about them. Abby continued listening but looked about the ballroom, admiring the beautiful gowns. She caught sight of a woman playing in the orchestra and thought it wonderful. That was the type of person she would enjoy becoming acquainted with, a woman brave enough to go against the norms of Polite Society and pursue what she loved.

She heard Magnus mention Trent Furnishings and turned her attention back to the circle around them.

Lord Motwell said, "So, you have been inspired by your travels and use your experiences when you design your furniture?"

"Yes, my lord."

"Where is your shop?" someone asked.

She gave its location in Mayfair, and several asked about what she designed. Abby described a few pieces and saw interest on the faces of those gathered about them.

"Miss Trent is quite busy now, working on a large project for the Duke of Bradford," Magnus inserted into the conversation.

"Bradford?" a woman asked. "You *know* the new duke?"

"Why, yes," she said, smiling genially. "His Grace commissioned me to furnish his entire London townhouse. It was empty of all furniture and so a blank slate. I have enjoyed working with him and the Duchess of Bradford on this project."

People began peppering her with questions. Even as she answered, she heard side conversations mention the duchess and how she had been mistreated by her husband, and how the new duke closely resembled the father he had never met.

Not wanting to press too hard, she concluded with, "I hope to see all of you at my shop sometime this Season."

Magnus quickly picked up on her cue and took her arm. "We should continue around the ballroom, Motwell. I still see many others

I wish to catch up on. If you will excuse us."

They left and continued making their way around the room, meeting so many in such a short time. One who impressed her, though, was the Duchess of Westfield, who was taller than most men and had fiery red hair and expressive gray eyes.

"Word has already circulated through the ballroom, Miss Trent, that you design furniture," the duchess said.

"I do, Your Grace."

"I am creative myself. I paint portraits."

"You do?" Surprise filled Abby. "That is marvelous. I would love to see your work someday."

"I will have you and Lord Ladiwyck come to tea soon," the duchess said. "You can see the portraits I painted of my husband at different stages of his life."

"I would be honored, Your Grace."

The duchess nodded approvingly at Abby. "We are alike, Miss Trent, in that we march to a different tune than most ladies in Polite Society. I am fortunate that my husband recognizes my need to pursue my passion for art. Most men wouldn't understand. For me, painting is as necessary as the air I breathe."

"I totally understand, Your Grace. If I could not sketch my ideas and see them brought to fruition, I would be most unhappy."

The duchess clasped Abby's elbow and leaned close. Quietly, she said, "It will take a special man to see how your talent must be nurtured. There may be only a handful of men—if that—who would allow you to continue with your business, much less without interference."

Her words startled Abby. "Oh, I am not looking to wed, Your Grace. I have only begun Trent Furnishings. I must devote all my time and efforts to it. My business is my sole focus."

The Duchess of Westfield smiled enigmatically. "You will attract the attention of many, Miss Trent. Good luck with your endeavor. I look forward to hosting you at tea very soon. Look for an invitation."

Her Grace's husband joined them and introduced himself. Abby found she liked the Duke of Westfield quite a bit.

"Apologies, Miss Trent," the duke said, "but I must steal my wife for the supper dance now. I hope to see you and Lord Ladiwyck soon."

The duke led his wife to the dance floor, and Abby watched as they began to waltz. She wished Elijah had been able to come tonight, because she would have wished to dance a waltz with him. It had startled her when he admitted he couldn't dance, until she thought about his upbringing and how he had worked odd jobs to help support his family before spending his entire adult life at war. His mother had told Abby she had taken her son in hand and taught him dance steps to prepare him for tonight's ball.

"Miss Trent, might I have what is left of this dance?"

She saw it was an earl she had been introduced to earlier in the evening, a widower who mentioned he had a young son four years of age.

"I would be most happy to, my lord," she replied.

While Abby enjoyed the music and the earl danced beautifully, her thoughts returned to Elijah. Dancing with him would have brought her joy.

She dined with the earl and a group of his friends, who asked her many questions about her travels and furniture designs. She danced most every dance after supper ended. Several men asked to call upon her tomorrow and she informed them she would not be receiving any visitors because she would be at work. Most of them seemed put off by her words, but a few promised to make their way to her Mayfair shop in the next few days.

By the time the ball ended, Abby was tired but pleased at how the night had gone. She had not been too assertive in discussing her work, yet she hadn't shied away from questions regarding it.

When they reached their residence, they bid the Bradford coachman goodnight and went inside.

"When are you planning to call upon Her Grace, Magnus?" she asked as they went up the stairs wanting to visit her friend.

"After breakfast if that suits your plans," he replied.

She agreed to accompany him to see the duchess and then went to her bedchamber. Ethel awaited her and helped Abby to undress.

"Did you enjoy your first ball, Miss Trent?" the maid asked.

"I did, Ethel. I met a good number of people and even danced a few times. All in all, it was a most pleasant evening."

She climbed into bed and instead of thinking about everyone at the Capwell ball, Abby fell asleep with the Duke of Bradford's image in her mind.

CHAPTER EIGHTEEN

Abby dressed with care, believing at least a few of those who attended last night's ball might come and visit Trent Furnishings today. She knew some in the *ton* found her to be an oddity, owning a shop and designing all its contents. That curiosity alone might bring in some to view her work on display. She supposed others would ignore her—if not directly, then any mention of her owning her establishment. It seemed the *ton* did not want their own to dirty their hands with honest labor. She had no use for a society which would disregard creativity and hard work, and yet because of her designs and the craftsmanship that went into them, the *ton* were the very clients she needed to cultivate to stay afloat.

"Business is tricky," she told herself, knowing she would have to dance a fine line in the world her customers inhabited. She would dip her toe into that world upon occasion. She had already decided that she would not attend tonight's ball, held at Lord and Lady Danby's, thinking it would be better to take a night away from society. Her absence either would not be noted or could draw others to be curious and tempt them to visit Trent Furnishings.

She joined Magnus at breakfast, noting he wore one of his new coats and cravats.

"Are we still off to see Her Grace after breakfast?" she asked.

"Yes. I do want to see how she feels today." He looked to Feathers.

"Have both the carriage and Samuel's cab readied so that we may depart after breakfast."

"Yes, my lord," the butler replied and exited the breakfast room.

"We could ride together, and then you could drop me at Trent Furnishings after our visit."

"I may wish to stay with Her Grace for a few hours," Magnus said.

Abby bit back a smile. "I see."

Magnus grinned. "I believe you do."

They finished their meal, and Abby joined Magnus in his carriage, Samuel following them. They alighted at the Duke of Bradford's residence and were greeted by Nelson.

"Ah, Miss Trent. I did not know we would be seeing you today."

"This is not business, Nelson, but purely a social visit. Lord Ladiwyck and I have come to call on Her Grace and see how she is."

The butler smiled. "Her Grace will be delighted to have your company. She is in the drawing room."

"She isn't resting in her bedchamber?" Magnus asked, his worry plain to see.

Nelson chuckled. "Her Grace is feeling much better today, my lord. She had His Grace carry her to the drawing room because she was bored in her own room."

"She is spirited," Magnus said proudly.

"That she is, my lord. This way, please."

Nelson escorted them to the drawing room, where they found the duchess stretched out on a settee, a book in her lap, a cushion beneath her ankle. She smiled as they entered.

"It is so good of you to come, my lord, Miss Trent. Forgive me for not rising. Please, have a seat."

They took chairs close to the duchess, and Abby asked, "What happened? Bradford said you had fallen. He was quite worried about you."

Her Grace smiled. "He has always been so concerned for my welfare. He is gone now, retrieving a light blanket. Wouldn't even let a servant fetch it. He had to do it himself."

"How did you fall?" Magnus asked.

She pursed her lips. "I really don't know. I was coming down the steps and assume I missed one because I went tumbling down. I suppose it was clumsiness on my part." She smiled. "Or eagerness to attend last night's ball and show all those harpies that I have a spine of steel."

"You would certainly have done so," Magnus agreed, grinning like a schoolboy at her.

The duke entered the room. "Ah, I see you already have visitors, Mama. Good morning, my lord, Miss Trent. It was so thoughtful of you to come see how Mama is." He draped the blanket over his mother's lap.

"We were eager to see Her Grace," Magnus said, gazing adoringly at the duchess.

"Sit, Bradford." She turned back to Abby and Magnus. "Tell us all about the Capwell ball."

"It was very crowded," Abby said. "I am hoping it was only because it was the first event of the Season. If all of the events are so congested, I may avoid them."

"Did you dance?" the duke abruptly asked.

She faced him, seeing his eyes were dark and intense. "Why, I certainly did, Your Grace. Magnus was clever enough to bring up Trent Furnishings, though, and I was able to answer questions about my designs and shop."

"Did you mention me?" he pressed.

"I did let it slip that I was in the midst of a large endeavor on your behalf. People are quite eager, you know, to meet you and make their acquaintance again with Her Grace. I still believe the idea of you hosting a ball would be ideal in order to show off my work."

"I quite agree," Her Grace said. "We are looking to hire a secretary for Bradford. Once we do so, we must consult the social calendar and see when might be a good time to allow others to see what you have done with the place."

"As long as your guests don't start looking into empty bedchambers," Abby reminded. "It will still take a good portion of the Season before that task can be completed. After all, yours is one of the largest townhouses in London."

"They aren't that important," the duke said. "If you have other requests come in, you should see to them first. We will not be entertaining overnight guests for quite some time."

"I will do my best to continue with the work here and balance out new commissions that come in," she said.

They spoke for an hour about the ball itself, with Abby mentioning that she saw a female musician in the orchestra. Magnus told of old friends he had renewed his acquaintance with, and they praised the buffet.

"When might you be able to be on your feet again, Your Grace?" she asked the duchess.

"Dr. Orr said a day or two. The swelling has gone down considerably, though, so I will most likely put weight upon it sometime tomorrow. I cannot let the Season pass me by. I've already sent Nelson to check the attics to see if a cane was left behind. I am not going to let a sore ankle keep me from social events."

"If Nelson cannot find a cane, Mama, I will buy you one," the duke promised.

"Oh, you could go to that store we shopped in, Miss Trent. You know, the one with the pearl gray gloves we both purchased. I believe I saw a cane or two there."

"I do remember. Let me look for it, Your Grace. It is only three doors down from Trent Furnishings." She paused. "While I am enjoying our visit, I do need to get to the shop in case some people from last night decide to come and browse."

"I will accompany you, Miss Trent," Bradford said. "I can leave you at your shop and proceed to find Mama a cane."

"That won't be necessary, Your Grace," Abby said. "Samuel is waiting outside for me and will take me to Trent Furnishings."

The duke's eyes darkened. "I would still like to come to your shop. It has been some time since I have been there. I would like to look through it again and see if there is anything to my taste."

Abby couldn't deny the duke. Besides, if others saw him there, it would definitely be good for business.

"Very well, Your Grace. I will see you there." She stood. "It was lovely seeing you, Your Grace. I am so glad you are not as bad off as we had expected."

"Her Grace should not have everyone abandon her," Magnus said. "I will stay with you, Your Grace."

The duchess beamed at him. "That would be lovely, Lord Ladiwyck."

Abby left the drawing room with the duke, who asked, "Might I ride with you?"

"Won't you need your carriage to return home?"

"It is not all that far from your shop to my townhouse, Miss Trent. A walk in the fresh air would do me some good."

"You are more than welcome to come with me then," she said.

They ventured outside, and Bradford helped her into her private cab. She told Samuel to head to Trent Furnishings. The cab seemed smaller than usual because of the duke sitting next to her. She swore the man radiated more heat than a fire burning in a hearth. His side, pressed against hers, made her belly dance as if a ballerina pirouetted inside it.

When they arrived at the store, he handed her down, keeping hold of her gloved hand a bit longer than he should. She told Samuel to return home because she would be at the shop all day and arranged a time when he was to return for her.

As Samuel drove off, the duke asked, "Won't you need more time to get ready for this evening's ball at Lord Danby's?"

"I am not going," she said breezily.

"Why not?"

Abby wanted to tell him it was because he wouldn't be there. Instead, she said, "I met a good number of future patrons last night. A few were cool toward me once they learned I am in trade. I think a brief respite from Polite Society is called for."

"Would you wait to make your return until Mama and I can accompany you?"

Her mouth grew dry at the request. "If that is what you wish."

"I do."

She led them into the shop, where they were greeted by Mr. Hogan, who informed them that Mr. Nix had gone to the workshop to supervise more of the storeroom's inventory being moved to the shop.

The duke walked around, hands clasped behind his back, pausing occasionally. Abby watched him pensively as he made a full circle and returned to her.

"I cannot seem to find fault in any of your work," he declared.

"You are looking for fault?" she teased.

His cheeks reddened. "That is not what I meant. I thought I was complimenting you. What I mean is that everything you design is functional. Practical. Yet it also has clean lines that flow well and turn a piece of furniture into a work of art. Do you ever make a mistake, Miss Trent?"

Only when I wish for a future with you . . .

"I try not to, Your Grace. Not every design comes out well, much less the first time. Many times, I start and stop. Ponder a design. Take up my pencil again, only to throw out the entire concept and begin again. Then there are times when my craftsmen bring my design to life, only to find it less than appealing."

"That is fascinating. So, you aren't perfect, after all."

Her hackles went up. "I never said that I was," she said defensively.

He smiled apologetically. "I meant no harm, Miss Trent. You have seemed quite perfect to me in every way ever since we first met. It is nice to hear you are as human as the rest of us."

"I do take pride in my work, Your Grace. I strive each time for the best design possible. It bothers me when I waste the time of one of my craftsmen."

"What do you do with these less than satisfactory pieces?"

"There is a place I donate the furniture to. They take in orphans. Some of it, they use. Some pieces, they sell."

"You are quite generous."

"I fear your opinion of me is too high."

His gaze burned into her. "And I fear you do not understand just how high it is."

They looked at one another a long moment. Abby yearned to reach out and touch him. Then the bell above the door jingled, breaking the spell. She turned away, flustered, and greeted the newcomer, whom she recognized from last night.

"Lord Motwell, what a delightful surprise," she said to the viscount.

"Am I your first customer today?" He glanced over her shoulder. "No, I see that I am not."

Abby indicated the duke. "May I introduce the Duke of Bradford? This is Viscount Motwell, who was a friend of my father and Magnus at university."

The duke stepped forward and offered his hand. The two men shook.

"I hear Miss Trent is furnishing your entire townhouse, Your Grace," the viscount said.

"She is—and has done a remarkable job of it. Perhaps you would care to see it sometime, Motwell?"

The viscount's eyes lit with pleasure. "That I would, Your Grace."

He hesitated and then added, "I knew your father. Not well. He was a member at White's, and I saw him there occasionally."

She watched Elijah's mouth hardened at the mention of his sire. "What of him?"

"I just thought you might want to know that he was a bloody scoundrel. I don't know of anyone who actually *liked* him. He was a duke, though, and so most toadied about him, flattering him and agreeing with everything he said or did." Motwell paused. "I think you will be the man your father never was."

"That is my goal," Bradford said.

"Let me look about Miss Trent's shop a bit and then perhaps the two of us might go to White's. I would be happy to introduce you around."

When Bradford hesitated, Abby said, "What a lovely idea, my lord. His Grace is only recently returned from the war in Spain. I'm sure he would be delighted to have you smooth the way with a few introductions."

The duke picked up on the sentiments Abby expressed. "I would like that, Motwell. Have your look about. I must run a quick errand, and then I will return. My mother has need of something."

Bradford excused himself and left the shop. Motwell turned to her.

"Don't worry, Miss Trent. I will take care of him as I did your father and Ladiwyck. It is something I am very good at. Now, why don't you show me about?"

By the time the duke returned a quarter-hour later, cane in hand, Trent Furnishings was full of browsers.

He came to her. "Where did they all come from?"

She chuckled. "Last night's ball." She noticed the furtive glances being thrown at the duke and the abundance of whispers.

"There are a large number of men present."

"I am not complaining," she said. "If they have come to buy, I will sell to them. If they wish to bring their wives, I am happy to meet with them."

He gazed across the shop. "You are going to be a success, you know."

She glowed at his compliment. "I think so."

"I suppose you no longer have need of me and our bargain."

Her spirits fell. Quickly, she said, "I could still use a bit of attention from you, Your Grace. One morning of browsers does not necessarily transfer into paying clients. Besides, our agreement was not one-sided. I am to help keep fawning females away from you."

He nodded solemnly. "That is true. Since you are not attending this evening's ball, would you and Lord Ladiwyck care to come dine with Mama and me? It would be a good test of my new cook's abilities, and I know Mama would enjoy your company."

"I must check with Magnus, but I believe we would be delighted to dine with you tonight. In fact, Magnus was going to stay with your mother a good portion of today. You may have to send him home in order to change for dinner."

"They do seem to enjoy one another's company," the duke agreed. "Shall we say seven o'clock, then?"

"We will be there," she promised.

Bradford went to Viscount Motwell, and the two men left the shop, which immediately buzzed once they departed. She was glad Lord Motwell had taken Elijah under his wing. It would be good for him to meet others at White's and know a few gentlemen before he and his mother attended their first event of the Season.

Immediately, she had everyone in the store vying for her attention. By day's end, Abby had orders for eight different items and promised to bring sketches to four others. It had been a good day. A very good day.

She only hoped this evening would be even better.

CHAPTER NINETEEN

ELIJAH CARRIED HIS mother to the drawing room, where the cane he had purchased awaited her. Her face was flushed with happiness because he had told her of the company they expected for dinner. He placed her on a settee and slipped a cushion under her ankle.

Nelson arrived and announced Lord Ladiwyck and Miss Trent, and he and Mama greeted their guests.

"How is your ankle, Your Grace?" the earl asked, causing Elijah to turn away and hide his smile, knowing Ladiwyck had only left two hours earlier.

"Ever so much better, my lord." Mama turned to Abby. "Dr. Orr came this afternoon and examined it. I think he was surprised how the swelling had gone down. He said I am to put weight on it tomorrow and to use the cane Bradford bought for me." She lifted it. "Isn't it pretty?"

Nelson came around with drinks for them, and the four talked for several minutes until the butler returned and announced that dinner was ready.

"Shall I carry you into the dining room, Your Grace?" Ladiwyck asked.

Mama beamed at the earl and agreed for him to do so. He lifted her with ease and moved across the dining room, Elijah and Abby following.

"I do think they might make a match of it," she said quietly.

"I agree." He frowned. "I wonder if I should tell her what I am up to."

"Up to?" She looked puzzled.

"I will tell you after dinner," he said. "Perhaps you can give me some advice."

He escorted her into dinner and thoroughly enjoyed the meal, both the food and their entertaining company. Abby praised their cook's efforts.

"Nelson and Mrs. Nelson have done a wonderful job in assembling a staff," Mama said. "I suppose we should leave you gentlemen to your brandy and cigars. Miss Trent and I can go to the drawing room."

"I have never been one for that custom," Lord Ladiwyck said. "Though I do enjoy a snifter of brandy, I am not fond of cigars. If His Grace does not mind, we can accompany you back to the drawing room."

They returned to the room, and the conversation turned to the decorating Abby had done throughout the house.

"I couldn't be more pleased with what Miss Trent has accomplished," Elijah said. Looking to her, he added, "I hope you are strongly considering taking on my other houses once you finish filling the guest bedchambers here. In fact, I would prefer you turn your attention to Marblebridge, truth be told. Once the Season ends, I wish to leave London for the country and would like a home with a bed to sleep in and chairs to sit upon."

"I would have to work a room at a time, much as I have done with this townhouse, Your Grace," she replied thoughtfully. "It would be important that I see the house, as well. I cannot furnish a place sight unseen."

"Then I hope you can find time to make a trip to Surrey."

"It is the Season, Bradford," Mama protested. "You cannot ask

Miss Trent to leave town now."

"Surrey is not that far, Mama. Marblebridge is only forty-five miles from London. We could reach it in about three hours."

"But then there would be time spent at the house, as well as returning to London," Mama pointed out. "You must also rest your horses, Bradford. They could not travel so far in a single day."

He sighed. "Very well. We could spend the night at the local inn, I suppose."

"You will also need a chaperone," Mama pointed out. "The two of you could not possibly travel together alone *and* spend the night away."

"If Her Grace is willing, perhaps the four of us could go together," Lord Ladiwyck volunteered. "It would be good to spend a day in the country and see your ducal estate, Bradford."

"We can consult the social calendar and see when would be a good time to be gone from town for a couple of days," Mama said.

Miss Trent sighed. "You and Magnus can choose a time, Your Grace. I barely know anyone in Polite Society and wouldn't know what event we could miss."

Elijah decided to take this opportunity to try and spend time alone with Abby. "Why don't you and Lord Ladiwyck look at the calendar now, Mama? The two of you know far more than Miss Trent and me about these things." He looked to Abby. "You mentioned that you knew how to play billiards, Miss Trent. Since I now have a billiard table, perhaps it is time I learned. While these two decide when we might go to Marblebridge, perhaps you would teach me a bit about the game."

He knew she had no polite way to refuse him. After all, he was a duke—and dukes seemed to always get their way.

Rising, Elijah said, "If you will excuse us."

Abby did the same, and he led her from the room.

In the corridor, he explained, "I thought it would be good to give them time alone. I also seek your advice on a certain matter."

"And here I thought you had nefarious plans for me," she teased.

He did—but Elijah would not tip his hand to her at this point.

He took her to the billiard room and closed the door, not wanting to be overheard by any servant. "I have hired a Bow Street runner," he revealed.

"Whatever for? I thought they investigated crimes."

"I needed to locate a missing person. For Mama. A man named Paul Baxter."

Elijah related the story his mother had, leaving nothing out.

"So far, Miss Slade has been able to trace Baxter to his next two jobs. The trail is cold at that point, though."

"Miss Slade? Your runner is a woman?"

"Yes, I was told she is the only one within the organization. She specializes in finding people. Frankly, I am surprised she's discovered as much as she has. The point is, I had hoped to reunite the pair after all these years. Mama seemed to still hold feelings for Mr. Baxter. I can see, though, that a strong friendship—if not more—is developing between her and Lord Ladiwyck. Even if Baxter is found, I don't know if I should tell her."

"It depends," Abby said. "Her Grace deserves to have some kind of closure from these long-ago events if Miss Slade locates Mr. Baxter. It should be her choice, however, whether she decides to embark upon a relationship with Mr. Baxter or chooses to allow things to remain in the past. She could still hold tender feelings for him and not act upon them. What if Baxter has a wife now? He may not wish to see his former love. I would see if your Miss Slade can locate Mr. Baxter first. Then you could visit him and see whether or not he is interested in having Her Grace contact him. If he is, then certainly you should tell her."

"I agree. I will approach Baxter first and see what his situation is before I speak with Mama." He smiled. "Thank you for listening. I haven't had anyone to talk to about this."

"I am happy to do so. I have grown very fond of your mother."

"She speaks the same of you, Abby."

She frowned. "You really shouldn't call me Abby. And we really shouldn't be alone here together. While playing billiards in a private home is an acceptable thing for a lady to do, she should never be alone with a single gentleman."

He caught her wrist. "Please teach me how to play now. No one is here but us. No other guests to stumble upon us and demand we wed merely because we were found alone together."

She looked at him a long moment. "All right. But we must light the oil lamps. I know most prefer candlelight to the smell of oil lamps, but it is a better light source in order for players to see the balls." She pointed above the table. "See, four lamps are set into a framework and suspended over the billiard table. That is how I knew the purpose of this room when it was empty. Note how these lamps have cone-shaped shades. That directs most of the light onto the table, while these receptacles stop any dripping oil from striking the table."

"I had wondered about that."

"Natural light is preferred in billiards. In fact, players usually lower the number of points needed to win a game based upon whether they play during the day or at night. And I hope I did not mislead you. This billiard table is the only item in your house I did not design or have crafted. I purchased it from an estate sale. Tables are custom made and covered with green wool baize."

He moved toward the table. "I see the baize is only attached at the edges."

"Yes, it tends to wrinkle. I made certain that Nelson purchased a square iron strictly meant for ironing baize. When you are entertaining, he should iron the baize immediately before a game is played."

"I had assumed it was your work because of the way the wood grain shines." He turned and pointed to the maces and cues which hung from a place on the wall. "What of these?"

"I purchased those, as well. You can see the ornate patterns at the end of each one. The maces are tortoise-shell, and the cues mother-of-pearl inlay."

Abby moved to the balls. "These used to be made of wood long ago, but over time, they would warp and not roll properly along the table. Nowadays, the tusk of a female elephant is used in making them. Ivory balls will not develop any dents or abrasions. They are crafted with great care because a nerve runs through the center of each elephant tusk. That same nerve must also run through the center of every billiard ball, so they are balanced and concentric. It takes a craftsman with great skill to produce these balls and table, which is why I had to look elsewhere. My employees' time is better spent crafting my designs."

Elijah lifted a ball, inspecting it. "What are the rules?"

She laughed. "Whatever two gentlemen can agree upon. Frankly, there are no set rules, just a few generalities. Even the points played to can vary and should be determined before a game is played."

"Give me a simple overview then."

She told him about the maces and cues and how most gentlemen nowadays stuck with using cue sticks, which had a small piece of leather attached to their tips, allowing a player to control the direction and speed of the ball with greater ease.

"You see there are three balls. We each get our own white cue ball." Lifting them both, she turned them until he saw a small, black dot on one. "That distinguishes between our balls. Basically, points are scored with strokes called a cannon or hazard. Cannons are scored when the striker's cue ball hits the other two balls in succession. You score hazards when your ball drives your opponent's ball or the red object ball into one of these pockets. I have learned in my travels that we English are the only ones who play on a table with pockets. Those on the Continent prefer playing without them."

Abby stepped back. "That is billiards, in a nutshell."

"Shall we play? I would like to see how to move this cue stick and what it takes to strike a ball and move it—and yours." He grinned shamelessly.

"You think because you are a man that you—even though you have never played—will be better than I am." She grinned back. "You are sadly mistaken, Elijah. I am excellent at billiards. Far more than Magnus, who taught me the game."

He liked that she had slipped and called him Elijah.

"I have no doubt that you will trounce me. I merely wish to learn the physical aspects of the game so one day I might try and compete with you."

She went to the cue rack and removed two sticks, handing him one.

"Hold it with your dominant hand. Not too firmly. You want to be relaxed, and yet maintain control of your stick. It's best to grip the stick with your thumb and index finger. Add your middle finger if you want more power behind your strike."

He did as she instructed while she placed the three balls on the baize.

"Lower your body to the table, legs relaxed and slightly bent. Line your body up with your cue ball and visualize where you wish for your ball to hit."

She let him test a few shots to give him a feel and observe what he did instinctually before teaching him how to make an open bridge with his other hand, which balanced the cue stick and gave him greater control.

"No, strike the ball. You are poking at it," she corrected. "Watch me, especially how I follow through with the shot."

Abby demonstrated, and Elijah tried again, deliberately hitting his ball the wrong way.

"Here, let me guide you."

She stepped behind him and had him grip the cue stick, placing her hand over his. The intoxicating scent of jasmine stirred his desire.

"Visualize where the ball should go," she urged as she slowly pulled his arm back and then pushed it forward.

This time, the cue ball sailed a true course, striking her cue ball and the red target ball, as well.

"That's it!" she cried. "You did it."

She released him and stepped away. Elijah was having none of that. He spun, startling her. Dropping his cue to the carpet, he latched on to her shoulders.

"What are you doing?" she asked, her chest heaving, her tempting, rounded globes rising and falling.

"Just as you said to envision where I wished my ball to go, I am imagining where I want my mouth to go." The corners of his mouth turned up. "I have several areas targeted."

With that, he lowered his mouth to hers.

Chapter Twenty

Abby had been fearful of being alone with Elijah. Not because of what he might do.

She'd been afraid of what *she* would with no others present.

She had thought it a poor idea to head to the billiard room but was curious why he had thought to seek her advice. It had shocked her that the Duchess of Bradford had once loved a man in her youth and risked everything to run away with him. The fact that her father separated the two lovers and then forced his daughter to wed a man decades older was bad enough. Then for her husband to banish her from Polite Society was another heavy blow. To think the duchess had raised her twins alone, all while longing for the man she loved, broke Abby's heart.

Once she had given Elijah her advice, she had reluctantly stayed to show him a bit about billiards. It had been difficult to touch him as she demonstrated what he should do, but Abby had kept her head about her.

Only the duke now turned the tables, his lips pressed to hers. Her body became a willing participant as she wrapped her arms about him, forcing him close to her. Their bodies collided, and heat surged through her. His fingers gripped her shoulders, making certain she wouldn't try to flee. Abby had no intention of going anywhere.

She was exactly where she wanted to be.

Weeks of being apart from Elijah had only made her want him more. Need rippled through her now. She tightened her hold on him, wanting him to touch her intimately again, as he had before. Abby had lain awake at night, thinking of the feelings he stirred within her and the pleasure he had given her. And now he was here again. They were alone.

His mouth coaxed hers open, his tongue sweeping inside, exploring, possessing, taking. She knew more about kissing now, thanks to him, and answered his call. His hands went to her waist and lifted her, setting her on the billiard table. Slowly, never breaking the kiss, Elijah leaned her back until she was lying atop it, her legs dangling from the edge.

His mouth left hers, his tongue moving to her breast, outlining the curve. Chills ran through her. He pushed the gown down, freeing her breasts, his mouth going to one. Finding the nipple, his teeth grazed across it, teasing it, causing her core to pulsate with need. Elijah licked and sucked until she nearly lost her mind. Then he moved to her other breast and repeated his actions.

He left her breasts and pushed against the table, coming to his full height, then he captured the hem of her gown and lifted it up, along with the layers she wore underneath it. He brought them to her waist, and she felt the cool air.

Elijah's gaze pinned her. "I have dreamed of your taste every night, Abby," he said, his voice low and rough. "Every. Night."

Then he disappeared. She could not see him because of all the material at her waist, but she felt his touch. His fingers dancing up her calves and thighs. His finger running along the seam of her sex. Suddenly, she was aware of his hot breath there and gasped as his tongue licked her. His hands slipped beneath her buttocks, steadying her, as his tongue plunged inside her. Soon, she was writhing on the billiard table, her head twisting and turning, as Elijah's teeth and tongue brought about the most exquisite orgasm. She made sounds that she never imagined she would make as waves of pleasure rippled through her.

Abby found tears streamed down her cheeks as he replaced her skirts and appeared once more. Elijah's hands captured her wrists, and he pulled her from the table. She landed next to him, and he wrapped her in an embrace as he kissed her. She answered the kiss, still stunned by what he had done, never imagining something such as this took place between a man and a woman.

Finally, he broke the kiss and rested his forehead against hers. They both panted, words impossible.

It took several minutes before their rapid breathing slowed. He lifted his head and gazed down at her.

"Thank you for the billiards lesson. I hope I will get better with practice."

"I suppose I should thank you, as well, for the . . . lesson you gave me," she said, not knowing what she should call what had happened between them.

Even though no words had been spoken, Abby knew without a doubt that she had fallen in love with this man. It wasn't just being moved physically by him. It was Elijah himself. He was smart. Funny. Honest. Vulnerable.

She could never share this with him, though. He had made it perfectly clear that he would never wed. Never choose to carry on the ducal line. If she told him that she loved him, he would feel trapped.

And he might vanish from her life forever.

He smiled at her now. "I am happy to give lessons in things I know about." His fingers caressed her cheek. "Or the ones I am learning about. You have a beautiful body, Abby. It is a pleasure to touch it."

"You have twice given me pleasure beyond comprehension, Elijah. Is there something I could do for you to make you feel that alive?"

"Yes, but we won't do that. Not now. What we should do is return to Mama and Ladiwyck. They will be wondering where we have gone."

She reached up to smooth her hair and saw it still seemed to be in place. She brought her fingertips to her lips, finding them swollen.

"I am afraid to see them. They might guess what we have been up to."

"Then let me put you in the carriage. You can go home, and I will tell Ladiwyck that a sudden headache came on. That I sent you home immediately. You can have the carriage return for him once you are safely home."

He leaned down and kissed her gently. "It would be for the best. Your lips are too swollen. They would give away what we have been up to."

"Billiards. That is what we have been up to, Your Grace," she said, returning to formality between them.

"Let me escort you to your carriage."

He did so, seeing her inside. She heard him tell the coachman to return for Lord Ladiwyck and then the carriage began to move. Abby looked out the window and caught sight of Elijah. It caused her throat to swell with emotion. She sat back against the cushion, wondering what she was going to do.

She had fallen in love with a duke. A man who had no interest in marriage or children. She chastised herself for being so foolish as to have come to love him. She had no time for love. She had a business to run. Designs to create. Furniture to be crafted. Sales to make.

What she should do is turn down Elijah's request to furnish his Surrey home. The less she had to do with him, the better for her. The unwise bargain they had agreed to must be forgotten. The duke would have to fend for himself and fight off all the scrambling mamas who thrust their daughters into his path. As for Abby, she did not need more attention cast upon her. Enough members of Polite Society already knew she had furnished the Duke of Bradford's townhouse from top to bottom. Orders were pouring in. She would help him find someone else to decorate his other houses. No, she must cut all ties with him. He was a duke. He could very well find someone on his own to furnish his country estates.

Abby knew protecting her heart now would become her primary mission. No more kisses with the Duke of Bradford. No more working with him. She must put an end to contact with him.

Because her very soul was at stake if she didn't.

ELIJAH AGREED TO escort his mother to Lord and Lady Prather's ball. A garden party was occurring earlier in the day at Lord and Lady Simms' residence, but he thought it too much for her to attend both with her ankle barely recovered. She had chosen the ball.

Once again, it had been arranged for Elijah's carriage to pick up Lord Ladiwyck and Miss Trent. His mother had seen to those arrangements, and he knew Abby would turn up out of respect for the duchess.

He hadn't told her he loved her. He was still fearful of frightening her off, knowing her views of marriage and how important Trent Furnishings was to her. Still, he hoped his actions spoke loud and clear regarding his affection for her.

When the time came, he escorted Mama to the waiting coach. She brought the cane with her, but she didn't seem to need it. She had said she would do no dancing tonight in order to give her ankle a rest.

"That does not mean I will always sit on the sidelines," she warned him. "It has been far too long since I danced—and I am not counting my time with you."

When Elijah revealed he did not know how to dance, Mama had sprung into action. She had said it was too late to call in a dance master and that she would teach him herself. While he would never be a confident dancer, she taught him several country dances and also the waltz. The waltz was easy to learn and simple to perform.

He planned to dance it tonight with Abby.

They arrived at Lord Ladiwyck's, and the earl and Abby joined them in the carriage. Elijah had thought to exit the vehicle and meet them, but the pair appeared before he could do so. He had wanted to sit next to Abby, who looked breathtaking in a gown of ice blue, but sitting across from her and soaking her in was the next best thing.

They arrived at the Prather townhouse and went through the receiving line. The hosts were taken aback when they met Mama and him, and he knew it would be a feather in their caps that they were the first couple to host the pair.

Entering the ballroom, Lord Ladiwyck took them about, introducing them to others. He saw the curious looks which turned approving. Elijah tried not to say too much and learn by listening.

Until Lord Longley approached them.

Elijah knew the face before the name because the man closely resembled Mama. Cold anger filled him as the man said to Mama, "I thought that was you. So, you are finally showing your face in town after all these years."

Mama stiffened and coldly said, "Longley." Then she turned her attention away.

The earl turned to Elijah. "Your Grace. I am Lord Longley. Your uncle."

Elijah forced his arm to remain by his side and not smash his fist into this man's face. "I know exactly who you are, my lord. You did not support my mother when she was in great need of support. You and your entire family showed her not one iota of kindness."

Longley sniffed. "See here, Your Grace, I—"

"There is nothing to see or listen to, Longley." He glared at the gentleman. "You—and every member of my mother's family—turned your backs on her. You sided with the odious, lying Duke of Bradford and let the Duchess of Bradford slide into oblivion. A young, innocent woman, one who carried her husband's twin sons. We learned to do without you. Quite well, as a matter of fact. You can bloody well go to hell, my lord, because this Duke and Duchess of Bradford want nothing to do with you."

He realized as he finished speaking that the ballroom had gone silent, listening in to his frank words to his uncle.

Longley, now purple in the face, started to speak—but Abby stepped in and quietly said, "You have been embarrassed enough tonight, my lord. You have received the cut direct from His Grace. I advise you to leave Lord Prather's without causing a scene. You have reaped and sowed this and must now live with the consequences of the choice that you and your family made long ago. Leave, my lord. Do not address either of Their Graces again."

Elijah could have kissed her right there in front of everyone. In Abby, he had found someone who championed him and his mother. A woman of great beauty, both within and without. One who would make for a most magnificent duchess.

And mother.

He wouldn't refuse her children. True, their children would contain a bit of his father's blood, but Elijah realized it would be the lessons he and Abby would teach them that would mold and shape them, not the blood they carried within them.

Longley slinked off, and Elijah said, "Thank you for defending us, Miss Trent."

"No one did so before," Mama added. "We appreciate your kindness, Miss Trent." She embraced Abby, and a murmur scattered throughout the *ton*.

"Shall we continue?" Lord Ladiwyck asked cheerfully.

They continued moving through the ballroom, names and faces beginning to blur simply because of the sheer number. He did pay attention, though, when he met another duke. They first came across the Duke and Duchess of Westfield. The duchess greeted Abby warmly, sharing that she and Miss Trent had their art in common. The duchess explained that she sketched people and then painted their portraits, while Miss Trent drew furniture and commissioned for it to be built. Elijah liked the forthright duchess and her husband and accepted an invitation to tea sometime the following week.

The Westfields, in turn, introduced the four of them to the Duke and Duchess of Linberry, who had been wed less than a week earlier.

"You were playing in the orchestra at the opening night's ball," Abby said. "I greatly admired seeing a woman as a member of the musicians."

The Duchess of Linberry smiled graciously. "It was my first time to play in public. I was both thrilled and terrified at the same time."

"My wife also writes her own music," the Duke of Linberry said proudly, his arm going about his wife's waist.

Though Elijah knew little about Polite Society, he realized these two duchesses were special women, pursuing what they loved, with the full support of their husbands. He hoped Abby might become friends with these women—and he with these men.

The Duchess of Westfield said, "Would you mind if Linberry and his duchess came to tea next week when you do, Your Grace?"

"Not at all," he replied. "I do hope your invitation extends to Lord Ladiwyck and Miss Trent, though. They are special friends of ours."

The duchess smiled. "Of course, they are invited, Your Grace. I had already asked Miss Trent to tea. We simply had not agreed upon a day or time yet since we both are so busy." She turned to Abby. "I hear your client list is growing by leaps and bounds."

"I am pleased with things, Your Grace," Abby replied demurely.

"The dancing will commence soon," Linberry said. "Might I sign your programme, Miss Trent?"

Jealousy rose within Elijah, but he saw Linberry only made a friendly overture, so he asked the Duchess of Linberry to dance, as well as the Duchess of Westfield.

When they parted from the couples, Mama said in his ear, "It is all well and good to dance with a duchess, Bradford, but they are married women. Find some unwed ones, and sign their dance cards."

Elijah knew exactly whose card he intended to sign next. Turning to his left, he said, "Miss Trent, might I sign your programme?"

"I apologize, Your Grace, but I have no more dances available."

"What?"

"As we went through the ballroom, I had several gentlemen approach me. You were busy meeting others while my dance card filled."

"I want a dance with you, Abby," he said quietly.

Frowning, she said, "And I told you I have no vacancies, Your Grace. I will see you at the end of the ball."

She turned and disappeared into the crowd.

Mama clucked her tongue, one eyebrow cocked. "If you truly want her, Bradford, you will need to do something about that."

CHAPTER TWENTY-ONE

A DISGRUNTLED ELIJAH went down to breakfast, opening the newspapers and thumbing through them without truly seeing what was in them.

He had escorted Mama to a rout two nights ago and another ball last night, Lord Ladiwyck accompanying them to both events.

Abby went to neither.

The earl explained that Abby was picking and choosing a few events here and there to attend because she was so busy. He mentioned how his townhouse had been filled with bouquets from gentlemen interested in her. Elijah had winced hearing this, not having thought to do the same. Lord Ladiwyck said Abby had told others she would not be receiving visitors during morning calls, yet several young swains had shown up at his doorstep, nonetheless.

How was he supposed to show her he was interested in her if she did not attend the events the *ton* held?

Elijah resolved to go and see her at Trent Furnishings this morning. He would pin her down on a date for them to travel to Marblebridge. If the opportunity presented itself, he would also tell her of his affection for her. It was hard for him to believe he couldn't just come out and tell her that he loved her. The thought of saying those words aloud, though, terrified him, especially when he believed Abby might reject him. If he remained silent, he could still believe he had a chance with her. Her growing popularity, though, might push him out of the picture.

No, he must go to her shop this morning—flowers in hand—and open his heart to her. If she rejected him, so be it. He would return to his original plan and never wed, allowing the dukedom to return to the crown. Yet a life without Abby in it seemed a desolate one. Elijah wasn't a praying man, but he prayed now that his feelings would be returned.

He greeted Mama and over breakfast, they discussed a good time to journey to Surrey. He told her that he planned to visit Miss Trent this morning to come up with a date convenient for them all to go to Marblebridge.

"Lord Ladiwyck has told me he can leave town with us whenever it is convenient," Mama revealed. "As far as the events we might miss, it really does not matter to me anymore."

"You like the earl, don't you?"

She blushed. "I find Ladiwyck charming and interesting. More than that, I find him to be kindhearted."

Elijah did not press her further, and he handed the newspapers to her and retreated to his study before having his carriage readied. He decided Abby might be tired of the professional bouquets arriving daily and had his coachman stop at a flower cart.

"I need flowers for a lady," he told the vendor. "A very special one."

She smiled, showing that she was missing a few teeth. "What is she like, my lord?"

"Stubborn," he blurted out, causing the woman to cackle. "Dedicated. Creative."

As he spoke, she began assembling flowers, weaving a ribbon about the stems and wrapping them in tissue.

"This should do it, my lord. Not the usual roses so many gents send. She'll appreciate these. And you."

"Thank you." He accepted the flowers and gave her a coin, seeing her eyes light up as she took it.

"Don't know if I have change for this."

"No change is necessary. If your flowers do not do the trick, though, I may be back."

They both laughed, and he returned to his carriage.

He arrived at Trent Furnishings and saw Samuel, Abby's driver, sitting in his cab in front of the place. That meant Abby had already arrived. Entering the shop, flowers in hand, the bell tinkled. He spied Abby with a customer. She held a sketchbook in her hand, and her face was animated as she drew and spoke to the man. Elijah had met the gentleman the previous evening and knew he was a viscount but could not recall his name. Jealousy flared within him, wondering if this man truly wanted to commission a piece from Abby or if he merely used that as an excuse to spend time with her.

Abby listened to something the viscount said and nodded eagerly, her focus returning to her sketchbook. She drew for half a minute and then turned it to face her customer. He nodded. A pleased smile appeared upon her face.

Nix, her clerk, greeted him. "Good morning, Your Grace. Is there something I might show you?"

"I need to speak with Miss Trent. Thank you."

He returned his gaze to Abby and saw she shook hands with the viscount. She spoke a few words, and he smiled broadly. Elijah heard her say the piece should be ready in about five days' time.

Then she caught sight of Elijah—and her face fell—causing his heart to do the same. Still, he waited for the viscount to exit the shop before he approached her.

"I have things to say to you, Abby," he began, thrusting the flowers at her. "Perhaps we might go to your office?"

She nibbled on her lower lip, clutching the flowers to her, and then said, "Yes, I have things to say to you as well, Your Grace."

Turning, she marched across the store, telling Hogan, her manager, that she had a quick meeting with the duke and would not be available to clients for a quarter-hour.

Elijah followed her to her office, and she swept inside, indicating for him to take a seat in front of her desk as she placed the flowers on the desktop. He did so, and she went to sit behind it, putting distance between them. He noticed she had left the door open, as well.

"I have things that I must say, Abby."

"Please, address me as Miss Trent," she said crisply. "I need to tell you that I will not be able to furnish Marblebridge for you."

"What? You have yet to even see the place," he protested.

"It does not matter what you want, Your Grace. I am too busy in town now to work on such a massive project away from London. My craftsmen are still working daily in order to complete your townhouse. By Season's end, every guest bedchamber will be filled. I have found, however, that I cannot turn away new business that is coming in because it will be the lifeblood of Trent Furnishings in the future. If I do not accept these clients now and work exclusively for you, I fear the *ton* will forget me. Therefore, I cannot accept the job of furnishing your ducal country estate. Or any of you other estates."

She rose, and he came to his feet, both hurt and stunned by her declaration.

Before he could counter her words, his eye caught sight of movement in the doorway. He turned and saw Hogan standing there.

"I hate to interrupt, Miss Trent, but there is a young woman here who insists that she speak to His Grace at once. She said it is of utmost importance."

"Is her name Miss Slade?" Elijah asked.

"Yes, Your Grace," the manager said.

His gaze met Abby's, and it was obvious she recognized the name.

"Show Miss Slade to my office, Mr. Hogan."

The manager left, and Abby said, "I will give you privacy."

She stepped away from the desk, and Elijah caught her wrist. "Please. Stay. This could be news of Paul Baxter."

He saw hesitation in her eyes, but she said, "If you need me to stay, I will."

Abby pulled away from him and returned to her seat behind the desk as Miss Slade appeared.

"Miss Slade, come in and close the door, please. Miss Trent is a family friend. You may speak freely in front of her."

He took a seat and motioned for Miss Slade to sit beside him.

She did so and then said, "I hope you don't find it presumptuous of me to have tracked you down, Your Grace. When I went to your home and learned you were out, I did not want to wait for you and draw the interest of Her Grace. It was important enough, though, for me to ask your butler where you had gone so I could speak to you."

"You have found Baxter."

"I have, Your Grace. He is here in London. In very poor health, I am afraid to report. He doesn't have long to live."

Elijah's gut twisted at this news. "Could you take us to him now? I want to speak to him." He turned to Abby. "Come with us. Please. You know I value your counsel in this matter."

"Of course." Abby turned to Miss Slade. "Is it possible to see Mr. Baxter now?"

The runner nodded. "Yes, Miss Trent. I can take you to him straightaway."

"My carriage is outside."

The three of them filed from the office and went to the vehicle, where Miss Slade gave the coachman an address. Elijah helped the two women into the carriage and sat beside Abby.

"Tell us what you can, Miss Slade, before we see Baxter," he urged. "I want to know everything you have learned."

"I had already shared with you two positions Mr. Baxter took after his dismissal by Lord Longley. He had a third and final position in

Berkshire, serving as the assistant steward for four years on a large estate before he took over as steward for another seven. He began experiencing health problems, however, and the earl who employed him gifted him with a small pension. Mr. Baxter chose to return to London, where he had a sister. She is a recent widow and took her brother in. Mrs. Smith is caring for him now."

Elijah thought aloud, saying, "I wish to do what I can to ease any suffering Mr. Baxter endures. Since his sister is taking care of him, I wish to make certain she is looked after once he is gone."

The runner nodded her approval. "That would be a good thing, Your Grace. Mrs. Smith has had to quit working in order to nurse her brother. The pension won't last long after his death, and Mrs. Smith might have difficulty finding work again."

They rode the rest of the way in silence and as the vehicle came to a stop, Elijah turned to Abby. "Would you go in with me? I need you there."

"I will."

He alighted from the carriage and handed both women down. They approached the door, and Miss Slade rapped on it.

Their knock was answered by a woman about fifty years of age, her face weary from the strain of caring for her dying brother.

"Good morning, Mrs. Smith," Miss Slade said. "This is His Grace, whom I told you about, and Miss Trent. They have come to see Mr. Baxter."

Mrs. Smith said, "Paul had a rough night and is resting now, but you may come in."

The trio entered, and Elijah looked about. The room was small yet tidy. He saw a cot in the corner and assumed it was where Mrs. Smith was sleeping, allowing her brother the only bed.

"Let me check on my brother."

They didn't speak, waiting for Mrs. Smith to return. When she did, she motioned to them to come to her.

"Paul is awake. I told him who you are and asked if he wished to speak with you. He does."

Elijah's fingers sought Abby's. Thankfully, she did not pull away.

"Mrs. Smith and I will stay here while you speak with Mr. Baxter," Miss Slade said.

He led Abby into the bedchamber. The room was tiny, barely fitting a bed. Propped against two pillows lay a man who was gaunt and pale. As they approached the bed, he gave them a weak smile.

"Hello, Your Grace," Baxter rasped. "You must favor... your father. I see none of your mother in you."

Abby squeezed Elijah's fingers encouragingly.

"My brother, Gil, is the one who resembled Mama. He was lost to us in the war."

"That must have broken... her heart," Baxter managed to get out.

"It did. Mr. Baxter, do not feel as if you need to speak. I beg for you to hear me out, however. The Duke of Bradford recently passed, near the same time as Gil, his heir. I became the new duke. Mama had never mentioned you to us as my twin and I grew up. She did recently, though, telling me how much the two of you had been in love and how Lord Longley prevented your elopement. Mama regretted being parted from you and told me she still had tender feelings for you. Might you be willing to have her come and visit you?"

A faraway look filled the ailing man's face. Elijah knew Baxter thought of happier times.

"I loved your mother with all my heart. I never looked at another woman after her. I heard of her marriage to the duke. I hope... I hope she was happy."

He did not see the point of sharing with a dying man how unhappy Mama had been. Once again, he asked, "Would you care to see her?"

"Selfishly, I would, though I am not much to look at these days."

Baxter began coughing ad brought a handkerchief to his mouth.

When he lowered it, Elijah saw the blood on it.

Baxter's gaze met his. "Bring her, Your Grace. Quickly."

He released Abby's hand and knelt beside this man's bedside. "I will do whatever it takes to make you comfortable, Mr. Baxter. I will also see your sister taken care of. She will never need to work another day in her life."

Baxter smiled. "Thank you," he whispered, closing his eyes.

Elijah rose and took Abby's hands in his. "We must go and fetch Mama now. Before it is too late. Will you come with me?"

"I can—or I could stay here with Mr. Baxter and Mrs. Smith."

"I would rather you come with me. You will know better how to comfort Mama. I will ask Miss Slade to remain behind."

They returned to the other room and made arrangements for the Bow Street runner to stay until they returned with the duchess. Going to the carriage, Elijah told the coachman to return home. Once inside, Abby laced her fingers through his. Comfort washed through him at the simple gesture. They did not speak.

When they arrived at his townhouse, she suggested, "Perhaps we should tell Her Grace this news away from the house. This will be a great blow to her. Having the privacy of the carriage might be wise."

"I agree. Stay here. I will bring her out soon."

Elijah left the vehicle, telling the coachman they would be returning to the previous address once the duchess accompanied him. Then, squaring his shoulders, he went inside his townhouse and was met by Nelson.

"Where is Her Grace?"

"She is in her sitting room, Your Grace," the butler replied.

"Have her bonnet and reticule brought downstairs. She will be accompanying me on an errand."

Going to the sitting room, he tapped on the door and heard her call out.

"Ah, Bradford. Come in. I hope you have good news for me and that you have offered for Miss Trent."

He closed the door. "No, Mama. I saw Miss Trent this morning but did not offer for her."

"You should do so soon," she urged. "Else you might miss your opportunity. She is a lovely woman. Not all of the *ton* appreciates her, though. There are those who disparage her for being in trade." Pausing, she added, "Now, if she were a duchess, all that talk would fade. A duchess sets the standard in Polite Society. I am certain you would allow Miss Trent to keep designing her furniture. She would make for a wonderful Duchess of Bradford and show others just how creative she is."

"I will think on it, Mama."

She sniffed. "There is no thinking to do, Elijah. Miss Trent would be perfect as your duchess. If you dillydally, you will lose her."

"Miss Trent is in my carriage now, Mama. I would like you to come with us somewhere."

Her eyes lit up. "Oh, have you purchased a special license? Am I coming to your wedding? We must stop for Magnus, you know. He would be distraught if he were not there to see the marriage take place."

Elijah noted her use of Ladiwyck's Christian name, but said, "No license had been bought, Mama. But we do need you to come somewhere with us. We will explain in the carriage."

She stood. "Very well then." Placing her hand on his sleeve, she added, "I do hope you will keep the idea of a special license in mind, Bradford. A gem such as Miss Trent will not remain available for long."

He brought her to the foyer, and she slipped into her gloves and tied her bonnet into place.

"I am ready," she told him.

Elijah doubted she would be once she heard where they were going.

CHAPTER TWENTY-TWO

ABBY WAITED FOR the duke and duchess, wondering what Elijah would say to get his mother into the carriage.

Her thoughts turned to the lovely flowers he had brought her. They were not the typical, huge bouquets she had been receiving regularly the past several days from men she had met at *ton* affairs. Instead, they looked to be off the street, sold by a flower vendor. A mix of crocus, daffodils, and forget-me-nots, with sprigs of heather blended in. The grouping was unusual. And thoughtful.

She could not continue to work for him, though. He must have wanted to arrange a time for them to go down to Surrey so that she might see his country estate. She had been clear, telling him she could not take on the job of furnishing Marblebridge. She feared if she did that her heart would be forever lost to him. Besides, it would make for bad business, having to turn away people who clamored for her designs. Yes, she could work on furnishings on the duke's many houses and make a great deal of money. In the long run, though, by the time she completed such all-consuming projects, the *ton* may have forgotten of the existence of Trent Furnishings with her gone from town so much.

No, she would remain in London. Keep busy. Already, more orders poured in. She would continue to go to the odd event, just to keep her name on the lips of others, even the gossips who no doubt talked about her for being in trade. Still, enough clients were making their way to her shop, praising her designs. Her business was definitely one which was word-of-mouth. She would depend upon talk about her furniture designs permeating the *ton*. She refused to leave town and be forgotten.

More importantly, she would not just be protecting her business.

She would be protecting her heart...

The carriage door opened, and the Duchess of Bradford appeared. She sat next to Abby, and the duke took the seat opposite them. As the duchess settled herself, Abby looked inquiringly at Elijah. He shook his head, letting her know he hadn't revealed anything about their destination.

"Mama, we are going to see someone whom you have not seen in a great many years," he began as the carriage started up.

"I don't know how you found someone I have not talked with since my return to town and *ton* affairs," the duchess said. "At the opening night of the Season, I saw so many from my own come-out group. It has been entertaining to meet them again after so many years. I am already coming to like several of them. We still must decide on a date for your ball, Bradford."

"Mama, slow down," Elijah cautioned. "I have something to tell you."

Abby slipped her hand around one of the duchess' and said, "We are going to see someone from your past, Your Grace. Mr. Baxter."

The duchess gasped. "Baxter? You found my... Baxter? Where? How is he?" Her eyes filled with tears, and they began to spill down her cheeks.

Abby slipped an arm about the older woman's shoulders as Elijah said, "You spoke of him so fondly. I commissioned Bow Street to find him. A runner did so today, and she is with Mr. Baxter and his sister now."

"He is here? In town?"

"Yes, Your Grace," she said. "Unfortunately, he is quite ill."

The duchess' mouth trembled. "Baxter is dying, isn't he?"

"Yes," she said.

Elijah told his mother about the places Baxter had worked after he left her father's employment and how his last employer had pensioned him off, due to his illness.

"We saw Mr. Baxter an hour ago, Mama," the duke said, handing her his handkerchief. "Miss Trent and I. The runner found me at Trent Furnishings, and we went directly to visit him." He paused. "He hasn't long to live, Mama. I told him you had thought of him warmly over the years. He agreed to see you."

The duchess wiped her cheeks. "I must be strong as I see him then. No tears."

"One thing, Mama. He said he hoped you had been happy in your marriage. I did not correct him."

"I understand. Baxter would have wanted the best for me."

"He knew you had wed, but nothing beyond that," Abby added.

"I will prepare myself." The duchess closed her eyes, keeping hold of Abby's fingers.

When they arrived, she opened her eyes. Abby could see the older woman drew upon deep reserves of strength as she squared her shoulders and took a deep breath.

"I am ready to see him."

They alighted from the carriage. Miss Slade answered their knock, telling them Mrs. Smith was sitting with her brother.

"So, you are the runner who found Mr. Baxter," the duchess said.

"I did, Your Grace."

The duchess embraced the Bow Street runner. "Thank you, dear. Having the chance to say goodbye to Baxter means a great deal to me."

Mrs. Smith appeared, looking a bit flustered. "Your Grace. Thank you for coming. My brother told me of you when he came here a few months ago." Tears streamed down her cheeks. "He loved you a great deal."

"I loved him, as well," the duchess confirmed. "May I see him now?"

"Certainly. He knows you are coming," Mrs. Smith said.

The duchess moved to the open door and then turned. "Come with me," she said, looking at her son and Abby.

They followed, the duchess entering first and going to the narrow bed. She smiled at Baxter, taking his face in her hands and kissing him softly before she perched on the edge of the bed.

Taking one of his hands, she wrapped both of hers around it. "I never thought I would see you again."

He smiled weakly. "I have seen you every night in my dreams, my love."

"How I missed you over the years, Baxter," the duchess said, her voice trembling. "You will never know how much."

"As much as I missed you. There was never another. It was always you."

"It was the same for me. My father arranged a quick marriage after your dismissal."

"I heard. I hope you were . . . happy."

"My greatest gift was the birth of my twins," she replied, avoiding the topic of her husband and his ill treatment of her.

Baxter smiled up at her. "Seeing you again . . . I can . . . go." His eyes closed.

No one moved or spoke. Abby watched as his chest rose twice—and then stopped moving.

They remained that way for some minutes. Then the duchess bent and kissed her former love's cheek.

"I hope you have found peace," she said, and then stood. "Thank you, Elijah. For finding him."

"I will see to paying for the burial arrangements. I also promised him I would see that his sister would be looked after."

The duchess left the room. Abby and Elijah followed, watching as she embraced Mrs. Smith, whose tears flowed freely as the duchess told her that her brother was now gone.

"Your brother was a good man. I loved him a great deal. I am only sorry for what my father did."

Mrs. Smith smiled. "He loved you, too, Your Grace."

"My son will handle his burial. Bradford will also see that you can go anywhere you choose. You may stay in London. Retire to the country. You will have nothing to worry about, Mrs. Smith."

"You are too kind, Your Grace."

The duchess sighed. "It is the least we can do for you."

"He liked the country. He would like to be buried there," Mrs. Smith said.

Elijah spoke up. "I have an estate in Surrey. Marblebridge. He shall be laid to rest there. If you would like, Mrs. Smith, I can find you a cottage on the estate so you could be near your brother."

The woman wept openly now. "Yes, Your Grace. That would be lovely."

"Pack your things then, Mrs. Smith. I will have a carriage come for you first thing tomorrow morning. We will take Mr. Baxter to Surrey and get you settled."

The three of them left, accompanied by Miss Slade.

"I shall write up my final report and have it sent to you, Your Grace," the runner said.

"It won't be necessary, Miss Slade. You have done all that I asked of you and more. I cannot thank you enough for finding Mr. Baxter in time for my mother to say her goodbyes to him."

"I am happy it worked out as it did," Miss Slade replied.

"May we drop you at Bow Street?" Elijah asked.

"No, I will take a hansom cab. You will have much to do before you leave tomorrow."

"Have Mr. Franklin submit the final bill to me then."

They returned to the carriage. This time, Elijah sat next to his mother, his arm around her, as Abby sat across from them.

"Is it wrong of me to want Magnus to come with us?" the duchess asked. "I don't wish to seem disloyal. We four had planned to go to Marblebridge soon anyway. We could see Baxter buried and Mrs. Smith settled there even as Abby looks over the house."

Abby's gaze met Elijah's. "Magnus and I will be happy to accompany you, Your Grace. Why don't we go to his townhouse now? You can speak to him about the situation in person."

Abby saw Elijah visibly relax. She would not mention having turned down his business and no longer needing to go to his country house. Instead, she and Magnus would accompany the duke and duchess to Marblebridge and attend Mr. Baxter's funeral for the duchess' sake.

They arrived, and she told Feathers of their departure tomorrow and asked him to have their things packed. Magnus was in the library, and the moment they entered, the duchess ran to him, falling into his arms. He embraced her, stroking her hair gently, calming her.

"Come. Let us sit," Magnus said, leading the duchess to a settee and sitting next to her, his arm about her.

"I told Magnus of Mr. Baxter shortly after we met," the duchess said. "How I once loved him and have worried about him over the years. I was fond of Mr. Baxter and do wish to attend his funeral, but we should tell you of our plans."

"Plans?" Elijah asked.

"Yes," Magnus said. "Her Grace and I have fallen in love. We will marry by Season's end and leave for India."

"India?" Abby asked, knowing it was one of the places Magnus enjoyed visiting most.

"Yes," the duchess said, tears in her eyes. "We have found each other later in life—and intend to make every moment of our future count. Magnus wishes for me to see the world, and we will start in India.

"I almost felt disloyal to poor Baxter when I saw Magnus," the duchess confessed. "I did love Baxter as a young woman. While the love faded, I have always remembered him fondly over the years. It was good to see him again and be able to tell him goodbye. But I love Magnus, and he loves me. We wish to travel the world together."

Elijah stood and offered Magnus his hand. "My mother deserves every bit of happiness that can come her way. I am grateful that the two of you have found one another."

Magnus rose and enthusiastically shook Elijah's hand. "Thank you for your welcome, Your Grace. I hope while your mother and I are off seeing the world that you will do me the favor of taking care of Abby."

The last thing she needed was Elijah hanging about her. "I am a grown woman, Magnus. I run my business. I do not need anyone—let alone His Grace—taking care of me." She stood, anger sizzling through her. "If you will excuse me, I have been away from Trent Furnishings a good number of hours today. I have work to see to. I will, however, accompany you to Surrey tomorrow."

Abby left, keeping a tight rein on her anger, knowing Magnus meant no harm in what he had said. She couldn't let Elijah hover over her, however. Her heart was already breaking, knowing he would never consider a marriage between them. She didn't need it trampled on further.

Determination filled her. She would comfort the Duchess of Bradford as best she could over the next couple of days. As far as the Duke of Bradford?

He could bloody well go to hell.

CHAPTER TWENTY-THREE

ELIJAH HAD THE foresight to send a rider ahead to his steward at Marblebridge, informing him of the visit. He asked Peabody to book rooms at the local inn for the four of them, as well as rooms for their valets and maids. Monk should be proud that Elijah had even thought to bring his valet along. Elijah also explained how they would need to hold a quick funeral service at the local church for a longtime, beloved retainer and that a cottage needed to be prepared for another who would retire on the estate.

He only hoped Peabody could work his magic by the time they arrived today. The steward had impressed Elijah with his efficiency and management skills. If anyone were up to the tasks spelled out in the letter, it would be Peabody.

Mama entered the breakfast room, glowing. She had ever since she had revealed her affection for Lord Ladiwyck. Although Abby's sudden retreat put a slight damper on things yesterday, Elijah had spent the remainder of the day with the couple. The earl talked of the distant places he would take his new wife. Mama seemed thrilled by the prospect of traveling. She had also confided to him on their way home that she was secretly glad to be losing her Duchess of Bradford title, having never wanted it—or the duke who came with it—in the first place.

"Will you be ready to depart after breakfast?" he asked as a footman seated her.

"Yes. My maid has everything ready. Where will we stay, Bradford? I'm sure there isn't a bed to be found at Marblebridge."

"I have written to my steward and asked him to secure rooms at the inn for us and our servants."

"That was thoughtful of you." She buttered a toast point and bit into it. "You are learning."

He chuckled. "Well, I *was* an army officer, Mama. I had many responsibilities and seemed to manage them well enough to be named a major. Actually, it was good preparation for becoming a duke, now that I think about it."

"What of Mrs. Smith and Mr. Baxter?" she asked.

"I spoke to Lord Ladiwyck regarding the matter. He sent his carriage to Mrs. Smith this morning, along with an undertaker, who was to prepare the body for travel. I mentioned to Peabody that we were bringing the body of a longtime servant to be buried at Marblebridge."

"Thank you for offering to have Baxter buried there. It will be nice to know where he is and visit his grave whenever we come to see you."

Elijah said, "I doubt that will be often. From what Lord Ladiwyck said, he has a good dozen places he wishes for you to see."

"Not all at once, thank goodness. He knows you and I were parted for many years and that after we visit a country or two, I wish to return to England. Ladiwyck spent years with Miss Trent for company so he will also wish to visit her, as well, anytime we come home." She looked hopeful. "It would be nice if we could do so in one place."

Sighing, he said, "I will work on that, Mama."

"So, you do have feelings for Miss Trent?"

"I do."

"What of your earlier statements?"

He knew she referred to him wanting to end the Bradford line. "If she will have me, then I would welcome any children that came from our marriage."

Mama beamed. "That's the spirit, Bradford. That alone might keep Ladiwyck and me in England more often than not."

They finished breakfast, and Nelson informed him that their baggage had been loaded into the rented carriage that would carry the servants. Samuel was set to drive it and follow them down to Marblebridge.

He escorted Mama to his carriage, and they traveled the short distance to the earl's residence. Elijah disembarked and waited on the pavement until Lord Ladiwyck and Abby made their appearance.

"Thank you again for coming with us to bury Baxter," he told the pair. "Mama appreciates your support."

"Now that you are aware of our feelings for one another, we have no intention of being parted," Lord Ladiwyck said.

"I know you will take good care of my mother." He turned to Abby. "Thank you for arranging your busy schedule so that you, too, could come along, Miss Trent."

"I think very highly of Her Grace. I am happy to spend time with her."

Elijah handed her up and allowed Ladiwyck to enter the carriage. Naturally, the earl took a seat next to his betrothed, leaving Elijah to sit with Abby. She seemed to have gotten over her foul mood of yesterday. He couldn't blame her. She was a grown woman, more mature than most because of her life experiences, not a child who needed looking after. Yet he *wanted* to care for her. He resolved to share his feelings with her before they left Marblebridge.

They arrived at the local inn, where Peabody met them.

"Your Grace, I just sent one of the stable lads to fetch the vicar, Mr. Zimmer. I have spoken to him about the graveside services you wish to be held. Mr. Zimmer can perform those this afternoon or tomorrow morning. It is your choice."

Elijah looked to his mother. "Which do you prefer, Mama?"

"Today would be best, Bradford. The sun is shining, and we cannot guarantee it will be tomorrow. Of course, we can also check with Mrs. Smith of her preference. After all, it is her brother we bury."

"Mrs. Smith arrived half an hour ago. I placed her in a private room upstairs," the steward told them. "If you would like, you can go there now. I will have the innkeeper bring you some refreshments after your trip."

They agreed it was a good idea, and the four went upstairs. Mrs. Smith once again thanked Elijah for not only assuming her brother's burial costs but also for giving her an opportunity to be in a place close to where he would rest.

"Mr. Peabody has told me of the cottage I will reside in, Your Grace," the widow said. "It truly sounds lovely. You are a most generous man."

"My boy is nothing like his father," Mama said fervently. "He is a good man. The same as your brother was."

The innkeeper and his wife brought up trays with food and ale for them. At first Mrs. Smith did not want to partake of anything, but the duchess encouraged her to do so.

"After all, we were almost family once, Mrs. Smith. I will always look upon you as a sort of sister."

"You humble me with your words, Your Grace. Paul would have been so happy."

As they were eating, Mr. Zimmer arrived.

"Mr. Peabody says you would like to have the service conducted this afternoon," the clergyman said after introducing himself.

"If that is convenient for you," Elijah said. "We can go straightaway to the graveyard once we finish here."

An hour later, their small group stood beside the open grave of Paul Baxter, the cemetery adjacent to the village church. Mr. Zimmer led them in a few prayers and then asked if anyone wished to say anything. Elijah watched Mrs. Smith shake her head, tears rolling down her plump cheeks.

"I would like to speak briefly," Mama said, surprising him.

His mother took a step forward, looking down at the coffin already in its final resting place.

Smiling wistfully, she said, "Paul Baxter was excellent at his duties," she began. "He had a generosity of spirit unmatched by others, as well as a kind heart. Above all, he was a good man. Good to me. We formed a bond over many things. Our love of music. Bird watching. Books. At one time, I planned a life with this wonderful man. But it was not meant to be."

Her voice broke on that last word, and Lord Ladiwyck quickly moved to her, slipping an arm about her shoulders. She glanced up at him and smiled. Elijah saw the love in that smile. Despite the hard life his mother had led, he knew she would be well taken care of by the earl.

He only hoped he might find the kind of love these two shared with Abby.

"I would have been proud to be Paul Baxter's wife. I am sorry for how our story ended so many years ago. I hope that you rest in peace, my beloved. Know that I have finally found happiness myself. God rest your soul."

Elijah swallowed hard, his throat thick with emotion. He wondered what Mama's life might have been like if she had made it to Gretna Green and wed Baxter instead of being forced to wed the Duke of Bradford. Of course, that meant he and Gil would never have been born. He knew she did not regret giving birth to her twins. At least she had once again found love with Lord Ladiwyck.

Surprise filled him when Abby's fingers encircled his. She squeezed them—and it gave him hope for the two of them. He would bare his soul to her soon and pray she would not turn him away.

The clergyman concluded the graveside service with another prayer, and Elijah felt a peace settle over him, knowing in some small way, he had righted at least one wrong done by his father.

Peabody stepped forward and said, "I would be happy to take Mrs. Smith to her cottage now, Your Grace." The steward told Elijah which one had been chosen. He knew two had been vacant on the property and thought Peabody had chosen wisely.

"Yes, if you will take care of Mrs. Smith now and see that she is made to feel at home, I would appreciate it." He turned and saw Mama and the widow embracing.

Peabody went and spoke a word to Mrs. Smith, and she nodded, leaving with the steward.

By now, Abby had released his hand, and she and Elijah moved toward his mother and Ladiwyck.

"I think we are going to take a stroll about the village," Ladiwyck told them. "We will see you back at the inn."

Deciding he needed privacy for his conversation with Abby, he shared, "I am going to take Miss Trent to Marblebridge. I would like her to see the place before we leave tomorrow morning." He turned to her. "Would that be agreeable, Miss Trent?"

He saw she was conflicted by his plans, especially since she had already informed him she would not be furnishing the house, and so he added, "Please?" causing her to nod.

The two couples left the cemetery, Mama and the earl turning right.

Elijah said, "The horses will be resting for tomorrow's journey. It is but a mile to Marblebridge if we cut through these woods. Are you game, Miss Trent?"

"I would enjoy the exercise, Your Grace, especially after our carriage ride here."

They went in the opposite direction from Mama and the earl, Elijah longing to take Abby's hand again but refraining from doing so. As they moved through the woods, he thanked her again for coming.

"I would do anything for Her Grace," she said. "We have grown most fond of one another." A small smile crossed her lips. "Although I do not believe I was needed much today, with Magnus here to comfort her. What do you think of their plans to travel the world?"

"The change will do Mama good. I believe Lord Ladiwyck's love will heal her in unexpected ways. She won't need the *ton* nearly as much as she will him. She admitted to me that she was looking forward to getting rid of the albatross around her neck—the title of Duchess of Bradford."

"Most women would loathe giving up such a title," Abby pointed out.

"I would say most women who hold the title of duchess are treated with respect. Mama received none of that from Bradford. I doubt many ladies of Polite Society could have taken on the burdens she did, much less have such a positive attitude in life."

"I know it must have been difficult for her, raising you and Gil with no outside help."

"She never gave us any indication that she was anything but happy. She was the best mother we could have had. I know she spent many lonely years, especially after we left for the war. Thankfully, she and Lord Ladiwyck were drawn to one another."

"Not only drawn together, Your Grace. They are in love."

"Yes, they are," he agreed. "I know she looks forward to marriage with the earl and the places he will show her around the world."

They cleared the woods and crossed a meadow, his grand country house standing in the distance.

"Does it feel odd to you that this is your home?" she asked. "Especially since you only recently saw it."

"I used to think home was a single-room cottage. Actually, home had always meant Mama and Gil. I haven't had a true home in a long time."

"You miss your brother, don't you?"

He nodded. "There is a special bond that exists between twins.

Once Mama purchased our commissions, Gil and I were fortunate to have been assigned to the same regiment and stayed together all those years we were at war. Losing Gil was as if I lost half of myself. Then the other half, too, was gone when I resigned my commission and returned to England. I knew my place in the world when I was a poor lad growing up in the country in Norwich. I knew my new place in the world once Gil and I entered His Majesty's army. I am adrift now, being a part of Polite Society and having no true connection to it."

"I understand a bit of what you are saying," she said. "I lost my mother at such a young age. There has always been a hole in my life because of that. Then Papa died, and Magnus and I left England for many years. I feel as if I am a citizen of the world—and yet a stranger in the country of my birth. I had never even been to London until we returned last June. While my designs give me purpose, I feel as if I, too, am a ghost between the world of the *ton* and the world of trade, not quite belonging to either."

He stopped and faced her, knowing the moment had come to speak to her about what was in his heart. The risk he now took in sharing his feelings was more dangerous than any of the times he had led his men into battle.

Taking Abby's hands in his, he asked, "Do you think two lost, lonely souls who don't seem to fit anywhere could find happiness together?"

Her eyes widened. "What are you saying, Elijah?"

"I am a misfit everywhere I go. Except when I am with you, Abby. I love you. I didn't want to love you. I didn't think I had any love left in me after losing Gil and being hardened by all the sights I have seen during my years at war. There is a goodness about you, Abby. Something that draws me to you. It goes beyond a physical attraction, though I will admit to you that my attraction to you is strong. The kisses we have shared have been earthshattering, moving me in ways that almost frighten me because they are so intense."

Elijah paused. "The most important thing, however, is that when I am with you, I feel as if I belong somewhere and to someone."

He released her hands and framed her face. "I love you so much, Abby. I love your independence and free spirit. I love how talented and determined you are. I see a life with you. If you are willing to try." He swallowed. "I want children with you, Abigail Trent. I thought never to have them. I didn't want to continue the line of a man I loathe. But it's not his line—it's *my* line. I had worried that my children would have Bradford's bad blood in them. I understand now how wrong I was. We would teach our children to be good and kind. To think of others before themselves. To make this world a better place."

Elijah searched her face. "I hope you will find it in your heart to give us a chance, Abby. Perhaps one day you might learn to love me as I do you."

"Elijah!" she cried. Her fingers touched his cheek. "I have loved you for some time. I fought that feeling because of what you had said about never wanting marriage and children. I buried myself in my work and hoped it would be enough." Her fingers stroked his face. "My life would be empty without you in it."

Her fingers slipped to his nape and pulled him down for a tender kiss. His arms went about her as they kissed in the warm sunshine, which felt as if it were a blessing shining down upon them.

He broke the kiss and told her, "I expect you to continue with Trent Furnishings. Designing furniture is a part of you. I would never strip away that part of your identity. We have met two other women, both duchesses, and they continue the pursuits which make them happy. I want you to know I support you in whatever you do, Abby. I want you to be happy."

She smiled at him, a smile so radiant that he felt he grew two feet taller. "I want *us* to be happy, Elijah. Knowing I have your love and support means everything to me."

They kissed again, long and deep, sealing the new bargain they had made between them. A bargain that would result in a lifetime of love and shared experiences. Tears stung his eyes. Tears of happiness and joy.

Abby broke the kiss and smiled up at him. "Why don't we go and see Marblebridge together now? After all, it will be where we raise our family."

Elijah threaded his fingers through hers "For part of the year, my love. While I think it important for children to be allowed to run free and enjoy the country air, I would not have you neglect Trent Furnishings. We shall divide our time between town and the country."

She glowed at his words. "Thank you, Elijah. For understanding that design is important to me. For knowing I need to exercise my creativity—even while I am your duchess and mother to our children."

He led his betrothed to the house. One which she would furnish and turn from a house into a home. One where their sons and daughters would grow and play. A home which would always be full of love and laughter.

Their home. Together. With their children. Grandchildren. Great-grandchildren. They would split time between both the worlds they would need to inhabit.

Home would always be where Abby was.

CHAPTER TWENTY-FOUR

ABBY HOPED THEY had not made a mistake in sending the note to the Duke and Duchess of Westfield, and anxiously awaited a reply as she sat with Elijah. Her hand was in his. Ever since they had admitted their love for one another, they were constantly touching. The *ton* would have been appalled with its members disdainful of any display of affection in public.

Still, they were not the only ones indulging in physical touch. Magnus and the duchess, who had been delighted to hear the news of Abby and Elijah's engagement, also were quite open with their own affection.

"Do you think we will hear from them soon?" she asked worriedly.

He leaned in and kissed her cheek, his breath warm. "I do. And if we don't? We could always go to tea with them as planned and follow through with our own plans afterward. Either way, we will be married by day's end." He paused. "Unless you have changed your mind."

She saw the teasing light in his eyes. "You aren't getting away from me that easily, Your Grace," she retorted.

"I do hope we can pull this off today," Magnus said, lifting his betrothed's hand and kissing her knuckles.

The duchess giggled like a schoolgirl, causing Abby and Elijah to exchange a knowing smile.

Nelson entered the drawing room. "A note has arrived from the

Duchess of Westfield, Your Grace."

"Ah, thank you, Nelson."

Elijah broke the seal and held it so Abby could also see what was written. She sighed with relief.

"Tell Cook it is on," Elijah said.

Nelson grinned. "Very good, Your Grace."

As the butler left the room, Abby and the Duchess of Bradford came to their feet.

"We both have a good dozen things to do," Abby said.

"Packing better be one of them," Elijah said, his eyes now smoldering with passion. "I will expect you in my bed tonight, Miss Trent."

Magnus laughed and turned to his fiancée. "You'd best do the same, my dear. I will tell Feathers to be expecting your luggage to arrive shortly." He rose. "Come, Abby. We shall return home. We both have a wedding to prepare for."

They headed to Magnus' carriage and once inside, he said, "I couldn't be more pleased for you. His Grace will make for a good husband. I suppose my new wife and I will see India and then come home for a bit. I would expect by the time we return, either a baby will be on the way, or you'll already have a newborn in a cradle."

She slipped her hand through the crook of his arm. "I hope so, Magnus. I plan to keep working, but I won't be at Trent Furnishings every day. Mr. Hogan and Mr. Nix are perfectly capable of handling the shop's sales and deliveries. And Mr. Bauer will be in charge of the craftsmen's work. Mr. Alexander has volunteered to come either to our townhouse during the Season, or travel down to Surrey once a month during the rest of the year so that I might meet with him and discuss my designs at length."

"I'm glad you have decided to continue your design work, Abby. It is unusual for a lady of the *ton*, but then again, you are a unique woman."

"Marrying a unique, loving man," she added.

Once home, Abby had Ethel pack her things and send them over to her fiancé's townhouse. She took a lengthy bath and then allowed Ethel to dress her in the ice blue gown Elijah had asked her to wear. He told her how beautiful she had looked in it and hoped she would wear it again for their wedding.

A knock sounded at the door, and Ethel answered it, returning with a small package.

"It's from His Grace," the maid said, beaming at her mistress. "Well, go ahead, Miss Trent—open it!"

Abby sat at her dressing table and cut the twine, unwrapping the brown paper. She found a black, velvet box inside and opened it, stunned to see a diamond necklace and earrings.

"My, His Grace has sent you a wedding present," the maid exclaimed.

She saw a folded page beneath the box and opened it.

My darling Abby —

I hope you will wear this gift as we speak our vows to one another. It is not a part of the Bradford estate but rather something I purchased for you alone, thinking it would enhance your gown. Perhaps one day you might wish to pass it down to our oldest daughter for her own wedding day.

I love you, Abigail Trent. With every breath, I count the seconds until we are together again. Together forever, never apart.

Your loving duke,
Elijah

She lifted the necklace from the box, the light catching the fire in the diamonds. She had never dreamed she would possess jewels so fine. Then again, Abby had never thought to marry, much less to a thoughtful man such as Elijah.

"Here, Your Grace, let me help you put it on."

Laughing, she handed the necklace to the maid. "I am not a duchess yet."

"Pish-posh," Ethel said. "You will be soon. Might as well get used to hearing it, Your Grace." The maid grinned shamelessly as she fastened the clasp on the necklace.

Abby put on the earrings and then looked at her reflection in the mirror. Yes, she saw beautiful jewels sparking at her ears and neck.

What stood out most to her was seeing a woman in love.

She thanked Ethel and went downstairs. Magnus awaited her in one of his new coats from Tibbets, a pearl gray. She could see he had taken care with his cravat.

"You look like a groom," she said, smiling.

"And you are a most magnificent bride." Magnus kissed her forehead. "Your parents would have been so proud, Abby. They are here, in spirit, watching over you."

They went to the carriage and returned to the Bradford townhouse. As they pulled up, she saw Elijah pacing along the pavement. He stopped in his tracks and smiled as he caught sight of her in the window and rushed to open the carriage door.

Clasping her hand, he helped her down the stairs. "You are breathtaking," he said, awe in his voice.

"Thank you for the diamonds. They are spectacular," she told him.

"They cannot hold a candle to your beauty," he said. "Lord Ladiwyck, you are looking rather dapper."

"The same to you, Your Grace," Magnus replied.

They entered the townhouse and went to the drawing room. The Duchess of Bradford waited there, dressed in a pale peach gown.

Magnus rushed to her. "You take my breath away, my love."

The duchess smiled. "And you are the light of my life, Ladiwyck."

They sat, nervously awaiting their guests.

Nelson entered the drawing room. "The Duke and Duchess of Westfield, and the Duke and Duchess of Linberry."

The two couples swept into the room. Abby couldn't help but

admire how regal the Duchess of Westfield was, so tall, her auburn hair swept up in an elaborate style. The Duchess of Linberry was just as impressive in her own way, petite and blond and yet full of confidence. Their husbands escorted their two wives to their group as the four of them rose.

Elijah began. "Thank you, Your Graces, for agreeing to the change of venue for tea. You see, we have a rather special occasion occurring today and hoped you might wish to become a part of it."

"A wedding. I knew it," the Duchess of Westfield cried. "Didn't I say so, Daniel?"

The Duke of Westfield smiled indulgently at his wife. "You did indeed, my love."

"When you asked us to tea," Elijah continued, "Miss Trent and I were not yet engaged. Neither were Mama and Lord Ladiwyck. But the events of the past few days have happened swiftly. Lord Ladiwyck and I are in possession of two special licenses—and they are burning holes in our pockets. If you and the Linberrys would be so good as to witness our wedding, we can all sit down for tea afterward." He grinned. "Or actually, a wedding breakfast at teatime. Ever since your note arrived, Cook has been creating a few dozen dishes for us."

The Duchess of Linberry smiled at Abby. "A double wedding. I think this is incredibly romantic." She slipped her hand through her husband's arm, smiling up at him. "And I married a most romantic man."

"Nelson, bring in Mr. Zimmer if you would," the Duchess of Bradford said. "I believe it is time for the weddings to begin."

The butler fetched the clergyman, and he placed everyone where he wanted before beginning the ceremony.

Abby felt love bursting from her as she and Elijah made their own vows first, followed by Magnus and the duchess. Blinking back tears, she watched her groom slip a wedding band onto her finger, and then Magnus followed suit with the duchess. A few more words and a

DESIGNS ON THE DUKE

prayer followed, and then Mr. Zimmer announced both couples were now husband and wife.

Elijah gave her a slow, sweet kiss, the first of thousands which would come over the years. When he broke it, she gazed into his eyes, seeing the love and joy within them.

"I love you, Your Grace," she said to him softly.

"I love you more," he responded and then kissed her again.

The teacarts were rolled in, and the four couples spent a wonderful two hours together, sampling all kinds of wonderful dishes. Abby and Elijah recounted their own romance, as did Magnus and his countess. They concluded with a tour of the house because her new husband wanted to show off how his duchess had furnished it. All their guests raved about the work Abby had done and pressed her and Elijah to give a ball to show Polite Society what she had accomplished in a very short time.

"We plan to do that very thing," her new husband said. "You all will be invited, naturally. Thank you for sharing in our day today." He held up a cup of tea. "To my new wife. To my mother and her new husband. And to new friends."

They all raised their teacups and then drank from them.

Elijah leaned down. "Happy?"

"Deliriously happy," she affirmed. "I am wed to the man I adore. What more could I ask for?"

Abruptly, he set down his teacup. "While I am glad you came and celebrated this day with us, my wife and I have . . . things to do now."

Everyone laughed as Abby turned bright red.

"Those *things* are most wonderful," the Duchess of Westfield said. "In fact, I think we shall leave and do a few *things* ourselves."

"Thank you again for making us a part of your happy day," the Duchess of Linberry said. "And we shall all be at another wedding in a few days' time—the Duke of Stoneham is marrying Lady Nalyssa Shelbourne at St. George's."

"I am afraid I do not know her," Abby said.

"Oh, you will have received an invitation to the wedding," Westfield said. "After all, you are married to a duke. Dukes seem to be invited to every social occasion. I think you'll like the Duke of Stoneham, Bradford."

Elijah smiled. "As long as my bride and I can make time for *things* now, we will be happy to attend this wedding at St. George's."

Everyone laughed, and Abby believed these two couples would become very dear friends.

They walked their guests to the Westfield carriage and waved goodbye. Magnus turned and embraced her.

"You have made me proud, Abby," he said. "You have stayed true to yourself and found a man who will be an equal partner to you."

The new Lady Ladiwyck embraced Abby. "I hope you might find it in your heart to call me *Mama*."

Tears misted her eyes. "I would be honored to do so. And I am Abby to you."

The women held one another tightly for a moment and then parted. Elijah slipped an arm about Abby's waist as the Ladiwycks climbed into their carriage and left.

Her husband kissed her head. "Come along, Your Grace. We have *things* to do. All night long."

The duke swept her into his arms and carried her into the house. No, not just a house.

Their home.

Epilogue

Marblebridge—February 1817

Elijah gave his daughter another ride around the nursery, crawling on his hands and knees as she clutched his hair, sitting astride on his back.

"Faster, Papa!" Alice cried and he did as requested, galloping—well, at least traveling as fast as he could on all fours.

He reached the end of the room, where Abby sat rocking their son, who was eighteen months old and as much a cyclone as his sister. They had named the boy Gil, after Elijah's brother, and little Gil's sunny nature was the same as his namesake's.

"Promise me the next one will be calmer," he said as Alice dismounted and then hugged his neck joyfully.

"I make no promises. I say they take after you with all the energy they have." She rose. "I'm going to put Gil down."

"Do I have to take a nap now, Papa?"

He picked up his little girl, who would be four next month. "Yes."

"I don't like naps," she whined.

His wife set the baby in his crib and came back, kissing their daughter. "If you promise you will nap now, Alice, we will draw once you awaken."

"Draw *and* paint. And I also get a biscuit."

Elijah's gaze met Abby's. "I say her negotiating skills come from you, love."

She bit back a smile. "Perhaps." Abby turned. "Nanny, will you see she gets down—and stays down?"

The governess smiled. "I will do my best, Your Grace, but I guarantee nothing."

They left the nursery, and Elijah led Abby to the billiard room.

"I hoped you might wish to play a game," he told her. "A new one. For every cue or target ball that lands in the hole, the other person must remove a piece of clothing."

Her brows rose. "Oh, is that so? Then I will have you bare naked in a matter of minutes, Your Grace," she said cheekily.

"You may continue to be better at billiards than I am, but I think this game might see both of us as winners."

They began to play, agreeing to as many points as possible until one of them had nothing on.

"Of course, we must even out things," Elijah explained. "You wear far more than I do so you must take off at least two items before play begins. No, three."

"I will take off everything except my corset and chemise—and I will *still* win," she predicted.

"Then let me assist you, Your Grace," he said, his voice growing husky as he picked her up and set her upon the billiard table.

Elijah proceeded to remove her slippers and stockings before ridding her of her gown, petticoats, and chemisette. Left in her corset and chemise, Abby merely smiled wickedly at him.

"Shall we play?" she asked.

He was getting better at the game. Five years of marriage had given him lots of practice.

At billiards . . . and other things . . .

They played for several minutes, with Elijah scoring a single point, causing him to aid Abby in the removal of her corset. He, on the other hand, had been forced to remove everything he wore—except for one item—his shirt. He enjoyed the admiring glances his wife flashed in his direction. Apparently, so did his cock, which now stood at full attention, begging for her touch.

"I completed the final draft of my encyclopedia," she said, drawing back her cue stick and making a clean shot, knocking his cue ball into the target ball and sinking the latter.

"You finished it? That's wonderful, darling."

"I will look for a publisher once we return to town. Mr. Alexander thinks he may know of someone interested in a furniture encyclopedia." She paused, a slow smile spreading across her beautiful face. "Especially one written by the Duchess of Bradford."

Elijah snagged her nape, pulling her close for a delicious, lingering kiss.

"A duchess of some note," he said. "You know how proud I am of you and all your accomplishments."

In the years they had been wed, Abby had completely furnished one of their houses each year. She had also continued designing furniture, and Trent Furnishings was thriving as never before. That was in addition to giving him two wonderful children, who were the essence of the joy they shared every moment of each day.

"Quit procrastinating," she said. "It is your shot."

"We are each down to a single item of clothing," he noted. "My next shot might see you removing that chemise and standing naked before me." He grinned wickedly at her.

"Or you might bungle it and have to remove your shirt, Your Grace. Then *I* will enjoy removing your last item of clothing and admiring that hard, muscled body I so enjoy touching."

His cock now ached, yearning for her touch. Elijah made a bridge with his left hand and then lined up his shot, trying to visualize where it should go. He couldn't because Abby now bumped against him, her arms snaking about his waist, her breasts pressing into his back.

"Bollocks!" he cried, muffing his shot.

He turned and pried her arms from him, peeling away his shirt and then lifting the hem of her chemise and pulling it over her head, throwing it onto the billiard table. Even after birthing two children, her figure was still willowy, though her breasts had grown in size. As always, the scent of jasmine enveloped her. Greedily, he yanked her to him, the kiss hard and long and satisfying.

Then he placed her onto the baize of the billiard table and climbed on it himself, her laughter pealing through the room. He made love to her with enthusiasm, still hungry for her after a thousand couplings. When he sensed her orgasm coming, he plunged deeply into her, pumping away, and they both cried out at the same time, riding the delicious, delirious wave of passion until they were spent.

Elijah collapsed against her, burying his lips against her throat, kissing her a final time before easing off her. He remained atop the table, though, on his side. She rolled to face him.

"Are you going to make a habit of taking me on this table?" she asked, her lips twitching in amusement.

"I haven't done so since . . ." His voice trailed off as he thought. "Christmas night, I think it was. A good six weeks ago." He grinned wickedly. "With my new rules of stripping off our clothing with each shot, I may think about doing so more often."

Her eyes gleamed with mischief. "Oh, I think the last time we made love here, you were quite successful."

"Successful?" He frowned. "At what?"

"What do you think?" she asked seductively.

He thought a moment and then suddenly knew. "We made another babe?"

Abby tenderly stroked his face. "We made another babe," she echoed.

Elijah pulled her to him, kissing her hungrily, the urge to celebrate strong enough to bring his tired cock back to life. They made love again, slowly and tenderly, and then he nestled his wife within his arms.

"I think we tore the baize again," she said cheerfully. "Who should tell Nelson that we need another one for the billiard table?"

He laughed and kissed her hair. "I think it is your turn to confess needing another one, Your Grace."

Abby smiled up at him. "Perhaps this time it will be twins."

"Boy or girl, one or two, I already love this babe more than life itself," he told her, kissing her belly. "And I love the mother more than I ever thought possible."

Elijah kissed his duchess, the woman who had made him whole again, and counted his blessings.

About the Author

Award-winning and internationally bestselling author Alexa Aston's historical romances use history as a backdrop to place her characters in extraordinary circumstances, where their intense desire for one another grows into the treasured gift of love.

She is the author of Regency and Medieval romance, including: Dukes of Distinction; Soldiers & Soulmates; The St. Clairs; The King's Cousins; and The Knights of Honor.

A native Texan, Alexa lives with her husband in a Dallas suburb, where she eats her fair share of dark chocolate and plots out stories while she walks every morning. She enjoys a good Netflix binge; travel; seafood; and can't get enough of *Survivor* or *The Crown*.

Printed in Great Britain
by Amazon